SARAH BENNETT has been reading for as long as she can remember. Raised in a family of bookworms, her love affair with books of all genres has culminated in the ultimate Happy Ever After: getting to write her own stories to share with others.

Born and raised in a military family, she is happily married to her own Officer (who is sometimes even A Gentleman). Home is wherever he lays his hat, and life has taught them both that the best family is the one you create from friends as well as relatives.

When not reading or writing, Sarah is a devotee of afternoon naps and sailing the high seas, but only on vessels large enough to accommodate a casino and a choice of restaurants.

You can connect with her via twitter @Sarahlou_writes or on Facebook www.facebook.com/SarahBennettAuthor

Spring at Lavender Bay

SARAH BENNETT

ONE PLACE. MANY STORIES

HQ
An imprint of HarperCollins*Publishers* Ltd
1 London Bridge Street
London SE1 9GF

This paperback edition 2020

First published in Great Britain by
HQ, an imprint of HarperCollins*Publishers* Ltd 2018

ISBN: 9780008389246

MIX
Paper from
responsible sources
FSC® C007454

Printed by CPI Group (UK) Ltd, Croydon CR0 4YY

Chapter One

'Sort this for me, Beth.' A green project folder thumped down on the side of Beth Reynold's desk, sending her mouse arrow skittering across the screen and scattering the calculation in her head. Startled, she glanced up to see a wide expanse of pink-shirted back already retreating from her corner desk pod. Darren Green was her team leader, and the laziest person to grace the twelfth floor of Buckland Sheridan in the three years she'd been working there. She eyed the folder with a growing sense of trepidation. Whatever he'd dumped on her—she glanced at the clock—at quarter to four on a Friday afternoon was unlikely to be good news. Well, it would just have to wait. Sick and tired of Darren expecting her to drop everything, she ground her teeth and forced herself to ignore the file and focus on the spreadsheet in front of her.

Fifteen minutes later, with the workbook updated, saved and an extract emailed to the client, Beth straightened up from her screen. Her right ankle ached from where she'd hooked her foot behind one of the chair legs and there was a distinct grumble from the base of her spine. Shuffling her bottom back from where she'd perched on the edge of the cushioned seat, she gave herself a mental telling off. There was no point in the company spending money on a half-decent orthopaedic chair when she managed to contort herself into the worst possible sitting positions.

Her eyes strayed to the left where the file lurked like a malevolent toad. If she turned just so, she could accidentally catch it with her elbow and knock it into the wastepaper basket sitting beside her desk. Brushing off the tempting idea, she grabbed her mug and stood up. Her eyes met Ravi's over the ugly blue partition dividing their desks and she waggled her cup at him. 'Fancy a brew?'

He glanced at his watch, then laughed, showing a set of gorgeous white teeth. 'Why am I even checking the time; it's not like I'm going to refuse a coffee, is it?'

Everything about Ravi was gorgeous, she mused on the way to the kitchenette which served their half of the huge open-plan office. From his thick black hair and matching dark eyes, to the hint of muscle beneath his close-fitting white shirt—the only thing more gorgeous than Ravi was his boyfriend, Callum.

Though she'd never admit it to anyone other than Eliza and Libby, she had a huge crush on her co-worker. Not that she would, or could, ever do anything about it, but that wasn't the point. Ravi being unobtainable and entirely uninterested in her as anything other than a friend and co-worker made him perfectly safe. And it gave her a good excuse for not being interested in anyone else. An excuse to avoid dipping her badly scorched toes back into the dating pool. Once had been more than enough.

Until she recovered from the unrequited attraction, there wasn't room in her heart for anyone else. She could marvel at the length of the black lashes framing his eyes and go home alone, entirely content to do so. He was the best non-boyfriend she'd had since Mr Lassiter, her Year Ten history teacher. He also provided a foil on those rare occasions she spoke to her mother these days. Lying to her didn't sit well with Beth, but it was better than the alternative—being nagged to 'get back on the horse', to 'put herself out there', to 'settle down'.

2

Eliza and Libby knew all about both the hopeless crush and her using a fake relationship with Ravi as a shield against her mother's interference. And if they didn't entirely support the white lie, they at least understood the reasons behind it. Just like they'd known everything about her since the first day they'd started at primary school together. They knew what her mum was like, and they understood why Beth preferred the harmless pretence of an unrequited crush. She'd never been one for boyfriends growing up, and the more her mum had pushed her, the more she'd dug her heels in.

Beth had been eight years old when her dad had walked out with not so much as a backward glance. Her mum had spent the rest of Beth's formative years obsessed with finding a replacement for him—only one who could provide the financial security she craved. Before he'd left, there'd been too many times her mum had gone to pay a bill only to find the meagre contents of their account missing. If Allan Reynolds hadn't frittered it away in the bookies, he'd blown it on his next get-rich-quick scheme. Given the uncertainty of those early years, she had some sympathy for her mum's position. If only she'd been less mercenary about it. A flush of embarrassed heat caught Beth off guard as she remembered the not-so whispered comments about Linda Reynolds' shameless campaign to catch the eye—and the wallet—of newly widowed Reg Walters, her now husband.

Determined not to emulate Linda, Beth had clung fiercely to the idea of true love. She had even thought she'd found it for a while, only to have her heart broken in the most clinical fashion the previous summer. Trying to talk to her mother about it had been an exercise in futility. Linda had no time for broken hearts. Move on, there's plenty more fish in the sea. She'd even gone so far as to encourage Beth to flirt with her useless lump of a boss, for God's sake. Beth shuddered at the very idea. In the end, she'd resorted to making up a romance with Ravi just to keep Linda off her back.

Beth clattered the teaspoon hard against Ravi's coffee cup, scattering her wandering thoughts. Balancing the tea and coffee mugs in hand, she returned to her coveted corner of the office. People had offered her bribes for her spot, but she'd always refused, even if sitting under the air-conditioning tract meant she spent half the summer in a thick cardigan. Her cubicle with a view over the grimy rooftops of London was worth its weight in gold. When her work threatened to overwhelm her, she needed only to swivel on her chair and glance out at the world beyond to remind herself how much she'd achieved. The ant-sized people on the pavement scurried around, travelling through the arteries and veins of the city, pumping lifeblood into the heart of the capital.

Moving to London had been another sop to Linda. Based on her mother's opinion, a stranger would believe Lavender Bay, the place where Beth had been born and raised, was akin to hell on earth. A shabby little seaside town where nothing happened. She'd moved there after marrying Beth's father and being stuck on the edge of the country had chafed her raw, leaving her feeling like the world was passing her by. When her new husband, Reg, had whisked her off to an apartment in Florida, weeks before Beth's fourteenth birthday, all of Linda's dreams had come true. She'd never stopped to consider her daughter's dreams in the process.

Though she'd never been foolish enough to offer a contradictory opinion, Beth had always loved Lavender Bay. The fresh scent of the sea blowing in through her bedroom window; the sweeter, stickier smells of candy floss and popcorn during high season. Running free on the beach, or exploring the woods and rolling fields which provided a backdrop to their little town. And, of course, there was Eleanor.

The older woman had taken Beth under her wing and given her a Saturday morning job at the quirky seaside emporium she owned. The emporium had always been a place of wonder to Beth, with new secrets to be discovered on the crowded shelves. Hiding out in there had also given her a haven from Linda's never-ending parade of boyfriends. Beth suspected she'd been offered the few hours work more to provide Eleanor with some companionship than any real requirement for help.

When it had looked like Beth would have to quit school because of Linda and Reg's relocation plans, Eleanor had intervened and offered to take her in. Linda had bitten her hand off, not wanting the third wheel of an awkward teenage daughter to interrupt her plans. It hadn't mattered a jot that a single woman nearing seventy might not be the ideal person to raise a shy fourteen-year-old. Thankfully, Eleanor had been young at heart and delighted to have Beth live with her. She'd treated her as the daughter she'd never had, and Beth had soaked up the love she offered like a sponge.

Under Eleanor's steady, gentle discipline Beth had finally started to come into her own, Desperate not to disappoint her mum in the way everyone else had seemed to do, Beth worked hard to get first the GCSEs and then A levels she'd needed in order to go to university. With no real career prospects in Lavender Bay, she'd headed for the capital, much to Linda's delight. Her mother's influence had been too pervasive and those early lessons in needing a man to complete her had stuck fast. When Charlie had approached her one night in a club, Beth had been primed and ready to fall in love.

For the first couple of years working at the prestigious project management company of Buckland Sheridan, she'd convinced herself that these were her own dreams she was following, and that her hard work and diligence would pay off. Lately she'd come to the realisation she was being used whilst others reaped the rewards. Demotivated and demoralised, she was well and truly stuck in a cubicle-shaped rut.

Raising the mug of tea to her lips, Beth watched as the street lights flickered on below, highlighting the lucky workers spilling out of the surrounding office blocks. Some rushing towards the tube station at the end of the road, others moving with equal enthusiasm in the opposite direction towards the pubs and restaurants, rubbing their hands together at the thought of twofers and happy hour. Good luck to them. Those heady nights in crowded bars with Charlie and his friends had never really suited her.

Checking the calendar, Beth bit back a sigh. She was overdue a weekend visit to the bay, not that Eleanor would ever scold or complain about how much time it had been since she'd last seen her. She'd tuck Beth onto the sofa with a cup of tea and listen avidly to all the goings on in her life. Not that there'd been much of anything to report other than work lately. Unless she counted the disastrous Christmas visit to see her mum and Reg in Florida, and Beth had spent the entire month of January trying to forget it.

Even surrounded by Charlie's upper-class pals she'd never felt more like a fish out of water than she had during that week of perma-tanned brunches and barbecues. She would much rather have gone back to Lavender Bay and Eleanor's loving warmth, but Linda had organised a huge party to celebrate her tenth wedding anniversary to Reg, and insisted she needed Beth by her side. Having people believe she had the perfect family had always mattered more to Linda than making it a reality.

With a silent promise to call Eleanor for a long chat on Sunday, Beth drained her tea and turned back to her work. The dreaded contents of the file Darren had dumped on her had to be better than thinking about than the surprise date her mum had set her up with on New Year's Eve. She glanced across the partition between their desks. Ravi might be gay, but at least he had all his own teeth and didn't dye his hair an alarming shade Beth had only been able to describe to a hysterical Eliza and Libby as 'marmalade'.

Ravi caught her eye and smiled. 'Hey, Beth?' He pointed to the phone tucked against his ear. 'Callum wants to know if you're busy on Sunday. We're having a few friends around for a bite to eat. Nothing fancy.' They exchanged a grin. Nothing fancy in Callum's terms would be four courses followed by a selection of desserts.

'Sounds great. Can I let you guys know tomorrow?' It wasn't

like she had anything else planned, but going on Darren's past record, whatever was hiding in the file he'd dumped on her would likely mean she'd be working most of the weekend.

Ravi nodded and conveyed her reply into the handset. He rolled his eyes at something Callum said in reply and Beth propped her hands on her hips. 'If he's telling you about this great guy he knows who'd be just perfect for me then I'm not coming. Not even for a double helping of dessert.' The only person more disastrous at matchmaking than her mother was Callum.

Her friend laughed. 'You're busted!' he said into the phone then tilted it away from his mouth to say to Beth in a teasing, sing-song voice, 'He's a very fine man with good prospects. All his own teeth!' She closed her eyes, regretting confessing all about the New Year's date to Ravi on their first day back after the Christmas break. He'd never let her live it down.

She shook her head. 'Aren't they all? I'll message you tomorrow.' Which was as good as accepting the invitation. There was always a good mix at their parties and the atmosphere would be relaxed. Leaving Ravi to finish off his conversation, she turned her attention to the dreaded file.

Three hours and several coins added to the swear jar on her desk later, she decided she had enough information together to be able to complete the required draft report and presentation at home. Darren had left the office on the dot of five, laughing with his usual pack of cronies as they made their way towards the lifts. He'd not even bothered to check in with her on his way out, assuming she would do whatever was necessary to ensure their department was ready for the client meeting on Tuesday. The project had been passed to him by one of the directors a fortnight previously, but either through incompetence or arrogance he'd chosen to do absolutely nothing with it.

Stuffing the file, a stack of printouts, and her phone into the backpack she used in lieu of a handbag, Beth swapped her heels for the comfy trainers under her desk and disconnected her laptop from the desk terminal. Coat on and scarf tucked around the lower half of her face, she waved goodnight to Sandie, the cleaner, and trudged out of the office.

The worst of the commuting crowd had thinned so at least she had a seat on the train as it hurtled through the dank Victorian tunnels of the Underground. The heating had been turned up full blast against the February chill but, like most of the hardened travellers around her, Beth ignored the sweat pooling at the base of her spine and kept her eyes glued on the screen of her phone. Music filled her ears from the buds she'd tucked in the moment she'd stepped on board, drowning out the scritch-scritch of a dozen other people doing exactly the same thing.

She never felt further from home than when crammed in with a load of strangers who made ignoring each other into an artform. In Lavender Bay everyone waved, nodded or smiled at each other, and passing someone you knew without stopping for a ten-minute chat was unthinkable. After three years in London, there were people she recognised on her regular commute, but they'd never acknowledged each other. Nothing would point a person out as not belonging faster than being so gauche as to strike up a conversation on public transport.

The anonymity had appealed at first, a sign of the sophistication of London where people were too busy doing important stuff to waste their precious time with inane conversations. Not knowing the daily minutiae of her friends and neighbours, the who'd said what to whom, was something she'd never expected to miss quite so much. Having everyone in her business had seemed unbearable throughout her teenage years, especially with a mother like Linda. But on nights like this, knowing even the people who shared the sprawling semi in the leafy suburbs where she rented a room for an eyewatering amount wouldn't be interested in anything other than whether she'd helped herself to their milk, loneliness rode her hard.

8

Cancelling the impending pity party, Beth swayed with the motion of the train as she made her way towards the doors when they approached her station. A quick text to Eliza and Libby would chase the blues away. The odds of either of them having Friday night plans were as slim as her own so a Skype chat could probably be arranged. Smiling at the thought, she stepped out of the shelter of the station and into the freezing January evening air.

Clad in a pair of her cosiest pyjamas, Beth settled cross-legged in the centre of her bed as she waited for her laptop to connect to the app. The piles of papers she'd been working from for the past hour had been replaced by the reheated takeaway she'd picked up on her way home, and a large bottle of ice-cold Sauvignon Blanc. With perfect timing, Eliza's sweetly-beaming face popped up in one corner of her screen just as Beth shovelled a forkful of chow mien into her mouth. 'Mmmpf.' Not the most elegant of greetings, but it served to spread that smile into an outright laugh.

'Hello, Beth, darling!' Eliza glanced back over her shoulder as though checking no one was behind her then leaned in towards the camera to whisper. 'I'm so glad you texted. Martin's obsessed with this latest bloody game of his, so you've saved me from an evening of pretending to be interested in battle spells and troll hammers.' She rolled her eyes then took a swig from an impressively large glass of rosé to emphasise her point.

Fighting her natural instinct to say something derogatory about her best friend's husband, Beth contented herself with a mouthful of her own wine. It wasn't that she disliked Martin, per se. It was almost impossible to dislike someone so utterly inoffensive, she just wished her friend didn't seem so unhappy. The two of them had made a sweet couple at school, but Beth had always assumed the attraction would wear off once Eliza gained a bit more confidence and expanded her horizons beyond the delicate wash of purple fields encircling their home town.

When Martin had chosen the same university as them both

though, her friend had declared herself delighted so Beth had swallowed her misgivings and watched as they progressed to an engagement and then marriage. They'd moved north for Martin's job and fallen into a kind of domestic routine more suited to a middle-aged couple. Eliza never said a word against him, other than the odd jokey comment about his obsession with computer games, but there was no hiding the flatness in her eyes. Beth suspected she was unhappy, but after her own spectacular crash-and-burn romance, she was in no position to pass judgment on anyone else's relationship.

Opting yet again for discretion over valour, Beth raised her glass to toast her friend. 'Bad luck for you, but great for me. I miss you guys so much and after the day I've had I need my girls for a moan.'

A sympathetic frown shadowed Eliza's green eyes. 'What's that horrible boss of yours done this time?' She held up a hand almost immediately. 'No, wait, don't tell me yet, let's wait for Libs. She'll be along any minute, I'm sure.'

Beth checked her watch before forking up another mouthful of noodles. It was just after half past nine. The fish and chip shop Libby helped her father to run on the seafront at Lavender Bay closed at 9 p.m. out of season. With any luck she'd be finished with the clean up right about now . . .

The app chirped to signal an incoming connection and a pale and harassed-looking Libby peered out from a box on the screen. 'Hello, hello! Sorry I'm late. Mac Murdoch decided to try and charm his wife with a saveloy and extra chips to make up for staying two pints over in The Siren.'

Beth's snort of laughter was echoed by Eliza as she pictured the expression on Betty Murdoch's face when her husband rolled in waving the greasy peace offering. Considering she looked like a bulldog chewing a wasp on the best of days, Beth didn't fancy Mac's chances.

Eliza waggled her eyebrows. 'She won't be sharing his sausage anytime soon.'

'Oh, God! Eliza!' Libby clapped her hands over her eyes, shaking her head at the same time. 'That's an image I never wanted in my poor innocent brain!' The three of them burst into howls of laughter.

Gasping for breath, Beth waved a hand at her screen. 'Stop, stop! You'll make me spill my bloody wine.' Which was a horrifying enough thought to quell them all into silence as they paused to take a reverent drink from their glasses.

Libby lifted a hank of her hair, dyed some shade of blue that Beth had no name for, and gave it a rueful sniff. 'So, I get why I'm all alone apart from the smell of fried fish, but what's up with you two that we're hanging out on this fine Friday night?'

'Work,' Beth muttered, digging into her takeaway.

'Age of Myths and bloody Legends.' Eliza said.

'Ah.' Libby nodded in quiet sympathy. She knew enough about them both that nothing else was needed. People who didn't know them well found their continuing friendship odd. Those bonds formed in the classroom through proximity and necessity often stretched to breaking point once they moved beyond the daily routine. Beth and Eliza had left their home town of Lavender Bay, whilst Libby stayed at home to help her father after the untimely death of her mum to cancer when Libby had been just fourteen.

They made a good trio—studious Beth, keeping her head down and out of trouble; warm, steady Eliza who preferred a book or working on a craft project to almost anything else; and snarky Libby with her black-painted nails and penchant for depressing music. She'd taken immense pride in being Lavender Bay's only goth, but both Beth and Eliza had seen beyond the shield of baggy jumpers and too-much eyeliner to the generous heart beneath it. Though it might be difficult to tell from the hard face she turned to the world, Libby was the most sensitive of them all.

A sound off-screen made Libby turn around. She glanced back quickly at the screen. 'Hold on, Dad wants something.' Beth took the opportunity to finish off her takeaway whilst they waited for her.

Pushing the heavy purple-shaded fringe out of her red-rimmed eyes, Libby stared into the camera in a way that it made it feel like she was looking directly at Beth. 'Oh, Beth love. I've got some bad news, I'm afraid.'

A sense of dread sent a shiver up her spine and Beth took another quick mouthful of wine. 'What's up, not your dad?'

Her friend shook her head. 'No. He's fine. Miserable as ever, grumpy old git.' There was no hiding the affection in her voice. Mick Stone was a gruff, some would say sullen, bear of a man, but he loved his girl with a fierce, protective heart. 'It's about Eleanor. She had a funny turn this evening as she was closing up the emporium, and by the time the ambulance arrived she'd gone. Massive heart attack according to what Dad's just been told. I'm so sorry, Beth.' Streaks of black eyeliner tracked down Libby's cheeks as the tears started to flow.

The glass slipped from Beth's limp fingers, spilling the last third of her wine across her knees and onto the quilt. 'But . . . I only spoke to her last week and she sounded fine. Said she was a bit tired, but had been onto the school about getting a new Saturday girl in to help her. It can't be . . .'

'Oh, Beth.' If Eliza said any more, Beth didn't hear it as she closed her eyes against the physical pain of realisation. Eleanor Bishop had been a fixture in her life for so long, Beth had believed her invincible. From the first wonder-filled visits she'd made as a little girl to the sprawling shop Eleanor ran on the promenade, to the firm and abiding friendship when she'd taken Beth on as her Saturday girl. The bright-eyed spinster had come to mean the world to her. All those years of acting as a sounding board when Beth was having problems at home, dispensing advice without judgement, encouraging her to spread her wings and fly, letting Beth know she always had a place to return to it. A home.

If she'd only known, if she'd only had some kind of warning, she would have made sure Eleanor understood how much she meant to her, how grateful she was for her love and friendship.

Now though, it was too late. She'd never hear Eleanor's raucous, inelegant laugh ringing around the emporium as she made a joke to one of her customers or passed comment on the latest shenanigans of the band of busybodies who made up the Lavender Bay Improvement Society.

The unpleasant dampness of her pyjama trouser leg finally registered, and Beth righted the glass with trembling fingers. Through the haze of tears obscuring her vision, she saw the worried, tear-stained faces of her friends staring back at her from the computer screen. 'I'm all right,' she whispered, knowing they would hear the lie in her voice if she spoke any louder. 'Poor Eleanor.'

Libby scrubbed the cuff of her shirt beneath one of her eyes. 'I don't think she suffered, at least. Dad reckoned she was gone before she would have known anything about it. At least there's that.' Her voice trailed off and then she shook her head angrily. 'What a load of bollocks. Why do we say such stupid things at times like this?' Noisy sobs followed her outburst and Beth ached at the distance between them.

Eliza pressed her fingers to the screen, as though she could somehow reach through and offer comfort. 'Don't cry, darling, I can't bear it.' She addressed her next words to Beth. 'What are you going to do about the arrangements? I'm sure Mum and Dad will be happy to host the wake. Eleanor doesn't have any other family, does she?'

Eliza was right. Eleanor had been an only child, never married and apart from some distant cousins she'd mentioned whose parents had emigrated to Australia somewhere under the old Ten Pound Poms scheme, there was no one. Which meant one thing—it would be up to Beth to make sure her beloved friend had a decent send-off. She sucked in a breath as she shoved her sorrow down as deep as she could manage. There would be time to deal with that later. 'I'll sort it out. I don't think it can be Monday as I'll have to straighten up a few things at work, but I'll be down on the first train on Tuesday morning. Can you let your dad know, Libs? See if he'll have a word with Mr Bradshaw for me.' There was only one funeral director in town so they were bound to be dealing with the arrangements.

Libby sniffled then nodded as she too straightened her shoulders. 'I'll give Doc Williams a call as well and then we'll track down whoever's got the keys for the emporium. Make sure it's properly locked up until you get here. You won't be doing this alone, Beth. We'll sort it out together.'

'Yes, we will,' Eliza added. 'I've got some leave accrued at work and Martin can look after himself for a few days. I'll call Mum and ask her to get my room ready. If there's not a spare available at the pub, you can bunk in with me for a couple of days.' The Siren had guest rooms as well as accommodation for the family, and although the bay would be quiet this time of year, they were one of the few places to offer rooms year-round so they got some passing trade from visiting businessmen and families of local people who didn't have room to accommodate their own guests. Eliza paused, then added softly. 'If you'd rather stay at the emporium, I'll sleep over with you.'

The thought of being in the flat above the shop without Eleanor's bright presence was something Beth couldn't bear to contemplate. She shook her head. 'No, I think with you would be best.'

'Of course, darling. Whatever you need.' Eliza's face crumpled. 'Oh, Beth, I'm so sorry.'

Beth nodded, but couldn't speak to acknowledge the love and sympathy in those words. If she gave in, she'd never get through the next couple of days. She stared down at the papers she'd set aside until the lump in her throat subsided. Darren would never give her the time off unless she got that bloody report finished. 'Look, I'd better go. I've got an urgent project to sort out for Monday.'

'Message me if you need anything, promise me?' Eliza raised her fingers to her lips and blew a kiss.

Beth nodded. 'Promise.'

'Me too. Love you both, and I'm sorry to be the bearer of such awful news.' Libby gave them both a little wave. 'I know it's terrible, but I'm so looking forward to seeing you both even under such awful circumstances. It's been too long.'

They signed off with a quick round of goodbyes, and the screen went dark in front of Beth. The greasy smell from her plate churned her stomach and she gathered it up, together with her glass and the bottle of wine. Trudging down to the kitchen, she thought about what Libby had said. She was right, it had been too long since the three of them had been together. They'd been drifting apart, not consciously, but life had pulled them in different directions. No more though, not if Beth could help it.

Now that Eleanor was gone, they were all she had left in the world. Crawling beneath the covers, Beth curled around the spare pillow and let her tears flow once more. The one person in the world she needed to talk to more than Eliza and Libby would never pick up the phone again. What was she going to do?

15

Chapter Two

'Stick another one in here, and stop mooning over that bloody girl, lad.'

Samuel Barnes dragged his eyes away from the corner table where his sister was huddled with her two best friends to fix a baleful stare across the bar taps. Honestly, he didn't understand what got into his grandad's head sometimes. He'd known both Beth and Libby since they were knee-high and they would never be more to him than surrogate sisters. And, even if he were inclined towards either of them—not that he was, of course!—he'd hardly be trying to hit on one of them at a wake. 'I'm not mooning, Pops, just checking the girls are all right. It's been a bloody tough day for all of them.'

Blue eyes, still as bright as the ones he saw in his own reflection every morning, twinkled back at him from his grandad's deeply lined face. The shock of curls on his head might be pure silver now, but Joe Barnes was still trouble in a tweed cap. 'My mistake. That's what happens when us old farts get dehydrated.' Pops waggled his empty pint glass and Sam took it from him with a shake of his head.

After placing the glass in a half-full rack beneath the bar, he selected a fresh one from the shelf above his head and pulled a fresh pint from that month's guest ale. Saucy Sal was proving to be a popular choice amongst the regulars, although that might have as much to do with the busty blonde winking out from the beer tap label as the golden-brown ale itself. Sam sighed; it was a long way from the vintage wines he'd recommended to customers at the Michelin-starred restaurant he'd worked at until the previous autumn. 'Make the most of it, Pops,' he said as he placed the pint on the towel in front of his grandad. 'I'm cutting you off after this one.'

'Cheeky whelp, you can't cut a man off in his own damn pub! You're not too old for a clip round the ear. We've got to give Eleanor a proper send-off, you know.' It had been a good few years since Sam's parents had taken over running The Siren from Pops, but he still acted like lord and master of the place given half the chance. Now, thanks to his dad's recent illness, Sam was the one with the dubious honour of being in charge, and Pops sought to take advantage of his relative inexperience at every opportunity.

'I know, but I don't want another complaint from the warden because you woke the other residents up with your singing and carrying on.' Sam struggled against the smile wanting to rise at the memory. They'd celebrated his dad's fiftieth birthday in as much style as he'd been up to. Sam had pulled out all the stops and cooked them all a four-course meal, choosing the perfect wines to complement each dish.

After a generous brandy nightcap, Sam had left his mum to settle his dad in bed whilst he walked Pops back to the sheltered accommodation flats about half a mile along the front. The fresh air had hit them both, and it hadn't been entirely clear who'd held who up, but Sam was accepting no responsibility for the rousing chorus of 'She was only a farmer's daughter' Pops had insisted on singing as Sam fumbled with the key to his grandad's door.

Pops waved a dismissive hand. 'Bah, she's as uptight as that awful perm on her head.'

This time Sam couldn't hold back his snort of laughter. 'What am I gonna do with you, Pops?'

His grandad winked then eased himself off the stool to join his cronies in their favourite spot. 'Well, you could fetch me a bite of something from that buffet. Your ma's done us proud again today. Eleanor would be right pleased with everything.'

Sam nodded. Pops was right. Mum had pulled out all the stops to make sure their erstwhile friend and neighbour had the send-off she deserved. He'd offered to do the catering, but his preferred style of cooking had been deemed too fancy for the occasion, and his mum had been happy to help, leaving him free to help Beth manage the logistics surrounding Eleanor's funeral.

A sudden lump formed in his throat at the realisation that feisty, funny Eleanor Bishop would never again perch at the corner of the bar to sip the single dry sherry she treated herself to on the way home from church on Sunday mornings. She'd been a fixture of the place his whole life, slipping him and Eliza a lemon sherbet or an Everton mint from one of the ever-present paper bags she kept behind the counter in the emporium.

When he'd found himself unexpectedly back in Lavender Bay, his dreams on hold, she'd been the first to welcome him back— and to offer a sympathetic ear during those first frustrating weeks as he juggled his own disappointment and his father's wounded pride. With regret, he let the memories go. There would be time enough to mourn her later, in private. Someone needed to hold the fort until they could usher the gathered mourners from the pub.

As no one else currently waited at the bar, he ducked under the side hatch and grabbed a plate from the end of the buffet table. After a quick glance to where the girls sat, he took a second plate. Heaping them both with sandwiches, sausage rolls and mini quiches, he delivered the first to his grandad's table to a champion's welcome, then made his way to Eliza's corner.

The girls had claimed it as their own from the first day they'd been old enough to drink. He could vividly recall a rare weekend visit home from his training placement at the Cordon Bleu in Paris when he'd found them ensconced with a bottle of wine, filling the bar with laughter. They'd been home from their second year at university, and seeing them so grown-up had been a shock to the system. Though Eliza and her friends were only three years younger, the age gap between them had seemed huge growing up. When he'd thought about them, they'd been this amorphous collection of pigtails, terrible taste in pop music, and annoying interruptions. That weekend, they'd diverged into distinct personalities, and that age gap had narrowed considerably.

He'd found Beth particularly distracting, but that had been a moment of madness. A surge of youthful hormones, alcohol and opportunity. The bottle of wine the girls had split had been followed by several large vodka and tonics, leaving them all a little unsteady on their feet. Worried about the way she'd almost fallen out of the door, Sam had followed her out, almost tripping over himself thanks to several pints and an enormous brandy Pops had poured for him.

When he'd straightened up, she'd been standing on the railing that lined the edge of the promenade, arms flung out like she was Rose standing on the prow of the Titanic. With her hair streaming out behind her, and a flush on her cheeks from the booze and the chilly wind, she'd looked as tempting as the mermaid who decorated the pub's sign swinging over his head.

He'd crossed to her without thinking, her name on his lips. Startled, she'd turned too fast and lost her balance to tumble the short distance into his arms. It might have been all right if she hadn't hooked her arms around his neck, pressing their bodies up close so he couldn't fail to notice the womanly curves, the way his hands slotted perfectly at her waist, as though the sculpted indent had been carved to fit only him.

Her fingers had knotted in the curls at his nape, and then they were kissing, hot and wet and frantic—a clumsy clash of lips and tongues. God only knows what might have happened had Libby not staggered out of the bar at the moment to screech in disbelief at the sight of them. Her shocked laughter had doused his passion as effectively as a dip in the sea and Sam had come to his senses. With a muttered apology, he'd fled back into the pub and brushed it off as a stupid mistake. Thankfully, that brief flutter of attraction had passed, and he'd tucked her firmly back into the like-a-sister-to-me box where she belonged.

Sliding the plate onto the table, he studied their red-rimmed eyes with a surge of brotherly concern. 'I thought you might be hungry.'

Beth glanced up at him. Her hazel eyes, which could morph from brown to green to blue depending on her mood, stood out huge in her pale face. Her chestnut hair had been dragged up in a high ponytail, the strands dull and lifeless. A jut of collarbone he'd never noticed before poked out from the too-loose neck of her navy blouse, and he had to shove his hands in his pockets before she saw them clench into fists. Voice husky with tears, she thanked him for the food.

His lip twitched, wanting to curl into a snarl. Beth had been hooked up with the same bloke for a few years now, so where the hell was he? What kind of man let the woman he loved get herself in such a state? There was no sign of the glossy confidence she'd attained during his years at university. She looked hollow, brittle.

The protectiveness he'd felt for Beth since the day she'd first skipped into his life at six years old, roared into life. At the grand age of nine, he'd been told old for the silly games his sister and her best friends played in the yard behind the pub, so had restricted himself to a lofty sigh or a weary shake of his head when they needed him to fetch a ball or help them sketch out a hopscotch on the concrete floor of the yard. Even back then, they'd known he would do anything for them and his complaints fell on deaf ears.

Pops had never understood Sam's fascination with fancy cooking, and had taken it upon himself to teach him the workings of the pub, whether Sam had much interest in it or not. They'd been down in the cellar one morning checking the barrels and making a note of what they needed to order that week from the brewery, when a high-pitched cry had reached their ears. Racing up the cellar steps, Sam had burst into the yard to find a tear-stained Beth on her hands and knees where she'd tripped over.

He hadn't been able to do much more than stare into her limpid hazel eyes before his mum had bustled over with a flannel to soothe the grazes on Beth's palms and shins, but it had been enough for him to make a decision. With no brothers or sisters, Beth didn't have anyone else to look out for her, so it would be his job from that day forward. It was true that little Libby Stone was an only child as well, but she'd always been as tough as old boots and would likely thump Sam if he tried to pull any of that big brother stuff with her. Beth had always been more delicate, more in need of his protection. Something her feckless parents had failed to give her.

The adult version of Libby wasn't any less scrappy than the mini one, and right now she was eyeing Sam in a way that made him want to squirm, or scrub at the heat he could feel rising on the back of his neck. With a knowing smile, Libby snagged a sausage roll from the plate in front of Beth and popped it into her mouth. 'So kind of you to think of us, Sammy.'

Having witnessed that momentary indiscretion between Sam and Beth, she'd been like a dog with a bloody bone, reading far too much into a something-and-nothing of a kiss. They'd both managed to forget about it, so why couldn't she? Fixing her with a warning glare, he gathered their empty glasses. 'It's a big brother's job to look after his girls. I'll get you a refill, shall I?' Not waiting for an affirmative, he returned to the bar, ignoring the derisive snort behind his back that could only have come from Libby.

Eliza followed on his heels. 'Better make those spritzers, Sam, and heavy on the spritz or we'll all be crying again.'

He lifted the hatch to let her join him on the business side of the bar, pressing a kiss to the top of the unruly sandy curls they'd both inherited from Pops, through their dad. 'How are you holding up, kiddo?'

Her arm slid around his waist, and she burrowed deeper into his side. 'Bloody awful. Poor Beth, she's been so brave all week she had me fooled into thinking she was coping all right with losing Eleanor, but she's absolutely shattered.'

His attention strayed once again across the room. Libby had an arm around Beth's shoulders and their heads were pressed close together as they whispered about something. He saw Beth shake her head, followed by a frown from Libby as the willowy brunette slipped out from beneath her arm and headed towards the bar. A couple of people stopped her on her way, no doubt offering some condolence or other which she accepted with a gracious smile and a few words.

Unable to stop himself, Sam stepped around Eliza to intercept Beth on the threshold of the door leading to the private areas of the pub. 'Everything all right?'

'What? Oh, yes, fine thanks, Sam.' Jesus, could she hear the lie in her voice as clearly as he did? He ground his teeth to choke back the words, forcing a smile he knew wouldn't reach his eyes. Luckily, she was too distracted to notice much of anything. Holding up the phone in her hand, she gave him a rueful grin. 'I just need to check in with work, my boss keeps texting me.'

From the little he'd overheard the girls talking about him, her boss sounded like a right knob. 'I thought you were on leave?'

'Me too.' She shrugged. 'It's a bit noisy in here, you don't mind if I pop in the back?'

Freeing one hand, he pushed open the swing door to the family area. 'Help yourself. Mum's in the kitchen, and I think Dad's having a lie down so the lounge will be quiet.'

Beth placed one foot on the bottom step, then paused to glance back at him. 'Thanks. I might go out in the yard, I could do with a bit of fresh air.'

'Of course.' Sam grabbed his jacket from the peg by the back door. 'Here, put this on, and mind your step. The sun doesn't get high enough this time of year so it's likely to still be icy in a few spots.'

A more natural smile played upon her lips, but she let him help her into the coat without protest. 'Thank you.'

The thick length of her hair was caught in the collar. He unhooked it, his fingers accidentally brushing against the nape of her neck. She froze at the unexpected caress, and feeling ten types of awkward himself, Sam tweaked her nose just as he had when she'd been a little girl. The weird tension between them snapped and she gave a little giggle.

He zipped the jacket up to her chin until she was all but swallowed up by the padded material. 'Don't get cold, all right? I'll see if Eliza can give me a hand rounding people up. They've all had a good feed and a couple of drinks on the house by now. More than enough to pay their respects.'

Her shoulders drooped, as though the promise of not having to face any more well-wishers had drained the last of her reserves. 'If you could, I'd appreciate it. I'm . . . I'm about at the end of my tether.' The hitch in her voice scrapped him raw. For all Eleanor meant to him, she'd been Beth's guardian and primary carer for the best part of ten years now.

Her features crumpled for a second before she forced her eyes wide open and heaved a breath. If she needed to be strong, to stand on her own two feet for just a bit longer, he would have to let her. Even if it felt like he'd swallowed a handful of glass. 'Consider it done, Princess.'

Growing up, the three girls had played elaborate games of dress-up. Eliza and Beth had always been princesses. They'd rope Sam in whenever they could, but never to play the heroic prince— that had been Libby's role. No, Sam had been relegated to playing the bad guy, a dragon to be slain by Libby's sword or an evil robber baron intent on stealing the kingdom. The flashback to those childhood days did the trick, just as he'd hoped and they both laughed. Her spine straightened, and she tilted her neck in a haughty angle as she gave him a mock-dismissive wave.

He nodded his head towards the door. 'Go and make your

call, and when you come back, I'll make you something special. Tequila Sunrise, perhaps?' The girls had snuck down to the bar one night when they'd been all of fifteen and experimented with cocktails, to their eternal regret and the permanent detriment of the bathroom carpet.

Beth pulled a face. 'Don't ever mention those again! Just when I start thinking you're a nice man, Samuel Barnes, you go and ruin it.' She was laughing though, and the smile she gave him was as soft as the words were harsh. A blast of cold air sent a shiver through him, so he shut the door behind her and nipped upstairs to let his mum know he was going to try and wind the afternoon up.

With the remains of the buffet cleared and the last few stragglers having at least moved closer to the exit, Sam made a start with wiping down the dark wood tables, one eye fixed on the door to the back. It had been at least twenty minutes since Beth had stepped outside and she'd yet to appear, leaving him in a quandary. He'd always acted on instinct, making decisions based on his gut, and it had served him well so far. His teachers had encouraged him towards university, advised him he could have his pick of subjects and tried to tempt him with the world beyond the bay.

He'd always known what he wanted though—working in the pub had given him a taste for the hospitality industry, but he'd had no intention of following family tradition. There'd been a Barnes behind the bar of The Siren since the place first opened to serve the once-thriving fishing community at the turn of the previous century. Sam hadn't been satisfied with pulling pints and making hotpots, though. Rushing home from school, he'd eschewed cartoons for the multitude of celebrity chefs gracing the airwaves with their grand creations. Pops had uttered a few choice words, but his folks had been nothing but supportive and encouraged him to dream as big as he dared. They'd all assumed there'd be years ahead of them before any decisions would have to be made about the future of the pub.

He'd planned everything meticulously, working hard to get the grades he needed for his catering course of choice. Winning the placement at the Cordon Bleu in Paris had beyond his wildest dreams, and having gained his Grand Diplôme, he'd landed a gig at a top-flight London restaurant. Several years of insane hours in that high-pressure atmosphere had been enough to alter his initial plans and he'd put the feelers out until he'd found the perfect fit. Tim Bray had transformed an average hotel restaurant in a small market town on the East Coast into one of the most sought-after bookings in the country. Sam had spent the last three years working for Tim, soaking up everything he'd taught him like a sponge whilst harbouring dreams of a place of his own one day.

Then his dad had taken ill. A nasty chest infection over the summer had deteriorated into bronchitis and eventually to a diagnosis of chronic pulmonary disease. The doctor had pointed the finger firmly at Paul's upbringing in a busy, smoke-filled pub. With his condition worsening, Sam's mum had been running herself into the ground trying to care for him and keep the pub going, leaving Sam little choice.

Deciding to put the best face on things, he'd convinced himself that running a seaside pub would at least give him the management experience he needed if he was ever going to have a place of his own. The bay had gradually worked its magic on him, and his plans had once again taken a turn from their original path.

For now, he was stuck in limbo as his dad refused to accept the limitations of his disease and talked constantly of getting back in charge. Sam couldn't see it happening, but his mum had begged him to patient, to give Paul time to adjust to the new reality of things. She knew Sam couldn't stay forever, had promised they'd find a long-term solution for the pub soon. He had worked too hard on his training to be willing to settle for making pub grub for the rest of his days. Just a few more months, six at most, and then he could get his life back on track.

A burst of laughter came from Pops' table and Sam glanced over to spot Libby leaning against his grandad's shoulder, laughing at some no doubt unsuitable comment from him. With her peacock hair and a heart the size of a lion's, it was easy for people to gloss over what Libby had endured in her short life. Unlike the rest of them, she'd never had a chance to explore life beyond the bay and he found himself wondering what regrets she might harbour beneath her bold façade.

Catching him staring at her, Libby jammed her hands on her hips. 'What?'

With a grin at the challenge in her tone, he crossed the bar to ruffle his hand through the bright strands of her hair, a gesture she claimed to hate, but always let him get away with. The spiky mop stood up in all directions after his ministrations. 'You look like a bloody parrot.'

'Cheeky sod.' She poked her tongue out. 'Did you come over here for something other than to bother me?'

'Have you seen Beth?'

Libby shook her head. 'She went to make a call.' Standing on tiptoe, she glanced over his shoulder as though expecting to see her. 'Isn't she back yet? Let me go and find her.'

Placing a hand on her arm to restrain her, Sam shook his head. 'I'll do it. Can you do me a favour and see if you can get Pops moving? I'll be back in a minute to walk him back.'

A familiar speculation glittered in her eyes. 'I'll look after Pops. You see to Beth.'

'Libby . . .' It was his turn to offer a warning. Really, she just needed to give it a rest.

With an unrepentant grin, she turned towards the table and gave Pops a nudge. 'Come on, it's your lucky night, I'm walking you home.'

Grumbling, Pops got to his feet. 'I don't need a bloody babysitter, girl.'

'Oh, hush. We can raid the ice cream fridge at Dad's on the way back.' Libby reached behind Pops to help him with his coat.

26

Trust Libby to have an ace up her sleeve. Pop's eyes lit with anticipation. 'Any Magnums?'

She hooked her arm through his and Sam stepped forward to open the door for them. 'Almond, or Double Caramel?' Sending Sam a wink, Libby waited for Pops to negotiate the large step down onto the promenade.

Leaning out, Sam watched them totter up the street, their conversation drifting back to him on a cold breeze.

'You know the way to a man's heart, girl. How come some young fella hasn't snapped you up?'

'No one wants me, Pops. I'm too much trouble.'

'Bah, if I was fifty years younger, I'd snap you up. Lads today, don't know they're born.' With a shake of his head, Sam ducked back inside; Pops could charm the birds from the trees.

His mission to find Beth proved unnecessary. In the few moments he'd been outside, she'd reappeared in the bar and been collared by Walter Symonds, a local solicitor. He wasn't a frequent customer at The Siren, but Sam knew his parents used him for business matters, and for the power of attorney agreement they'd set up when Pops moved into Baycrest, the retirement home at the top of the promenade. There'd been an almighty row about it, mostly caused by his grandad's pride, but having encountered the realities of another resident with dementia, he'd soon changed his mind.

Whatever Walter had to say to Beth had left her nonplussed, going by the pensive expression she cast at his retreating back. Sam stepped to one side as the solicitor approached the door. 'Please pass my compliments to your mother, Samuel. Annie's done the community proud today.'

'I will, thank you. Have a good evening.' Sam crossed quickly to Beth's side. 'What did he want? He hasn't upset you, has he?'

Beth raised a hand to rub one side of her face. 'Mr Symonds? He's asked me to call and see him tomorrow. I told him I don't have the final costs together for the arrangements, but he said it's not about that.' She shrugged. 'He was a bit cryptic, to be honest. At least he's agreed to open the office early, I need to head back to London first thing. I've promised I'll be in the office by lunchtime.'

So soon? She looked dead on her feet. She hadn't stopped since arriving back in the bay. Surely a day or two more wouldn't do any harm? 'You're on annual leave, for God's sake! What's so bloody important that you have to drop everything and rush back?' His concern added a harder edge to his voice than he'd intended, and he regretted the outburst the second he saw her stricken expression. 'I'm sorry, the last thing you need is me adding to the stress of your day.' He touched the back of her hand. 'I'll leave you in peace, give us a shout if there's anything you need.'

Her fingers closed around his for a second before her hand fell away. 'I'm . . . I'm so tired.' The words were barely a whisper, more an aside to herself than anything directed at him. She inched up the next couple of steps. 'I've got a busy day tomorrow, so I'm going to turn in. Thanks for your help today.' Turning on her heel, she hurried up the rest of the flight.

Someone needed to take care of her. With Eleanor gone, they'd all have to pitch in to make sure Beth understood she didn't have to cope with everything by herself.

28

Chapter Three

'I'm sorry, can you say that again?' The walls of Mr Symonds' office seemed to close in around her, and Beth tightened her grip on the bag in her lap.

The solicitor peered at her over the rims of his glasses. 'Miss Bishop has left everything to you, Beth. The shop, the flat above and all its contents, the contents of her savings and bank accounts. Everything.'

'But, why me? Surely there are some relations somewhere who are her proper heirs.' She knew Eleanor had been an only child—something they'd shared in common—but she was sure there'd been mention of some distant cousins . . .

'No one she'd had any contact with in a considerable period of time. Miss Bishop was of sound mind when she drew up her will, my dear, I can assure you it's all entirely legal and above board. She put all her affairs in order last year.' Mr Symonds removed the tortoiseshell framed glasses perched on the end of his nose and placed them on the blotter in front of him. 'I assumed it was something she might have mentioned to you, given the closeness between the two of you. I didn't mean to shock you like this.'

Assuming his request to meet had been to deal with a few

formalities and she'd be in and out, Beth had turned down Eliza's offer to accompany her. A decision she regretted now. She tried to swallow away the lump in her throat. 'We hadn't spoken much lately. Things have been very busy, and I wasn't aware she'd been unwell.' When the doctor had talked her through the events leading up to Eleanor's death, he'd mentioned her suffering from angina—something her old friend had singularly failed to mention to her. Whenever she'd asked after her health, Eleanor had sworn that beyond the usual aches and pains of old age she was fit as a fiddle. And Beth had taken it at face value.

'Would you like a cup of tea, my dear? You've gone quite pale.' She nodded and the solicitor all but leapt out of his high-backed leather chair to hurry to the kettle resting on a side table. Beth turned her head to stare out of the window and across the dark brown fields. Unlike the emporium and the pub, Mr Symonds' office was located off the seafront, facing across the rolling hills which gave the area its name. The barren soil would soon give way to green shoots, and later turn into a sea of purple in every hue from the palest lilac to a rich, imperial shade.

Closing her eyes, she pictured the lavender farm in full bloom, a heat haze shimmering over the fields carrying the heady scent of the plants on the breeze. The thing she loved about Lavender Bay more than anything was the smell of it—comforting and rich, with a unique tang from the salt air of the sea. She'd bought perfumes, oil burners, even pillow sprays back in London, but had never found anything close to matching it.

The rattle of a teaspoon against china disturbed her thoughts, and she opened her eyes to find Mr Symonds leaning over to place a cup and saucer in front of her. 'I've added milk, would you like a bit of sugar, too? Might make you feel better.'

She smiled at the genuine concern on his face. Poor man must get people blubbing and wailing all the time during appointments like this. 'No, I'm fine, thank you. Just a bit shocked, as you said. I . . . it never occurred to me for one moment that Eleanor intended me to inherit the shop, or anything else for that matter. I'm not quite sure what to do, to be honest. My life is in London.'

And what an amazing life it was. A disappointing job with a terrible boss, a single room in a rundown house in the suburbs. Such a far cry from the perfect flat, the perfect boyfriend, the perfect life she'd thought she'd had once. She was so far from her ambitions and expectations, and with no idea of how to get out of the rut. But no, they'd never been her ambitions or expectations, they'd been her mother's.

It had taken only a few days back in the bay to underline the fact that the people she socialised with in London were little more than acquaintances. The girls from the office, a couple of her housemates. They'd go for a drink or maybe a trip to the cinema occasionally, but if she never saw them again, she wouldn't feel the loss of their company. Not any more than they would hers, no doubt. It didn't matter how many times she told herself, and her friends, that she was over Charlie's betrayal, there was no denying the fact she hadn't moved on—only moved into hiding. The only people she cared for were Ravi and Callum, and half the time she felt like she was imposing on their good natures.

Mr Symonds settled back behind his desk, then pulled open one of the drawers to rummage inside. 'There's a letter from Eleanor which might help to explain things. I thought you might want to read it later, when you have some privacy.'

He placed the thick cream envelope on the desk between them, his hand hesitating over it for a moment, before he withdrew and folded his arms across his chest. 'I also feel I should let you know that I have a standing offer from an interested party regarding any property in the bay which may come up for sale.'

Beth blinked. 'Sale?'

'Well, yes. There's no mortgage entailed on the premises. If you did decide to sell it, you could realise a fair amount of money. We'd have to get you a proper valuation, of course, but this party is willing to offer five percent below market value for a quick settlement. There'd be no agent's fees to pay so you'd likely make more than if you listed it on the open market.'

Confused, Beth took a sip of her tea as she tried to sort through the fresh onslaught of information. It was hard to focus on anything other than the envelope containing Eleanor's last words to her, but she forced herself to try. 'Are you telling me someone has already offered to purchase the emporium?'

The solicitor steepled his fingers beneath his chin. 'No, not exactly. There's a developer chap who's keen to invest in the bay. He left me with an instruction to advise him of any property which becomes available on the promenade. I've made him aware the owner of the emporium has passed away, and he asked me to table the offer. There's no expectation, you understand, but I feel duty bound to pass this information on to you.'

And duty bound to collect the conveyancing fee on any sale, no doubt. Beth dismissed the uncharitable thought almost as soon as it arose. Mr Symonds had been nothing but kind to her since this whole terrible situation had started. As soon as he'd heard she was working on the arrangements, he'd told her the expenses would be covered by a funeral plan Eleanor had taken out, which had been a great relief. 'Can I have a little bit of time to think about things?'

'Yes. Yes, of course.' He opened the top drawer of his desk again, this time retrieving a business card. 'Give me a call next week.'

The promenade lay in the opposite direction to the train station, but Beth found herself moving on autopilot until she wound up standing opposite the emporium. The duck-egg blue signage board above the window was faded and flaking, with several of the gold embossed letters missing. Dirt obscured the bottom half of the plate glass and what stock she could see through the occluded window looked dusty and neglected. A pile of post lay scattered across the floor behind the door. Pressing her nose closer to the window, she could see past the dirt and cobwebs to a happier time.

She remembered standing in the shop just after her mother left for Florida, excitedly tearing the paper away from an enormous package Eleanor had presented her with. 'What on earth is it?'

Eleanor, resplendent in one of the bright floral dresses she favoured and the ever-present rope of pearls at her throat, smiled at the younger Beth. 'As soon as I saw it at the auction house, I simply had to have it.'

Beth smiled as she continued to unwrap the item. A flash of yellow, something darker nearer the top. She tapped her knuckles against it. Whatever it was, it was made of wood. After tearing free the last shreds of paper, she stepped back, mouth rounded in surprise. 'It's . . .' There were no words to describe what her eyes were showing her. Six feet tall if it was an inch, a giant banana curved from a square base, the ugliest carved monkey she'd ever seen clinging to the top of it. No, there were no words. None that she could say without hurting Eleanor's feelings at least. 'It's . . . unique.'

'Isn't it marvellous?' Eleanor clapped her hands together. 'We can stand it just inside the door, use it to display things.'

A woman's shrill voice interrupted her thoughts, dragging Beth back to the present. 'I hope they'll finally do something with this place.' The prim comment came from somewhere behind Beth.

Resentful of the intrusion, she turned to glare at the speaker. A middle-aged woman with an unfortunate perm and too much foundation smiled back at her. The scarf at her throat looked expensive, as did the camel-coloured wool coat she wore over a drab, calf-length skirt and sensible, heeled boots. She didn't know the woman, but thought she recognised her from the church the previous day.

There was still enough of the lessons in good behaviour drilled into her by Eleanor remaining that Beth forced herself to speak, though conversation was the last thing she wanted. 'Excuse me?'

Adjusting the handle of the leather handbag looped over her

forearm, the woman nodded at the emporium. 'I was just saying, I hope the new owners, whoever they are, do something about this place. Poor Eleanor, we all know she tried, but she was quite past it in the end. The place is an eyesore and really not in keeping with the tone we're aiming for.'

So much unpleasantness delivered with a pearly-white smile and a demure cock of the head. Beth barely knew where to start. 'And who is "we" exactly?'

'Oh, the Lavender Bay Improvement Society, of course. I'm Hester Bradshaw, chairwoman and founder.' She held out a hand tipped with neat, short nails painted in some neutral tone.

Beth stared at it, fighting the automatic response to shake hands. She wanted nothing to do with this woman, or her acid tongue. 'I wasn't aware the bay was in need of improvement. Excuse me, I have a train to catch.'

Undeterred, Hester settled into step beside her. 'Oh yes, the Major and I noticed when we moved here that things had been let go a bit. It's such a lovely part of the coast, and it benefits the whole community if we can improve the calibre of the visitors coming here.'

So, it was as she'd suspected. Mrs Bradshaw was a recent transplant to the bay. As Eleanor had been want to observe, it was always the incomers who wanted to change things. They only saw coastal towns and villages at their best, during the height of the summer season, and formed a romanticised ideal of life there. Once they made the move, they suddenly began to notice the peeling paint, the air of shabbiness brought on by slow years of decline and lack of investment. The residents of Lavender Bay had always maintained a sense of pride in their town, but it was almost impossible to compete with the all-inclusive cheap resorts on the continent that came with a lower cost of living and almost guaranteed sunshine.

Reaching the end of the promenade, Beth took a sharp turn to the left, increasing her pace as the street began to climb upwards. With any luck, she could outpace her unwanted companion.

Those boots of hers must've hidden a sturdy pair of calves, because Mrs Bradshaw continued to match her stride for stride. 'You know the area, do you?'

'Yes.' Goodness, if Eleanor could hear her, she'd be in trouble.

Impervious to her monosyllabic response, Mrs Bradshaw continued to prattle. 'I haven't seen you around the bay, and I like to think I know most people. I must say I was surprised to find a stranger so involved with the arrangements for Eleanor's funeral. The flowers weren't what I would have chosen, but you young people have such different ideas.'

Parking her wheeled suitcase, Beth forced a smile so false it made her mouth ache. 'Yellow roses were Eleanor's favourite which is why I chose them. She bought a bunch every week to decorate our kitchen table.'

Mrs Bradshaw blinked rapidly, her mouth opening and closing like a fish. 'Well. I hadn't realised that. The two of you were close then?'

Suddenly overwhelmed with the memory of a smiling Eleanor pulling a roast chicken out of the oven, Beth squeezed her eyes tight against a threatening flood of tears. When she could trust herself to speak, she opened them to find a look of sympathy on the other woman's face. She likely hadn't meant any harm, was probably one of those people who spoke without thinking through the consequences.

Beth owed her nothing, but knew Eleanor had valued kindness above all things. 'She practically raised me. Although I'd moved away, we were still very close.'

Mrs Bradshaw shook her head. 'I'm sorry, my dear. As the Major says, I'm inclined to let my tongue run away from me. I meant no offence.'

'It's all right. I hadn't noticed how the emporium had deteriorated. Hopefully, I can do something about that.' Though what she might do, she had no idea. Selling the place would be the wisest option, but she couldn't bring herself to think about it.

Taking her leave of a chastened Mrs Bradshaw, Beth made it past the smiling greeting of the guard at the ticket barrier and into a corner seat of the waiting train, before collapsing into a flurry of choked sobs. 'Oh, Eleanor.'

Agreeing to rush back to work had been a huge mistake, but the pressure from Darren had been unbearable, not to mention shaded with hints he'd have to reconsider his support for her application for a supervisory position. Gritty-eyed, she avoided the concern radiating from Ravi on the other side of the partition and tried to focus on the screen in front of her. The lines of text wavered so she clenched her fist beneath her desk until the pain from her nails digging into her palm distracted her from the need to cry.

Turning her attention back to the matter in hand, she worked her way through the trail of emails that had been flying back and forth. The clients had liked the presentation and returned with a long list of detailed questions about the proposed contract. A flicker of hope kindled in her stomach; they wouldn't have bothered to probe so deeply into the deal unless they were very interested. There was a lot of dross in the emails, but also some pertinent information for the response piece.

Scrolling back to the latest message, Beth highlighted all the text and dumped everything into a blank word document. The hubbub of conversations, ringing phones and the ever-present tap-tap of fingers on keyboards melted into the background as she began to work her way through, deleting the superfluous headers and footers, highlighting sections of text she thought she might need and annotating comments with the name of the contributor to ensure she didn't lose track. Warming to the task, she reached for her headphones and plugged them into her phone, clicking on a familiar playlist she knew by heart which would melt into the background.

Once she felt sufficiently caught up, she moved on to the draft response document Darren had tasked another member of their team to prepare. Scanning the first few paragraphs, Beth assumed she'd opened an early version of the file and stopped to double check their shared drive. With a sick feeling in her stomach, she tugged loose one of her earbuds and reached for the phone. 'Marco? I'm trying to find the latest version of the Sampson response doc.'

'Hello to you too, Beth.' She rolled her eyes to the ceiling at the snippiness in his voice. Marco had been with them only a few months, but was already Darren's blue-eyed boy. What he lacked in work ethic and ability, he more than made up for in sycophantic crawling. He deferred to Darren in everything and was one of his regular drinking buddies.

'Sorry, Marco. It's been a rough couple of days, you know.'

He sniffed. 'Yes, I do bloody know. You left us right in the shit when you buggered off without a word.'

'A very good friend of mine died, it's not like I was on holiday.' Beth swallowed the urge to snap further, terrified she'd break down and start crying again. 'If you could just confirm which version I should be working on, please.'

Marco sighed like she was asking him to sacrifice his first born. 'It's in the J: drive, version 1.3. Darren and I have put a lot of effort into it, so it shouldn't need much work, just the last couple of responses which came through overnight.'

Beth stared at the file extension name on the document in front of her. Shit. She would be better off starting from scratch, because there was no way she could do anything with the incoherent crap they'd cobbled together. 'Okay, thanks. Just remind me when this needs to go up to the director.' Crossing her fingers, she prayed she had at least another full day to fix the mess.

'It went up to Bruce earlier today. Like I said, it only needs a bit of tarting up.'

Beth swallowed a laugh at the way Marco dropped the name of the director of key accounts. As if he'd call him anything other than Mr Turner to his face, pompous git. The implication of his words sank in. The nonsense on her screen had been submitted to the director . . . She choked at the very idea.

Undeterred by her coughing, Marco continued to speak. 'Darren was well impressed with the amount of work I've put into it, so I used a bit of initiative.' Good God, he actually sounded pleased with himself. Wondering if it was worth putting a call into the director's office to try and intercept the email, she almost missed Marco's next boastful words. 'Between us, the boss has given me the head's up that the supervisor's job is as good as mine.'

Her vision narrowed as a strange roaring filled her ears. All that work she'd put in, all the late nights and weekends and for what? To be usurped by some useless idiot who knew how to suck up? Knowing she'd been silent too long, she forced herself to speak. 'Well, I guess I should offer you my congratulations.'

'Cheers, Beth. Don't worry, I won't make you call me Mr Travelli when you're reporting to me.' The nasty edge to his laugh made her stomach flutter, but thankfully he hung up before she had to respond further.

She replaced the receiver, picked it up again and dialled the first three digits of the extension for Nadia, Mr Turner's PA, before stopping. Why was she even bothering? She could make some excuse about the wrong file being sent, spend the rest of the afternoon trying to turn the rubbish in front of her into something halfway decent and get exactly zero bloody credit for it. Anger bubbled in her gut. After everything she'd done, this was how Darren repaid her loyalty? She stood so quickly her chair rolled back, causing the wheels to bang against the filing cabinet behind her desk.

'Everything all right, Beth?'

Turning to meet Ravi's concerned gaze, she shook her head. 'Not really, Rav. I need some fresh air.' Beth hurried over to retrieve her coat from the rack before he could press her for more details.

'Come on, come on . . .' Tapping her foot, she waited impatiently for the lift to arrive. Needing to keep moving, she was on the verge of abandoning her wait in favour of the fire escape beside it when the indicator bell dinged. The doors slid open, enveloping her in a waft of beer fumes and ribald laughter.

A man stepped backwards through the doors, intent on his conversation with the rest of the lift occupants and Beth was forced to side-step to avoid being banged into. She recognised the slicked-back hair, the dark suit with gangster-wide white stripes and her stomach lurched. 'Yeah, yeah, mate, I'm sure she said that.' His sarcastic drawl was greeted by another howl of laughter.

Beth reached for the handle for the stairwell door and had it halfway open when he spotted her. 'Hey, Beth. You finally decided to grace us with your presence then?'

Shoving a hand in her pocket, her fingers brushed against the crisp rectangle of the envelope containing Eleanor's letter. 'I need some fresh air.' She threw the comment back over her shoulder and took a step into the stairwell.

Darren barged his way through the door, his voice echoing loudly off the concrete walls. 'You must be joking, you can't have been at your desk more than five minutes. Bruce wants a copy of the response document ready for him to review tonight.'

Grabbing the handrail with her free hand, Beth backed down another couple of risers, wanting to put some distance between herself and the whole bloody mess. 'But Marco's already sent him a copy of the draft . . .'

Her team leader's face drained to an unpleasant shade she could only equate to the colour of lard. 'He did what?'

Beth shrugged. 'Maybe I got the wrong end of the stick, but I'm sure that's what he just told me.'

'Christ!' Darren spun on his heel, holding the door wide as he did so. 'Come on, come on. We need to get this sorted out.'

A strange sense of calm settled over her as Beth stood her ground. 'Did you promise Marco the supervisor's position?'

Her boss glanced back over his shoulder. 'I haven't got time for that now, we need to get this cock-up sorted out before Bruce sees that draft.' His lack of denial told her everything she needed to know. Stroking the edge of the envelope in her pocket, Beth took a deep breath as the full significance of her conversation with Mr Symonds sank into her exhausted brain. She had choices; options. Freedom.

Releasing the handrail, she trotted back up the stairs to a visible smile of relief from Darren. 'Good girl. Go and grab your laptop and meet me in my office. I'll try and head Bruce off at the pass.'

Beth watched him jog towards the tiny walled-off space in the corner before returning to her desk. She undocked the laptop, flicked off the monitor and tugged open her top drawer. A jumble of Cup-a-Soups, pens and sticky notes stared back at her and she slid it closed again then bent to collect her handbag. She'd come straight from the station, so her suitcase stood next to the window. Bag over her shoulder, laptop under her arm and the handle of her case in the opposite hand, she smiled across the partition at Ravi. 'I'll call you later.'

'Ooo-kay. You sure you're all right, mate?'

'Never better, I promise.'

Conscious of the stares following her, Beth marched towards Darren's office. Leaving her case outside, she approached his desk to dump her laptop on a pile of folders. She unhooked the ID card from around her neck and let the lanyard slither through her fingers.

'I've managed to intercept Marco's email, though I owe Janice a large G&T.' He glanced up from his screen. 'Well, pull up a chair then.'

'No.'

It took a few seconds for her refusal to register, and Beth could actually see the moment it dawned upon him. 'What did you say?'

'I said no. Nope. Pass. Uh-uh. Forget it. Not happening.' She couldn't stop the flush of heat surging over her skin, but she held her head high.

Darren rocked back in his chair, a flinty hardness settling in his eyes. 'Is this some kind of joke?'

'Working my arse off for an idiot like you for the past two years in the futile hope I'd one day earn a fraction of the respect you dish out to your drinking buddies and sycophants? Oh yes, it's a huge joke. A bloody laugh riot, and all at my expense. Well, no more. I quit.'

There was burning bridges, and there was dumping a gallon of petrol and aiming a flamethrower at it. Throwing up on his desk would only spoil the dramatic effect of her announcement so she gulped hard against the wave of panicked nausea.

His shiny face turned so red, she wondered for a moment if his head might pop under the pressure building beneath the skin. 'You can't fucking quit. If you take one step towards that door, I'll sack you.'

The panic melted away and, smiling, she took a deliberate pace backwards. 'Perfect. At least now I won't have to serve my notice. See ya.'

She made it across the office, the echoes of Darren's ineffectual bellowing ringing in her ears, down in the lift, across the lobby and halfway down the street before the first tear dripped hot upon her cheek.

Chapter Four

1st January

My dearest Beth,

I'm sitting in the window seat as I write this, listening to the waves on the shingle below. Thankfully, the Lavender Bay fireworks display was much less impressive than that malarkey on the telly, so it's silent as the grave now. Funny how we use phrases like that without a second's thought to their true meaning, isn't it?

I know what you're thinking, and yes, I'm properly wrapped up, Miss Fusspot. I've got that beautiful, soft throw you sent me for Christmas tucked around me and I'm snug as a bug. You shouldn't have bothered, you know, but I'm glad you did none the less. You should be saving your pennies, not wasting them on me. And it will be a waste because I'll not get much use from it . . . but enough of that for now.

It won't be midnight yet where you are, will it? Here am I shivering in my slippers and I bet you've been cooking yourself on the beach all day. I hope you're having a lovely time in Florida with your mum. Whatever her faults, she always tried to do right by you so I'm trying not to resent her too much for stealing you away from me this once.

Our lovely Libby popped around to see me earlier. She's such a darling girl, even with that mad hair of hers. Honestly, Beth, you should see her—it's as scarlet as Santa's suit. Poor Mick, she does drive him to distraction with her appearance. I wonder if he understands it's all a front and beneath that hard shell she's more soft and vulnerable than either you or Eliza. I know you see it too, so you must promise to take good care of her when I'm gone.

And so I find myself coming back to the point again, no matter how hard I try to avoid it, because if you're reading this then it means my time is up. Hopefully, you won't be reading this letter any time soon, and I've just got a silly case of the new year blues, but there are things I want you to know, things I should have explained to you, but have never quite got around to.

Dr Walsh keeps telling me to slow down, but what's the point in that? We've been managing my angina for the past couple of years, and though the pills don't work like they used to, there's life in this old dog yet! He wants to me have surgery, but I can't abide the idea of being cut open like that, and there are lots of people more deserving of the over-stretched resources of our lovely NHS than an old biddy like me.

It's all right though, I'm quite ready. Oh, I shall miss you like the devil, and this place I've been lucky enough to call home for the past eighty-odd years, but I think I'm just about done.

I know you'll be sad, my darling, and I wish more than anything I could be there with you now to give you a hug. You've brought so much joy to my life, I bless God every day for bringing you into this world. I've missed you, and I don't say that to make you feel guilty, but it's the truth. I can't help but worry about you, Beth, because I know something's happened and I wish you would talk to me about it.

Libby let slip about Charlie, but I don't want to force you to talk about it, so we keep having those silly conversations when you tell me everything is fine, and I pretend to believe you. It's like you've lost your sunshine, and I know how that feels. Perhaps you think I'm too old to understand a heartbreak, but of all the things I've forgotten over my life, that pain is the one thing which never seems to fade.

And that's why I want to warn you, darling, not to let it take you over the way I once did until being on your own becomes a habit you cannot break. I loved him so much you see, so I never let myself get over it—and that's a regret I'll live with for whatever days and weeks remain to me. It might seem impossible now, but you must let the disappointment go. <u>Promise me</u>!

I'm going to be awful and make a dying request to you. I know it's self-indulgent and I'll play on your guilt if I have to, because this is important. Look for love, Beth. Keep your heart and your mind open, and don't let your fear of being hurt hold you back. Life's hard, it hurts so much sometimes it can be tempting to hide from it. Be as bold and vibrant as I know you can be, dearest, and know I'm looking down and cheering you on.

And so we come to the emporium. So many happy memories, I hope for you as well as me, but it's okay to let it go. I'm leaving it to you with no strings attached. Keep it if you wish, but don't you dare hang onto it just because you think that's what I'd want you to do. I'll come back and haunt the bloody place if you do!

If you are happy in London, then sell up with my blessing and use the money to give yourself a safety net. If you're not, then maybe consider giving the bay a second chance. There's so much to love about the place, so please think about coming home and letting it give you the comfort you need, even for a little while.

Right, enough rambling from me. I'm going to make myself a cup of cocoa, with as many marshmallows as I can cram into my mug. The best thing about this aging lark is I don't have to worry about my waistline anymore!

With all my very fondest love, now and always.

Eleanor xxx

Chapter Five

It was a crisp, cold morning, the type Sam knew from experience would draw walkers to the beach to watch the white-tops crashing over the rocks at the end of the bay. With any luck, the fresh salt air would encourage a few appetites. He made a mental note to stop in and see Pete at the butcher's to add some extras to the meat order. He could already smell the rich scent of gravy oozing from the steak and kidney puddings his mum could knock together in her sleep. If he wanted one of those puddings, he needed to get on with his morning run. After adjusting the thin wool gloves on his hands, he tugged a knit cap down over his curls and began to jog along the promenade.

Come rain or shine, he never missed his run. It helped to clear the cobwebs away and set him up for the day. His route took him along one half of the prom, past the wide windows of Baycrest's breakfast room where he turned up into the streets behind the seafront, around past the station and back down to the other end of the prom. The loop was a couple of miles in total and he loved the quiet solitude of the town before it woke for the day.

Slowing his pace as he approached Baycrest, he turned his head to check who was up and about. Pops was an early riser and this morning he was settled at one the small tables next to the window, sharing a pot of tea with Mrs Taylor. Sam had a theory about the pair of them, but he kept his face straight as he returned their waves of greeting and kept moving. Much as he'd adored his Nan, she'd passed a long time ago and if Pops could find some comfort in his twilight years, then good on him as far as Sam was concerned.

Halfway down Church Street, the hat and gloves were off, tucked inside the neck of his tracksuit top. Although it was too early for opening, the lights were on inside the butcher's shop and he knocked on the window to get Pete's attention. Bending at the waist whilst he waited for the older man to unlock the door, he stretched out his hamstrings with a few toe touches. The bell above the door rattled, and he straightened up with a smile. 'Morning, Pete.'

The butcher grinned. 'Morning, Sam lad. Bit of a brisk one this morning.'

Sam nodded. 'But clear as far as the eye can see so I'm hoping for a few extra drop-ins. Can you do me about three kilos of braising steak and a dozen lamb kidneys?'

Pete's eyes lit up. 'You going to talk your mum into making puddings for lunch?' When Sam nodded, the butcher grinned. 'Make sure you save us a plate, I'll be in around half one.'

'Sounds good. I'll join you if you don't mind and we can maybe run through the menus for the next couple of weeks?'

Pete stuck out his hand. 'Sounds good. Billy should be in within the next half hour, I'll get your order together and he can drop it in to you, if that works?' They still did things the old-fashioned way in Lavender Bay, and the butcher's young assistant could often be seen peddling around the streets on a bike with a huge basket mounted on the front of it packed with paper-wrapped parcels of meat.

'That would be a great help, thanks. We've got a new guest beer in, I'll stand you a pint.' With a wave, Sam picked up his pace once again.

By the time he turned the corner and began making his way back along the prom, he'd bumped into half a dozen local traders and sold them all on the promise of his mum's steak and kidney pudding. It was a tightrope sometimes balancing the needs of the locals with the influx of tourists, but his parents had always stressed the importance of maintaining a good network of contacts. They shopped local whenever possible, and that loyalty was returned in kind. Each encounter also drove home to him how much resistance he'd be facing when it came to any changes he wanted to make at the pub. Folks around here were plain and hearty, and liked their food the same way. So for now it would be steak and kidney pud, rather than the cassoulet of venison he might prefer to make.

Jogging over to the railing which separated the edge of the promenade from the short drop down to the beach, Sam propped his foot on the lower rail and bent over his knee to stretch out his calf. A few dog-walkers dotted the dark sand, but other than that it was quiet.

Switching his leg stretches to torso twists, Sam froze mid-movement when he spotted a light shining in the window of the emporium. The fate of the place had been the subject of much gossip and speculation, and he, along with the rest of the town, had been expecting a 'For Sale' sign to appear soon. Curious, he crossed the promenade to peer through the dirty glass. The dust covers had been removed from a couple of the display cabinets, the cloth pooled on the floor. He cupped his hands to his eyes, but there was no sign of life inside beyond the light and the signs of disturbance. He knocked on the window and waited.

The lack of response worried him—the bay had its fair share of drifters and troublemakers, what if one of them was looking to take advantage of the empty shop? He tested the handle, pausing when it turned easily in his palm to glance upwards. The old-fashioned brass bell still hung over the door and opening it would provide warning for whoever might be inside. Hopefully it would be enough to scare them away. Sam checked his pocket, found the reassuring shape of his phone and sucked in a deep breath. Using his shoulder, he shoved open the door sending the bell clanging wildly.

A loud thump, followed by a ripe curse in a familiar female voice, came from beneath the large wooden counter across the room. 'Ow, bollocks and shite!'

'Beth?' Sam hurried closer as her familiar auburn hair, coated in a fine layer of dust, appeared from beneath the counter. The delicate features of her face were scrunched into a frown.

'Sam? What the hell are you doing here?'

He couldn't help laughing at the fierce demand. 'Shouldn't that be my line?'

Pushing to her feet, Beth folded her arms over her chest. 'Considering you're the one trespassing in my shop, then no, it's most definitely my line.'

'Your . . .?' Mind reeling from the shock of seeing her so unexpectedly, it took him a moment of two to put the pieces together and then he wondered why he hadn't thought of it before. 'Eleanor left the emporium to you?'

Beth used the back of her hand to push a stray length of her hair back from her face, leaving a dirty streak high on her cheekbone in the process. 'Yes. I had no idea, but it was a gift I couldn't ignore and came at just the right time because I couldn't stick that job a moment longer.' Her eyes widened in horror and she clapped a hand to her cheek. 'Oh, God! That sounded awful, like I wished Eleanor dead or something.'

Tears pooled in her eyes and he reached out to cup her shoulders. 'Hush, now. It didn't sound anything of the sort. Were things really that bad?'

Beth nodded her head, sending the tears spilling over onto her cheeks. She sniffed, then laughed at the ungainly noise. 'I hated it. I never realised how much until I was standing in my boss's office telling him to get stuffed.'

Sam squeezed her shoulders. 'From what Eliza's told me about him, he deserved it.' He glanced around, taking in the dusty shelves, and the ridiculous wooden banana with the cheeky-faced monkey perched on the top. Everything his eyes touched upon reminded him of Eleanor, and he had to admire Beth's courage at taking the place on. How much harder must it be for her, having spent so many years working side by side with her old friend and mentor.

As though she heard his thoughts, Beth sighed. 'I don't know if I can face being here either, to be honest. Mr Symonds told me there's a buyer who's interested in the place and Eleanor said she wouldn't mind if I sold it . . .'

Sam frowned in confusion. 'I thought you said you didn't know she planned to leave the emporium to you?'

'Oh, I had no idea, but she wrote me a letter which she left with her will.' Her hand strayed to the pocket at her hip, as though she carried the letter with her. 'It's not just the shop, she left me everything.' Beth hung her head. 'But I'm not sure I can fill her shoes, or if I should even try.'

The raw pain was visible in every line of her body and Sam curled an arm around her back to draw her close against him. 'She believed in you, Beth. Was so proud of everything you've achieved. She was always full of your latest news when she dropped in next door for her sherry.'

Beth gave a bitter laugh. 'And what exactly have I achieved? A failed career, a failed relationship.' Well, that explained why she'd been on her own at the funeral. The air seemed to escape from her and she sagged against him for a few moments before straightening up again. 'I don't think I'm very good at anything, no matter how hard I try.'

This lacklustre, deflated attitude wasn't like Beth, and although he wouldn't say anything to her, it had him worried. She'd always been quiet, but he'd never known her to be lacking in confidence. 'You don't have to rush into making any decisions, do you?'

Taking a deep breath, she shook her head then stepped back to look at him. 'You're right. I can save the big decisions for another day. I'll focus on getting the place spruced up a bit and try and work out where everything stands. No one's going to notice much if the place isn't open before Easter.' Like a lot of seaside towns, Lavender Bay was heavily reliant on the influx of holidaymakers at peak seasons to make ends meet.

'Good idea. If you need help with anything, you only have to ask.'

'I'm sure you've got your hands full running things next door.' Beth drew her bottom lip between her teeth. 'I was so sorry about your dad. I didn't get much of a chance to speak to him when I was down, how is he?'

Sam set his hands on his hips as he scrubbed the toe of his trainer through the thin layer of dust coating the wooden floor of the shop. 'Miserable. Keeps trying to do too much which only sets him back.' It was his turn to bite his lip. 'I'm not sure it's going to work out me trying to run things when he won't give me any breathing space.' He cut himself off with a sharp gesture. 'Jesus, you don't need to listen to me whining, you've got enough on your plate.' If he started talking about all the doubts churning inside him, he might not stop. And he meant what he'd said, she had enough to deal with.

Beth looked like she wanted to protest, but to his relief she let it drop. Her eyes dropped to his trainers, then back up. 'Have you been out for a run? Bit brave of you in this cold wind.'

It was a lame attempt at changing the subject, but he grabbed at it with both hands. 'Yeah, I have a regular route around the town I do every day. I try and get out into the countryside a couple of times a month—Dad opens up on a Saturday morning which gives me some extra time. There's some great routes out beyond Gilbert's farm, you should come out with me.'

She planted her hands on her hips and cocked her head. 'Is that your idea of asking me on a date, Samuel Barnes?'

'You must be joking!' She'd mentioned the boyfriend was out of the scene, but she'd never shown any interest in him that way. Well, other than that one time . . . When she didn't respond, he feared he'd insulted her. 'Not that any man wouldn't be thrilled to go out with you, Beth. Not me, of course, that would just be weird. But other men . . .' Sam forced his jaw shut with a snap, though there was nothing to be done about the heat rising on his cheeks.

Gales of laughter met his blundering words, and he wasn't sure whether to be relieved or just a touch insulted. 'Oh, God, the look on your face!' Beth waved her hands helplessly as another paroxysm of giggles wracked her.

Abandoning any thought of salvaging his ego, Sam let the infectious bubbles of her laughter raise his own smile. The glimpse of the girl he knew was too good to resist, as was the chance to continue the conversation about them dating. Best to clear the air, make it clear they were both on the same page and all that. 'Come on now, Beth. You know a date with me would be a much classier affair than a run around the block. At the very least I'd shout you a saveloy and chips, maybe even an ice cream to follow.'

Clutching her clasped hands to her breast, she fluttered her eyelashes at him. 'You sure know how to spoil a girl.' She heaved a sigh and he was pleased to see the tension seep from her frame. 'And you always manage to make me feel better. Thank you.'

Sam sketched a bow, which no doubt looked ridiculous in a tracksuit. 'That's what I'm here for.' Her smile faltered a little, so he hurriedly changed the subject. 'So, has the place changed much since the last time you were working behind the counter?'

She shook her head. 'Not really. When I walked in and caught that first hint of Penhaligon's Bluebell perfume it was like I'd never left home.' Glancing over her shoulder, she looked towards the stock room behind the shop. 'I keep expecting Eleanor to step out from the back.'

'As soon as the clock hits five-thirty, I find myself reaching for the sherry,' he confessed, and she turned back to him with a laugh.

'For medicinal purposes only,' they said together, and he shook his head. Eleanor's death had left a huge hole in so many lives—his own included.

It was quiet now, but the Easter holidays were less than two months away and families would be piling onto the beach and strolling the promenade. The emporium was such a fixture of the town, he couldn't imagine it without the doors wide open, revolving stands of postcards and trinkets standing out front, and inflatables dangling from strings hooked over the ceiling beams. The children loved to jump up and try and head the balls, animals and bright rubber rings—it was a rite of passage for locals and visitors alike and no one had cheered louder than Eleanor when one of them leapt high enough to touch one.

If Beth decided running the place was too much to deal with, he hoped someone else would take it on. 'Do you know anything about the potential buyer you mentioned? Do they intend to keep the place as it is?'

Beth shook her head. 'Mr Symonds said they had a standing request for any kind of property that might come up.' Her brow furrowed. 'A developer, I think he said. If they didn't keep it as a shop, what do you think they might do?'

A heavy weight settled in his gut. A developer would be interested in only one thing when it came to a prime seafront location. 'Flats would be my guess.' There was a real demand for high-end apartments in seaside towns like Lavender Bay. He'd noticed on his return last year how things had already begun to change.

The collection of shops he remembered from his youth had been altered irretrievably. At least three of the traditional buildings along the prom had been converted into glass and steel monstrosities with oversized balconies. The traders' association had discussed lobbying the council to fight any future developers' plans, but investment was desperately needed so they walked a tightrope between wanting to preserve the special atmosphere of the seafront and the depressing sight of empty, boarded up buildings.

City folk with too much money and a desire for an ocean view were pushing the prices through the roof, making it increasingly difficult for the younger locals to get a foot on the property ladder. At twenty-eight, living with his mum and dad was not Sam's idea of a good time, but he had no other option. Dad needed assistance sometimes at night, and he couldn't in good conscious waste money on rent when there was a perfectly good room for him at the pub. He knew from a conversation they'd had before Christmas that Libby felt the same kind of frustration sharing the flat above the chip shop with her dad, and they weren't alone. At least Beth would have the luxury of privacy in the apartment above the emporium—not that she'd see it that way under the terrible circumstances.

A look of dismay crossed Beth's face. 'Oh, that would be awful. The place just wouldn't be the same without the emporium. I can't possibly sell it, if they're going to knock the place about.'

'Why don't you run it?' Yes, he'd told her to take her time before making any decisions, but the idea of having Beth on his doorstep once more was growing more appealing by the minute. She knew the town, knew how the shop ran and it wouldn't take her long to get back into the swing of things.

'Me?'

He nodded. 'Why not? There's nothing holding you to London anymore, is there?'

'Only a dingy bedsit.' Her eyes glanced upwards. 'It might need a bit of redecorating, but living upstairs would be a palace compared to my current digs.' He could see the idea begin to take root in her imagination, all she needed was a little bit of encouragement.

'It'd be worth a try, at least. And if you did decide to sell it, then showing it as a going concern would make it all that more attractive to potential purchasers.' He nudged her shoulder. 'Besides, if you're living here at least I can keep an eye on you, make sure you're not getting into any trouble.'

Beth laughed. 'Don't start that big brother rubbish, again. If you're going to be sticking your nose in, I'll sell the place to the next person who walks in the door!' The sweet smile she gave him took any sting out of the words, and Sam laughed as he held his hands up in mock surrender.

'All right, all right, I'll leave you to it.' He crossed back towards the door, and she followed on his heels. Once outside, he turned to face her. 'Come next door for your lunch, yeah? Mum will be chuffed to see you, and I'm going to talk her into making some steak and kidney puddings for lunch.'

She pulled a face. 'God, I hate kidney. I'll pass.'

The fine bones on her face stood out too prominently for his liking. A few homecooked meals certainly wouldn't go astray and he knew his mum would make a fuss over Beth. 'I'll get her to make one with mushrooms instead of kidney, that suit you?'

Beth shook her head with a rueful smile. 'You're not going to take no for an answer, are you?'

Sam grinned. 'If you don't say yes, I'll set Libby on you.'

It was her turn to hold her hands up. 'Lord, no! She's going to be furious as it is because I didn't tell her I was coming back to the bay. Didn't even know myself until I was slinging stuff into a suitcase and booking a ticket last night.' She leaned out the door of the shop, casting a furtive glance up the prom as though expecting to see her friend marching towards them. 'I'd better give her a ring.'

'I'll leave you to it.' He fished out his keys and took the handful of steps to the entrance to the pub. When he glanced over his shoulder, she was leaning against the frame of the door, arms folded across her chest. The canopy above cast her face in shadow, leaving her expression unreadable.

A quick check of his watch told him he'd better get a move on if he wanted to get everything ready before they opened up for the day. He jogged up the stairs to where the family's private rooms covered the upper two floors of the building. 'Mum?' he called. 'Are you busy?'

Annie Barnes poked her head out from the kitchen. Unlike the rest of them, she had ruler-straight hair which just brushed the tops of her shoulders. Years spent on the go running the place had kept her figure trim, though the late nights had etched dark rings beneath her brown eyes. 'Hello, love, what can I do for you?' She must have seen something in his expression because she stepped out onto the landing to face him. 'What have you been up to now?'

Sam hooked an arm around her shoulder and pressed a kiss to her temple. 'Drumming up a bit of business, that's all. I'm just going to jump in the shower.' The bell rang and they both glanced down the stairs. 'That'll be Billy. I thought we could add a special to the menu today.'

Annie raised an eyebrow. 'Oh, you did, did you?'

He pressed another kiss to her head. 'You know how much everyone loves your steak and kidney puddings.'

'Bloody hell. I was going to put my feet up and catch up on my soaps.' Sam laughed. His mum hardly ever watched the telly, and he doubted she'd seen an episode of *Eastenders* since Eliza had moved out. She rolled her eyes at him, but there was a twinkle in her eyes. 'Okay, but you're on prep so I'd better see you in the kitchen in five minutes at the latest.'

'You've got it boss.' He flicked her a little salute as he backed down the hall towards the bedroom. 'Oh, and make one of them steak and mushroom. Beth's back and I've promised her lunch.' He shut the bathroom door against the sudden barrage of questions. Once he'd had his shower, he'd give his sister a call and let her know about the offer to buy the emporium.

Beth had a lot of big decisions to make, she'd need her friends to talk to.

Beth was back, and maybe it was up to him, Libby and Eliza to give her reasons to stay.

Chapter Six

Beth had barely put the phone down before the bell over the front door was rattling and she found herself swept up in a peacock-coloured embrace. 'You're here, you're only bloody well here. Oh, God bless Eleanor!'

Libby's arms dropped away as she bent over to clutch her knees, panting for breath. 'Man, I need to get some exercise.'

'You should join Sam on his morning run.'

Her friend glanced up through the bright strands of her fringe. 'You've been here, what, twelve hours, and you already know what Sam does in the morning?' With her elfin features and an evil grin, Libby looked like a demonic pixie. Beth gave her a shove, sending her into a staggering laugh.

'Shut up! He stopped in a few minutes ago, I guess he must've seen the light on. Don't you ever get your mind out of the gutter?'

Libby shook her head. 'Nope. When there's so little action to be had around here, my dirty thoughts are all I have to keep me warm at night.'

Beth couldn't help but laugh. 'God, Libs, you're incorrigible. And besides this is Sam we're talking about.' She gave a shudder. Sam Barnes was like a brother to her, thinking about him like . . . well, like that didn't feel right. There'd been that embarrassing night when she'd thrown herself at him, but that had been the vodka and the moonlight. He'd thankfully forgotten all about it and they'd gone back to their comfortable, familiar friendship.

'Ah, yes. Sam with his broad shoulders, those beautiful curls just begging a woman to sink her fingers into and a bum so tight you could bounce a coin off it. We definitely shouldn't be thinking about a gorgeous, eligible bachelor like Sam.' Libby rolled her eyes.

An image of Sam in his jogging clothes from earlier came unbidden into Beth's mind. His hair had twisted all over the place, tossed by the wind and just a little damp around his face. The zipped-up hoodie he'd been wearing had covered his upper body, but his long shorts had displayed a pair of fine, muscled thighs and lean calves dusted in light hair. His blue eyes had sparkled with mirth when they'd laughed together, like the sea at the height of summer . . . She shook her head. 'I'm going to hell,' she groaned.

Libby slung an arm around her neck and winked at her. 'Well, at least you've already sampled the goods so you know he's a good kisser.'

Beth clamped her hands over her ears. 'La, la, la, la, I can't hear you.' They collapsed into giggles. Oh goodness, it felt good to laugh. When was the last time she'd let loose like this? Been comfortable enough to tease and be teased? She couldn't recall. When was the last time she'd been around people she could trust? Other than the funeral, it had to be when she was still with Charlie. Not that he'd proven himself to be trustworthy in the end. Anything but, in fact. A tight knot formed beneath her breastbone, leaving her almost breathless.

Libby paused mid-laugh. 'Hey, who burst your balloon?'

Beth bit her lip hard against the sting at the back of her eyes. 'It's nothing, really.' If she kept on telling herself that, maybe one of these days it might be true. 'Anyway, Ms Stone, I'm going to put the kettle on and we're going to put our feet up and have a chat.' She caught the mischievous glint in her friend's eye. 'But not about Sam and his skills as a kisser! That was a one-time aberration.'

'Pffft! You're no fun. You know I only get vicarious thrills these days.' It was said in good humour, but there was an edge to Libby's voice that unsettled Beth. She didn't like the idea of Libby being lonely.

Beth made herself busy, flipping on the kettle and opening the cupboard to hunt up a couple of mugs. Her hand hovered over the bone-china floral cup Eleanor had always used, sucking in a deep breath at a stab of fresh loss and pain. It had been like that since she'd let herself in the back door of the building the previous evening. She'd crept around the flat upstairs, feeling like an intruder and regretting her hasty decision to jump on a train. She'd slept in her old room, not able to face the master bedroom still cluttered with Eleanor's possessions.

A week lying around on her bed, staring at the damp patch in one corner of the ceiling hadn't produced any clarity so she'd hoped a change of scene might help. Quitting her job had been a stupid, impulsive move, but she couldn't bring herself to regret it. A few half-hearted web searches had produced a ream of vacancies for jobs she could do with her eyes closed, but she hadn't submitted her CV to a single one of them. It was like being suspended in jelly, or wrapped in cotton wool. Everything muffled and muted—one step removed from her reality. That one week had been all she could stand before the inertia had threatened to drive her up the wall.

Lavender Bay had been the obvious choice, but now she was here it felt wrong. London wasn't home anymore either, hadn't been since the day Charlie had sat her down and explained in calm, cool tones that their life together, the life she'd tried so hard to fit into, just wasn't working for him.

Beth was adrift, and she hated it. Her forehead thunked against the frame of the open cupboard. 'Tell me what to do.'

'Take out a mug, drop in a tea bag and pour the hot water over it.'

A strangled laugh escaped her. 'Oh, Libs.'

Warm arms encircled her waist. 'Take out a mug, drop in a tea bag and pour the hot water over it. One step at a time, Beth.'

She nodded, catching her forehead on a sharp edge where the lining on the cupboard had chipped away. 'Ouch.' Libby let her go and she stepped back, rubbing her forehead.

'Here, let me.' Libby reached past and grabbed the first two mugs, including the floral one.

'Not that one, it's Eleanor's . . .'

'Well, technically, it's yours now.' Libby set about making their drinks, squeezing the teabag in the floral cup until the liquid inside turned the perfect shade of creamy-brown. She thrust it at Beth. 'Here, take it.'

When Beth made no move to take it, Libby huffed in frustration. 'What is going on with you? I can't believe you've been sitting on all of this—' she waved the mug, causing a slop of tea to spill over the edge '—and you didn't say anything.' Libby turned away to dump the tea back onto the side of the small kitchenette. 'Shit. I'm sorry, I didn't mean to shout.'

'It's all right, we're all out of sorts, aren't we?' Sinking deeper into the chair, Beth wriggled her bottom to avoid the loose spring Eleanor had never got around to having fixed. She traced a pattern over the crocheted arm protectors, her fingers adopting the old habit without thought. Everywhere she looked, everything she touched was as commonplace to her as breathing. She knew this place. Being here could be easy if she only gave herself a chance, and if she could bear the weight of her grief.

Her thoughts drifted to an earlier conversation. 'Sam thinks I should reopen the emporium.'

'Oh, does he now?'

Beth rolled her head towards Libby, drawn by the sly humour in her tone. 'What?'

Libby blinked as though she couldn't believe why she was even asking. 'What do you mean what? This is Sam we're talking about. Of course, he wants you to reopen the place.'

Beth thought about it. If the pub was to continue to succeed, Sam needed the seafront at Lavender Bay to be as appealing as possible to visitors. It made sense, she supposed, that he would prefer to have an open, thriving business rather than a boarded-up shop, or noisy development works. Especially when the shop in question was right next door to his own establishment. 'I suppose it makes sense for him and the other owners on the prom to want the emporium open.'

Libby opened her mouth, closed it again, then shook her head. 'Yeah, that's why.' She settled into the chair opposite Beth. 'So, are you going to do it? It'd be nice to have you around again.' She held her hand out across the gap between their chairs. 'I've missed you, B. You and Eliza, both. Skype is great and all, but it's just not the same as you being here, you know?'

'Oh, Libs.' Beth took her hand, squeezing her fingers tight. What kind of a best friend was she to sit there bitching about things when she had so many options, and poor Libby had none? The early death of her mother had left Mick and Libby both devastated and they'd clung to each other. Libby felt responsible for her dad, and the chip shop didn't make enough money to both pay for her to go to university and hire a replacement for the many hours she put in behind the counter. Libs had laughed it off, saying the idea of more study was her idea of hell, but she must have resented not even having a choice about it.

A horrifying thought occurred to her. 'Did you hate us when we left?'

'What? No! Well, maybe a little bit. You were both having such a good time, making all these new friends, falling in love . . .'

Beth snorted. 'Yeah, and that worked out just bloody brilliantly, didn't it?'

'Hey, at least you were getting some action. What did I have, a few spotty boys more interested in a free bag of chips than getting off with me? And that hasn't improved over the years. Lavender Bay isn't exactly a hotbed of passion, so I've never even had the chance to get my heart broken. God, the last bloke I went out with, I didn't even like him, I just wanted someone to pay me some attention.'

'Oh, Libs, when was this?'

Libby shrugged. 'A couple of months ago, I got drunk in the pub. He was a travelling salesman, called Barry.' She covered her face with her hands and groaned. 'Barry. Oh, God, you should have seen him, all greased-back hair and groping fingers. I don't know what I was thinking.' Her friend dropped her hands with a laugh. 'And old too, he must have been thirty if he was a day.'

'Ancient,' Beth said, drily, thinking of their own impending birthdays. She and Libby were both spring babies, and would be turning twenty-five within a couple of weeks of each other. Eliza was a late summer child. One day later and she would've been in the year below them, and they wouldn't have the special bond the three of them shared.

'Well, he seemed old. Mature, like he might know what he was doing, you know?' Libby waved her hand vaguely. 'I was so drunk, and mad, and frustrated. I just wanted to feel special, for once in my boring bloody life, so I let him walk me home.'

Beth cast her mind back, remembering her own early days at uni, the constant seesaw of emotions between breathless anticipation and abject terror as every new boy she met was sized up as a potential date. Freshers' week had been a cocktail of hormones, vodka and terrible decisions, but there'd been some spectacular kisses too. Something else Libby had missed out on by staying home. 'So, how was it?'

Libby grinned. 'Technically, it was very good. Emotionally . . .' She heaved a sigh. 'It was a disaster. A total washout. You know like how the books talk about fireworks and flutterings?' Beth nodded. 'Well, not a thing. It was hardly more exciting than those practice kisses we used to do on our hands.'

Beth threw back her head and laughed. 'Oh my God, I'd forgotten about those!' They'd read somewhere in a teen magazine about a practice technique which involved making a mouth shape with thumb and forefinger. The three of them had slurped and snogged their hands, trying to work out the mechanics. Eliza had gone so far as to suck up a red mark and had to make up a story about banging herself on a desk at school after Annie spotted it. Thinking about Eliza inevitably drew her thoughts back to the original subject. 'What makes you so sure he wasn't just a bad kisser?'

'Because I've had some really bad kisses, and some pretty spectacular ones too. He knew his way around a pair of lips, trust me. It just felt empty, and a bit weird. I knew he expected more, and I almost felt like I should go back with him to his room.' A bleakness settled over her, and Beth worried about where the story was taking them. Libby's face brightened. 'Thankfully Dad chose that moment to put the rubbish out. Nothing like the sight of him with his dressing gown flapping around his knees to cool a man's ardour! I beat a hasty retreat and hid at home for the next few days until I knew his holiday had ended. After that, I kind of gave up trying.'

Libby pushed herself out of the chair and retrieved their cooling tea from the counter. She held out the floral mug to Beth, tutting when she hesitated. 'It's just a cup of tea, not a legally binding contract.'

Acceding to the point, Beth accepted the drink. 'I'm just not sure . . .'

Libby slipped back into her seat, crossing her legs so her body was angled towards Beth. 'What else are you going to do?'

'Well, there's this really interesting damp patch on the ceiling of my bedsit. In another few weeks it might reach the corner.' They laughed again. 'Truth is, I have no plan, no clue what I want to do and it's scaring me half to death.'

Her friend reached across, steadying the sudden shaking in

Beth's arm. 'Baby steps, B. Let's start with cleaning this place up and then we can go from there. I don't know about you, but all these dust covers are depressing the hell out of me. Eleanor would hate to see everything coated in dust.'

Beth nodded, dislodging a tear from her cheek which plopped into her cup. Damn, she needed to stop crying at the drop of a hat. Sucking in a deep breath, she dashed the rest of the moisture from her face and sat up straight. 'Right. You're right. Let's get this place spick and span.' A thought occurred to her. 'What about the chippy?'

Libby waved it off. 'Dad'll be fine to cover lunch.'

Lunch. She'd forgotten. 'Oh.'

'What?'

'Nothing, only Sam made me promise to go next door for lunch. Annie's doing steak and kidney puddings.'

'Yuck! You hate kidney almost as much as I do.' Libby pulled a face.

'He said he'd get her to make one with mushroom for me.' And wasn't that just like Sam, always making sure everyone got what they needed?

'Oh, is he now?' Libby said in a sing-song voice, a wide grin on her face.

Beth drained the last of her tea and stood up. 'Keep stirring like that and you'll need a wooden spoon.'

Libby stood up to join her. 'I'll settle for a duster for now.' She rummaged under the kitchen sink, giving a crow of triumph as she withdrew a long feather duster. 'Ooh, I've always wanted one of these. Those cobwebs don't stand a chance.'

Grabbing a packet of cleaning wipes, Beth followed her out onto the shop floor. Together they removed the rest of the dust covers, folding them carefully as opposed to her earlier half-hearted efforts when she'd just dragged them onto the floor. The glass-fronted cabinets and shelves looked exactly as she remembered, down to the placement of the contents. Souvenirs and

Libby winced. 'Me and my big mouth. I'm sorry, B, forget I even mentioned it.' She fiddled with the dial until she found a station full of the latest hits. 'That's more like it.' Libby shook her hips hard enough to give Beyoncé a run for a money as she brandished the feather duster.

The loud music was nothing Eleanor would've stood for more than two minutes. Beth swallowed away the lump in her throat. Trying to keep everything the way her old friend had had it would only make things worse. If she was going to think about running the place—even for a little while—she would have to put her own stamp on things. With the music blaring away, they set to on the floor and windows singing and laughing at the tops of their voices. As the dust cleared and the happy atmosphere settled, the old ghosts receded to their dark corners. For now.

Chapter Seven

'Where's the rest of the wine?' Sam frowned as the drayman from the brewery unloaded the last of the stock into the rear yard. 'I ordered two-dozen from the new quality range featured in the latest promotion.'

The man dumped a tray of soft drinks on top of the nearest stack then pushed back the cap on his head to scratch at his fringe. 'Didn't see nothing other than the usual wines on the manifest. Let me fetch it from the cab.'

'All right. I'll be back in sec.' With a lurking sense of suspicion Sam jogged inside and up the stairs. 'Dad, have you seen the orders folder?' He stuck his head around the corner of the kitchen door to find Paul sorting through the previous night's takings—the takings Sam had already tallied, checked and made up ready to pay in later. His gut tightened in annoyance at the sight.

Not making any attempt to disguise what he was doing, his dad waved his pen in the direction of an open folder on the other side of the table. 'Is there a problem?'

Sam started leafing through the paperwork. 'I'm not sure, I ordered some new wine but it's missing from the delivery.'

Paul capped his pen. 'Oh, I cancelled that. People don't want to waste their money on over-priced plonk. This isn't your fancy restaurant where customers will pay over the odds for a pretty label.'

'Jesus Christ.' Sam rubbed his forehead, trying to ease the headache he could feel brewing. 'And it didn't occur to you to mention that to me?'

'Mind your tone. It's still my name above the door to this place. And no, it didn't occur to me to tell you I'd cancelled it any more than it occurred to you to run the idea past me in the first place.'

Ouch. He had a point, but still . . . 'I talked to Mum about organising a gourmet evening, something a bit different to draw people in whilst it's quiet. When I saw the deal, it seemed like an ideal chance to get some decent wine in. I was going to plan the menu around it.'

'Hello?' A shout came from down below, cutting off whatever response his dad might have made.

'Shit. I left the drayman, hang on a minute.' Still seething with frustration, Sam ran back downstairs to apologise for the mix-up and sign off the delivery. He waved the man off, then secured the tall metal gates protecting the rear yard.

The stacks of cans, bottles and casks of beer seemed to mock him when he turned to face them. He should go upstairs and have it out with his dad, but in the mood they were both in, one or other of them was likely to say something they'd regret. A bit of manual labour would help him work off the edge of his temper. Unhooking the keys from his belt, Sam unlocked the double doors to the cellar and began to transfer the new stock down the short flight of steps.

He'd just about finished when the side door next to the rear gates opened and his mum came bustling through, a number of empty carrier bags folded in her hands. 'Well, that's Beth's freezer all stocked up. Good idea of yours to give her some of our leftovers, there was only half a lump of cheese and some tomatoes in her fridge. Some homecooked food will do her the power of good. She's making really good progress next door, I'm so proud of how well she's coping. Everything all right with you, love?' She beamed at him on her way inside, then suddenly drew to a stop. 'No, you're not all right if that thundercloud lurking on your brow is anything to go by.'

Sam couldn't help but smile. His mum had always had a funny term of phrase, and he hadn't heard that one for years. 'Just a misunderstanding with the stock, nothing to worry about.'

Annie picked up the manifest from the top of the last remaining stack. 'Did the brewery make a cock-up? That's not like them.'

Hefting a couple of the trays, Sam shook his head. 'Dad cancelled that new wine I talked to you about.'

'Oh. I see.' The edge of the manifest crumpled in her fist. 'Stubborn old fool.'

Arms aching, Sam put the trays back down then moved to give her a quick hug. 'It's okay. I should have talked to him about it.'

Annie patted his back. 'And he needs to recognise how much you've given up to help us, darling.' She looked up at him, the lines of strain on her cheeks clear at such proximity. 'I don't tell you often enough how much I appreciate it. How much we both appreciate it. I'll have a talk with him, okay?'

Sam nodded. 'We've been doing crisis management for what, six months now? There's too many blurred lines. I know he's finding it hard to deal with taking a back seat, but it's like he doesn't trust me to do anything.' And now he sounded like a whining child. He puffed out a breath. 'It'll be fine, Mum. I'll admit I was looking forward to playing around in the kitchen again, but it's no big deal. Don't say anything to Dad, yet.'

'Well, if you're sure . . .' Annie didn't sound convinced.

'I am. Let me have a think about things and then we can all sit down when tempers aren't running hot.'

'Okay, but not too long. I don't like seeing you unhappy.' She cupped his cheek. 'Please try and remember than none of this is about you. Your dad is so proud of you, and he's always been your biggest fan. We'll talk him around.'

Not feeling as confident as her about that, Sam made himself smile. 'Sure thing, Mum. I'll get the last of this stock sorted and then make a start in the bar.'

'Good boy.'

He shook his head. 'You're still going to be calling me that when I'm fifty, aren't you?'

Annie laughed. 'Of course. You and Eliza will always be my babies, even if I have to stand on a chair to look you in the eye these days.' She patted his hand before turning towards the back door. 'I'll fetch you a cup of tea in a bit.'

She was never going to stop fussing, so why fight it? 'Cheers, Mum.'

Although she'd promised not to say anything, it was clear from the sheepish looks his dad was casting him from his seat next to Pops that Annie had bent his ear. It was a quiet lunchtime, a few locals scattered around the place. Mind turning over how to tackle the problem with his dad, Sam polished a few glasses, one ear on the latest gossip being passed back and forth.

Things continued to move apace at the emporium, giving the locals plenty of gossip fodder. The latest talking point was the apparently shocking decision by Beth to repaint the emporium's window frames and front door in scarlet red. A new sign had been ordered, according to Pops, who'd heard it from one of his pals up at Baycrest whose nephew was a carpenter and joiner.

'I hear she's replacing the canopy as well.' Hester Bradshaw sniffed to show him what she thought of that as she and the Major waited for him to pour their usual gin and dubonnet and half an ale. 'I admit the place was looking very shabby, but I'm not sure red is quite the thing for Lavender Bay, do you, Ronnie?'

The Major harrumphed and stroked his fingers over his moustache. 'Not the thing at all. It'll look like a bloody stick of rock.'

'Or a tube of toothpaste,' she added through lips so tightly pursed they reminded Sam of a dog's rear-end. Giving her a non-committal smile, he wondered what she said out of earshot about the pub sign swinging over The Siren's front door. It had been commissioned by Pops, way back in the day, and if the namesake mermaid it featured didn't draw sailors to their doom with her beautiful voice, her generous boobs would certainly draw them off course.

His mum wandered in from the back to join him, lifting the tea towel from where it was draped over his shoulder and began to polish the already-spotless glasses waiting on the rack beneath the bar. 'Evening Hester, Ronnie, how are you this evening?'

'Mustn't grumble.' The Major raised his half-pint in salute and sucked the foam through his thick moustache.

'I was just telling your son about the new *colour scheme* next door.' Mrs Bradshaw whispered the two words as though she was saying something obscene.

Annie flicked her tea towel at a non-existent spot of dust, the gesture dismissive. 'Well, I for one think it looks wonderful. I'm delighted to see Beth making a few changes around the place. Hopefully her efforts will spur a few others into having a spruce up.' She turned to Sam. 'Speaking of which—it's about time our front had a makeover. I'm bored of that white everywhere. What do you say?'

He stroked his chin, pretending to give the matter serious consideration whilst he tried to disguise the grin tugging at his lips. His mum could be a right wind-up merchant when she got in the mood, and the sparkle in her eyes told him what she thought the Major and his interfering wife could go and do. 'I think you might be right, Mum. Something vibrant—a nice sunny yellow, perhaps? Or something bolder like an azure-blue.' He glanced towards Hester whose cheeks had turned an alarming shade. 'Puce, perhaps?'

His mum covered a laugh with a cough, giving him a nudge with her elbow as she leaned past him to grab another already-clean glass. 'Mmm . . . yellow. You could be onto something there, Sammy.

I'll have to have a chat with Emma up at Bunches and see about redesigning the baskets and pots. Lots of orange marigolds . . .'

Sam bit the inside of his cheek. The cascading floral display outside the pub was his mum's pride and joy. She spent hours planning the designs with her friend from the florist's and they were always subtle hues of lilac, pink and blue. If Hester stopped and thought about it for a moment, she would know Annie was pulling her leg. But that would require a sense of humour, something the woman sadly lacked.

The Major tucked his hand under his wife's elbow and steered her away from the bar before she had an apoplexy. She was still chuntering away about tasteful design and calling an emergency meeting of the improvement society, but Sam let it drift into the background. It seemed like everyone in town had an opinion on the changes Beth was making, perhaps it was time he checked it out for himself.

He turned to his mum. 'Will you be all right here for a bit on your own?'

She raised an eyebrow, but didn't say anything more than, 'Yes, love.'

On a whim, he took a detour upstairs to dig around in the freezer. His hand closed on a Tupperware box and he withdrew the delicate pistachio macarons he'd made a few weeks previously. Sam pushed against the wooden gate in the fence surrounding the rear of the emporium and was stopped short by the resisting lock. Pausing to rub his shoulder, he stared up at the back of the building. Eleanor had never kept the gate bolted, but he should have thought that Beth might do so. The first-floor sash window had been pushed up and the strains of a radio competed with a metallic bang and the kind of language even Pops might blush at.

The swearing paused, and Sam cupped his free hand to his mouth and called out. 'Hey, Beth, are you there?' It was a stupid question. Of course she was there, for there was no mistaking the slight husk in the stream of invective that followed.

'Useless, no good bloody bastard!' Beth shoved her head out the open window. Her normally shiny hair had been yanked up into an untidy knot, and there was not a scrap of make-up on her sweaty face. 'Whatever it is, Sam, I don't have time.'

Feeling abashed, he stepped back. 'Sorry, I just thought you might fancy a brew and a bit of a treat.' He held up the Tupperware container like a peace offering.

The deep frown between her brows softened. 'What's in the box?'

Sam shook his head, taken another couple of steps back towards the pub. 'Never mind. You're obviously busy so we can catch up some other time.' He turned away.

'What's. In. The. Bloody. Box?'

He bit his lip. He knew he had her, but forced himself to shrug. 'Just some macarons I baked the other . . .'

'Don't move! You stay right where you are, Sam Barnes!' He grinned—she'd always had a sweet tooth. Not ten seconds later he heard the soles of her shoes slapping against the cobbles of the back alley then the bolt scraped back.

The front of her T-shirt was soaking wet, the thin cotton moulding to her breasts. She followed his gaze, then quickly folded her arms across her chest. 'Sorry. I'm just having a spot of bother with the sink. You did say macarons, right?' Keeping one arm banded across her front, Beth reached with the other for the box in his hand.

Feeling like a letch for staring, Sam let her take it without resistance. She prised open the lid to inhale the rich scent of the sweets with a throaty moan that made the skin on the back of his neck prickle. His eyes strayed to the front of her wet top then skittered away. 'Having a spot of bother?' He waved a hand towards her saturated clothes, careful to keep his gaze fixed over her left shoulder.

'What?' Beth dragged her attention away from the macarons. 'Oh, shit, the sink!' Her trainers squelched as she turned and ran back towards the shop. Sam followed hard on her heels.

They hit the threshold of the upstairs kitchen together and stopped. The cupboards beneath the sink stood open, bottles of cleaning products and cloths scattered all over the place. A steady flow of water leaked from one of the pipes lining the back wall adding to the rapidly spreading pool which covered most of the black-and-white checked floor tiles. 'Jesus Christ, what happened?'

'The dishwasher wasn't working properly, so I tried to check the connections, but the tap has seized. I thought I'd turned the stopcock the right way.' Her explanation ended in a small wail of despair. Sam edged past her, feet splish-splashing through the puddle. Knowing there was no other way around it, he grit his teeth in preparation for the shock of the cold and sat down in the water so he could lie back in the cupboard and examine the problem.

The on-off tap for the cold-water pipe was stuck fast, as she'd said. 'Shit.' He ran his eyes frantically over everything, trying to trace the pipe back to the source. The stopcock Beth had mentioned was wedged in the far corner and there was too much crap on the shelves between him and it.

Sam dragged his eyes from the tangle of pipes to see Beth still hovering in the doorway. 'Look, this will take me a minute or two. You'd better grab some towels to mop up before the water starts soaking into the carpet out there.'

'What? Oh, God!' Beth stared down at the rapidly spreading puddle for a second then dashed away.

Using his arms to sweep the bottles aside, Sam wriggled out of the cupboard and back into the other side. His fingers closed on the stopcock, and he muttered a prayer of thanks as, after a grunt of effort, it gave way in his grasp and the hiss of water from the pipe slowed, then stopped. He dropped his head back in relief, cursing as the cold water soaked into his hair.

Sliding back out, he narrowly missed cracking his head on the edge of the shelf as Beth dashed back into the room to throw an armful of bath towels onto the floor. Dropping on her hands and knees, she spread them out, the pale pastel shades deepening in seconds as the towels absorbed the worst of the water. She sat back on her knees with a sigh of defeat. 'This is hopeless. I'm hopeless.'

'Nonsense. A small plumbing mishap is hardly an excuse to throw a pity party. You've taken on an awful lot with this place, so it will take a while to get your head around everything.' Ignoring the uncomfortable chafe of wet denim against his legs, Sam crawled about on his hands and knees, using the towels to soak up the last of the water. With the worst of the mess sorted, he set about gathering them back up, holding the sopping wet bundle in his arms. 'Let's dump these in the bathtub and then we can wring them out.'

Beth led the way and Sam paused at the kitchen door until she'd cleared the hallway before rushing after her, trying not to drip too much water onto the carpet. He chucked the towels in the bath with a soggy thud, sending splashes up the tiled wall. 'I'll tell Dad you need a remedial class,' he said, hoping to get a laugh. Paul had insisted on teaching both him and Eliza the rudimentary basics of plumbing, car maintenance and anything else he could think of that they might need to know. Beth had joined in with a lot of the lessons.

She held her arms out to the sides. 'Look at the state of me. Oh Lord, look at the state of you! You're soaked through as well.'

Sam pushed the wet curls off his forehead. 'It's just a bit of water, no harm. Come on, grab the end of this and twist.' He held out the corner of one of the towels, then grabbed the other end. Working in opposite directions, they squeezed the worst of the water out, hooked it over the shower screen, repeating the action with the rest of them. 'They should be all right to go in the tumble dryer now.'

Beth shoved a loose strand of hair off her face. 'Thanks, Sam. Sorry to be a whiny baby earlier. You're very good at all this practical stuff.'

He went to tuck his hands in the front pockets of his jeans, grimacing at the cold, wet denim. 'I've had lots of practice, after

76

so many years in all those different kitchens—and my fair share of cock-ups along the way. It must be the day for whining, I had a right session myself earlier.'

She cocked her head, concern drawing her brows together. 'Something wrong?'

'Just a few stresses with Dad, that's all.'

Beth laughed. 'Let me get changed and stick the kettle on and we can commiserate together, yeah?'

'Sounds good. Can you lend me a towel to dry off ?'

Beth winced. 'Those are all the towels from the airing cupboard, sorry. Hold on a sec, I'll grab you something to put on and we can put your stuff in the dryer.'

It would probably be as easy to nip home and change, but she was gone before the thought occurred to him. Oh, well. He tugged off his sodden T-shirt and began to wring it out over the bath. 'Here, you can use thi . . .' He turned as Beth's voice trailed off to find her holding out an oversized white bathrobe, her mouth open in a perfect 'o' shape.

Her eyes roamed down over his bare chest before flicking back to his face, the look of surprise on her face expanding as though suddenly realising what she'd done. A bright flash of colour heated her pale cheeks. 'Sorry, I'll leave you to it.' The robe dropped to the floor and she dashed back out.

There was no getting around it, Beth had definitely been checking him out. Not quite sure how to feel about it, especially given his own roving eyes earlier, Sam quickly stripped the rest of his clothes and tugged on the thick, fluffy robe. The luxuriant material drew the clammy cold from his skin in moments. After squeezing the worst of the wetness from his clothes, he folded them into a neat pile. Grabbing a hand towel from the railing to dry the back of his hair, he wandered out of the bathroom to see if he could make her blush again.

Having been in the flat numerous times over the years to help Eleanor out with one thing or another, he knew his way around.

Sam walked to the end of the hallway and tapped on the door to the master bedroom which stood slightly ajar. When there was no response, he eased it open a fraction wider and stopped dead. Other than a thin film of dust, nothing about the room had changed since Eleanor had occupied it.

A flannel night gown, the kind that buttoned to the neck and had elasticated frills on the sleeves lay across the end of the floral bedspread. He could recall the one and only time he'd been in the room—to reseal the edge of the window when it had begun to leak the previous winter. Eleanor had scoffed at him when he'd asked her where her duvet was, insisting sheets and blankets were preferable to being 'choked by some huge marshmallow monstrosity'. The plain flannel garment was about as far removed from something he could image Beth wearing as the fur-lined tapestry slippers sitting neatly beside the bed. The pots and jars on the dressing table looked untouched.

So where was Beth sleeping? Backtracking, he checked the larger of the two spare rooms and found it too dusty and unused, the mattress stripped bare, the pillows uncased. The third bedroom—a single with faded boy band posters still decorating the walls—had a neatly tucked in quilt on the bed and a suitcase on the floor, its contents spilling out into a small circle around it. What on earth was she doing, cramming herself in there? Utterly bemused, Sam made his way back to the kitchen.

Beth had found a mop from somewhere and was tackling the last of the water on the floor. Her own wet jeans had been replaced with a soft pair of yoga pants which clung invitingly to the delicious round curves of her bottom. The bathrobe did nothing to disguise his rising interest in the view she presented, so Sam side-stepped to shield his lower half behind a kitchen chair before speaking. 'Do you want me to stick these in the dryer?'

She set the mop aside and held out her hands. 'Here, I'll do it. I've already put my things in there. I got distracted clearing up. Can you put the kettle on whilst I sort this out?'

'Sure.' Sam made a pot of tea, then rescued the box containing the macarons from the hallway. Beth opened the window to hang the hot air pipe outside then switched on the dryer. She gathered cups mugs and plates from the cupboard and joined him at the table. He poured their tea, adding a splash of milk to his mug before doing the same to hers after Beth nodded. Her eyes strayed to the still-closed Tupperware box, and he placed a hand over the top of it. 'If you want one of these, you have to promise to be honest with me about a few things.'

Her head shot up to meet his steady stare. 'Like what?'

'Like whether you regret giving up your life in London to run this place, and if you don't, why are you camped out in your old bedroom?'

A stubborn frown etched between her brows, and he thought for a moment she would refuse to answer. He knew what it was like to be thrown a curve ball by circumstances, and he didn't want her ending up feeling trapped the same way he had lately.

With a sigh she folded her arms and sat back in her chair, every line of her body rigid with tension. 'They'd better be bloody good macarons.'

Sam grinned then removed one from the box, placed it in the centre of a plate and slid it towards her. 'They're very good, I promise. The toast of Paris once upon a time.'

Beth rolled her eyes at his boast. He watched carefully as her teeth sank into the gooey treat. Her eyelashes fluttered, then closed as she chewed the small bite. She swallowed, and opened her eyes, her pupils dilated to fill most of the deep-brown irises. 'Oh, bloody hell. You weren't kidding.' She stuffed the other half of the macaron into her mouth.

The funny little noises she made had him crossing his legs under the table, and he slid the plate away from her. 'Right, if you want more then start talking.'

Chapter Eight

Feeling uncomfortable at his level of insight, it was on the tip of her tongue to tell Sam to mind his own business, but the taste of the macaron still lingered, and she knew just how stubborn he could be. If she wanted more of that pistachio heaven, she'd have to give him some information in return. She sipped at her tea whilst shuffling through possible answers in her mind. There had to be a way to satisfy his nosy big-brother instincts without baring her soul to him.

Placing her mug down, she folded her hands together on the table and looked at him. He had that one-eyebrow quirk thing going on which was straight out of Annie's playbook. 'You look just like your mum. Everyone makes the connection with your dad and Pops because of the hair and those eyes, but when it comes to bone structure and certain mannerisms I see much more of Annie in you.'

Sam raised both eyebrows this time, and she could tell she'd caught him off guard. 'I never really thought about it, but you're right. Eliza looks much more like Dad than I do.' He sat quietly for a few moments as though contemplating the idea before a look of determination narrowed his eyes. 'Nice distraction attempt, no macaron.'

She couldn't help but laugh. 'I honestly wasn't trying to put you off, you just had this expression which was pure Annie. I don't regret leaving London. There was an accumulation of things—Charlie dumping me back in the summer, Eleanor dying and leaving me this place, and everything at work coming to a head. I wasn't happy there anymore.'

'What happened with Charlie?'

Surprisingly, the question didn't bother her. After so many months of pain over the break-up, all that was left now was confusion. 'I'm not a hundred percent sure. Things seemed to be going all right, maybe we'd gone off the boil a bit, but isn't that what happens in most relationships after a while?' She stared into her tea. 'He came home one night and out of the blue told me it wasn't working for him. Packed a case and told me he'd give me a bit of time to find my own place then walked out the door.'

'And that's all he said? Wanker.' She had to smile at the outrage in his tone.

'I know it sounds ridiculous, but I was so blindsided by it I didn't know what to say until he was halfway out the door. I tried to contact him for a few days, but he ignored my calls and messages. It was his flat and the rent was way beyond my salary, so I found some digs and moved out.'

Sam reached across the table to grasp her hand. 'You must have been devastated. I had no idea.'

'Well, yes and no. I was shocked, of course, and it was difficult being on my own because most of the friends I'd made in London were through him, so I was cut adrift from them too. I told Eliza and Libby, and Mum.' She glanced up, saw the understanding in Sam's eyes and pulled a face. 'You can imagine how well that went down.'

'Things are still the same between you two, then?'

She nodded. 'Yup. Charlie had everything going for him as far as she was concerned, and I'd let him slip through my fingers.'

Beth buried her nose in the dregs of her now cold tea. Sam

81

was too damn easy to talk to. He'd always been this steady presence growing up, taking care of her just like he did Eliza. Like a favourite jumper, being around him always made her feel cosy and warm—comfortable. Charlie had never put her at ease in the same way, and she wondered if perhaps that had been part of the problem. 'Have you ever been in a situation where you feel like there's a private joke you're missing out on?'

Sam opened the box and placed another macaron on her plate. He took another one and lifted it up to study it. 'When I first moved to Paris, no one in the kitchen was allowed to speak to me in anything other than French. I'd done all right with it at school, but the leap from basic conversation to full-on technical discussions, especially in the high-pressure of a busy service, was a nightmare. After the first week I was ready to quit, but then one of the guys took pity on me and we went for a drink after work. Turned out he wanted to improve his English, so we used to meet up and teach other. If it hadn't been for him . . .'

'You speak French?' She couldn't keep the surprise out of her voice, then immediately felt like an idiot. Of course, he'd be able to speak it after living there for a year.

'Mais oui, mademoiselle.'

Bloody hell, that accent! A flush started at her toes and swept all the way up her body to set her cheeks on fire. Sam Barnes wasn't the sort of man who spoke to her in seductive French tones. Or maybe he was. She risked a quick glance at him, hoping her shock wasn't written all over her face. He'd always had those pretty eyes, but she'd taken them for granted, just part of a Sam-shaped whole.

Oh, God, if she wasn't careful, she would end up making a prize fool of herself. Lusting over the boy next door was not a sensible life plan, and that was what she needed. She'd spent too long trying to please everyone else—her mum, Charlie, that wanker Darren—it was time to stop being a passenger in her own life and take some control. Besides, Sam still saw her as a little girl with scraped knees who needed rescuing. Forcing her thoughts back to the topic in hand, she nibbled the edge of the macaron on her plate. 'When I met Charlie, he had this established group of friends, they'd grown up together, gone to the same fancy private school, their parents holidayed together—you know?'

Sam picked up his empty cup and rose to switch the kettle back on. Leaning against the board, he folded his arms then nodded to her. 'A kind of upmarket version of us lot?'

That brought a smile to her lips. 'Yeah, only they went to the Caribbean, not the beach on their doorstep. Anyway, we met not long after I moved to London, so I didn't really know anyone else. It was natural for us to socialise with them.' She stopped, not sure she was making much sense. No one had ever been unkind, though it had taken a while for a couple of the women in Charlie's circle to warm to her . . . 'They had these little conversational shortcuts, talked about people and places I didn't know. I know it was my own insecurities, but I never felt like I quite fit in.'

She studied the chipped ends of her fingernails; her perfect manicure had been the first thing to surrender under the onslaught of cleaning the shop floor had required. Making a mental note to visit the local beauty parlour to get them trimmed off, she accepted the refilled tea from Sam with a wonky smile. 'I thought coming back here would be better, but I'm not sure I fit in here anymore. It might be my name on the deeds now, but this place is still Eleanor's. I'm trying to get past it, which is why I thought the change in colour scheme would be a good idea. But now I can't bear to go out the front door and look at it because I think she would hate it if she was here. I tried to cancel the order for the sign and the new awning, but it's too late.' Beth let her head slump to the table.

The warm weight of his hand settled on her hair. 'Didn't Eleanor say you should do whatever you want with the place?'

Beth nodded miserably.

'I took a peek before I came over and I think the red looks brilliant. A real zip of colour. You can't keep this place the same. Not without turning it into a mausoleum, and Eleanor would be horrified at that.'

She knew he was right, but still . . .

Sam squeezed her hand. 'Hester Bradshaw hates it.'

Beth lifted her head at the mention of the local busybody. 'Really?'

He nodded, solemnly. 'Really, really. Full on dog's bum pursed lips and puce-faced hates it.'

She was probably going straight to hell, but it made her feel much better. 'What about other people?'

'It's generated a lot of interest, you were the main topic of conversation over the bar at lunchtime.'

She shuddered, just imagining what some of the talk would be like, about how she was dishonouring Eleanor's memory by changing things so quickly. 'Oh, boy.'

'They'll move on soon enough. Once the season kicks off, there'll be plenty for them to talk about.' Her tummy did a funny flip because he wouldn't know it, but he'd hit on the next big thing that was keeping her up at night. Was she actually going to go through with opening the shop up?

The list of independent suppliers and artists she'd drawn up in a fit of enthusiasm sat unactioned beneath the counter downstairs. There was always something else to do, something more pressing on her time—or so she kept telling herself. The floors were spotless, the cabinets sparkling, windows sanded, washed and painted.

What she hadn't bothered to do was anything with the stock itself. She'd come across things on the shelves that needed getting rid of because of damage or age, but had found herself resolutely dusting them off and putting them back. Thinking about the stock meant really making a commitment to the place. All the cleaning and tidying up—and even the decorating—felt justifiable because it would increase the marketability of the place. She could pull the escape cord, put down the paint brushes and throw up a 'For Sale' sign tomorrow if she felt like it.

As though sensing the nerves and uncertainty bouncing around inside her, Sam placed his hand on top of hers. The touch steadied her, and she focused on the neatly trimmed ovals of his nails. They looked a damn sight better than hers, a result of all those years working in a kitchen she guessed, though he'd always taken pride in his appearance. He squeezed her fingers, bringing her rambling thoughts back to the problem at hand. 'I'm not ready to make a commitment.'

He laughed. 'That's a big step up from holding hands.'

It was the perfect thing to say to shake her out of the doldrums, and Beth couldn't help but smile. 'Silly bugger. I was talking about the emporium.' Although come to think of it, she really liked the feel of his hand on hers—warm, but not clammy. She turned hers over so they were palm to palm and he threaded his fingers through hers.

A perfect fit. Beth stared at their joined hands, watching with a kind of distant fascination as her thumb stroked the side of his finger almost of its own accord. 'How do you always know the right thing to say?'

'I wing it.'

It was her turn to shake her head this time. 'Don't do that. Don't deflect.'

Sam eyes deepened to a stormy blue-grey, and her world narrowed down to two points of connection—the intensity in his eyes and the warm heat of his hand in hers. Her breath caught, and she could feel all her good intentions crumble to dust.

His mouth opened, drawing her attention from his eyes to his lips and then he sat back in his chair, breaking an invisible thread between them as the action pulled their hands apart. He blinked and the storm in his eyes had passed, leaving only the calm cerulean-blue of the summer sea. 'I'm not the one who's deflecting. You still haven't told me why you're sleeping in your old room.'

Nonplussed, she tucked her hand into her lap, curling it into a ball as though she could keep hold of the sensation of the calluses on his palm pressing into her skin. 'If I pack Eleanor's things away then it's not just an acknowledgement that she's gone, it's me deciding to stay.'

Sam grunted, a small noise of understanding. 'I know what you mean. I came rushing back here when Dad got ill, and once it became clear his recovery would be limited, I let myself start to dream I could maybe make a future here. But he's not ready to let go and as selfish as it might sound, I'm not sure how much longer I can put my life on hold.'

Her heart ached at the raw pain in his voice. 'I don't think you're being selfish, at all. Is your dad's condition permanent then?' She remembered the many tearful conversations she'd had with Eliza when Paul had first fallen ill.

'It's manageable, if he follows the doctor's orders.' Clearly, that was a big if. 'His lungs are shot to pieces, so he won't ever get his fitness back to the level needed to run the pub. It's a really physical job.'

'You guys have been butting heads, I take it?'

He snorted. 'Like a pair of prize rams at the country fair.' Sam scrubbed at the tangle of curls on his forehead. 'I just wanted to try something a bit different, keep my eye in, but he was having none of it.'

Beth listened as he told her about his idea for a gourmet night and his dad's negative response. It was tough enough for her to make changes to the emporium with Eleanor gone. Trying to do it with Eleanor peering over her shoulder would be close to impossible. No wonder Sam was frustrated. And as for his dad . . . Paul had always been this vital presence when they'd been growing up—a big bear of a man whose booming laugh had seemed to fill the whole beach as he'd tossed them into the sea with endless patience for their cries of 'Again, again!'

She stood up and opened the tumble dryer. Scooping out the

tangle of warm clothing, she began to smooth and fold the material as she ordered her thoughts. 'It must be really hard for him.' When Sam frowned, she held up her hand. 'Let me finish. Your dad's always been a hands-on guy, the one everyone relied upon to fix things.' He'd moulded his son in the same vein. 'Having to sit back and watch you doing all the things he feels he should be able to do must be killing him. And then to have you making changes on top of that . . .'

Sam stood up so fast the legs of his chair scraped on the tiled floor. 'So what? I'm supposed to just fill in for him. Keep everything exactly the way it's always been? I'm suffocating!'

Hurrying over, she placed a hand on the thick towelling covering his heart. 'No! No, Sam, that's not what I'm saying, not at all.' She stroked the front of the dressing gown, trying to soothe his raw feelings. 'Maybe you can find a way to do what you want to without changing the essence of what The Siren is.'

His shoulders slumped. 'I don't see how that's possible.'

Neither did she. Returning to the laundry, she finished folding their clothes as she racked her brain for a solution. She pictured the pub in her mind's eye—the familiar layout of the main bar, the sprawl of rooms above that were a mixture of family rooms and guest accommodation, the old skittle alley where she, Eliza and Libby had played when bad weather kept them confined indoors. The wooden floor had been perfect for bouncing a ball or skipping on. Eliza's parents hadn't minded them scuffing up the place, it hadn't been used for years. Oh. 'What about the skittle alley?'

'What about it?' Frowning, he settled back into his chair and stared up at her.

Trying to contain the bubble of excitement growing in her belly, she clutched the pile of clothing in her arms against her chest and grinned. 'You could turn it into a restaurant. I can just see it! Those wooden floors resealed and buffed to a high shine; a smattering of tables for two with crisp white tablecloths. You could even use the old scoreboard to display the menu.'

His frown shifted into something more thoughtful. 'It's not very big.'

'That's the point! You could make it something really exclusive, a proper dining experience for discerning customers. Somewhere people go for special occasions. You'd still be on hand to help your folks with the heavy stuff, but you'd have your own baby too.'

His chair skidded back again, and Beth found herself wrapped in a bear hug. 'That's bloody brilliant!' Sam pulled back to look down at her, his blue eyes sparkling. 'You're bloody brilliant!' He smacked a kiss on her lips. The look in his eyes softened, warmed and his head lowered towards hers again.

Time seemed to slow down, as she watched the thick lashes framing his eyes sweep closed, felt the tickle of his exhaled breath tease over her skin and then, finally, the brushed of his lips over hers. Stunned, she waited to see what he'd do next. Waited for him to realise his mistake, to remember who she was—his sister's best friend.

When she didn't pull back, he seemed to take her quiescence as permission to kiss her again. A firmer contact which he stepped into and she tilted her head unconsciously to give him better access. Apparently satisfied with the angle, he settled in, fluttering tiny kisses at the corners of her mouth, teasing her lower lip with just the tip of his tongue, withdrawing every time she tried to chase the contact.

A corner of her mind urged her to stop, that there were a million reasons she shouldn't be letting Sam kiss her, but those objections were cancelled out by the warmth spreading through her, turning her veins to honey, curling her toes and scrambling her brains with the sheer rightness of his lips on hers.

The years fell away, and she was back on the promenade, the wind whipping her hair around her face, giddy from the fresh air and the warm promise of Samuel Barnes stealing the air from her lungs. Letting the bundle of clothes drop to the floor, she wriggled her arms free from between them and threw them around his neck, her fingers diving into the thick, unruly hair at his nape.

A soft groan escaped his throat and he tugged her closer until their bodies were pressed together from shoulder to knee. His hand slid from her back to gather the thick length of her ponytail as he tilted her back, the press of his mouth turning from a request to a demand. She couldn't think, couldn't do anything other than whisper his name as she opened for him and his tongue swept in. Her own grip shifted down to his shoulders and she clung to the broad strength in them, her knees threatening to give way.

Breaking for air, Sam's hot breath ghosted against her cheek. His lips followed, tracing a path to the sensitive skin beneath her ear, sending goose bumps shivering over her skin. 'Beth?' The way he said her name was a caress in itself.

'Yes.' She didn't care what he was asking, couldn't think beyond the racing of her heart, the pulse of need echoing in lower parts of her body.

'Beth?' The husky note of seduction was gone, replaced by something closer to disbelief. No, no, no, no, no. His hands released her hair, her hip and the entire front of her body felt a sudden chill as he stepped away. 'Oh hell, Beth, I'm sorry.'

He looked so shocked, she had to laugh even as she battled against a wave of disappointment and the tingling aftermath of the best kiss of her life. 'It's not as though you took advantage of me, Sam. I was right there with you.'

A smile quirked the corner of his mouth. 'Yeah, you sure were.'

Heat flooded through her at the appreciation in his tone, but he was already turning away from her as he adjusted the belt knotted around the waist of the bathrobe. Spotting his clothes in a heap on the floor, she swept them up and offered them to him when he glanced back at her.

He stretched his arm out to take them, as though he didn't trust himself to get too close to her again. 'I . . . I should probably get dressed.'

'Okay.' She spent the time whilst he was in the bathroom giving herself a pep talk. Yes, it had been an amazing kiss, but getting involved with Sam was a singularly bad idea. The emporium needed all of her focus, and if he decided to go forward with the idea to convert the skittle alley, he'd be flat-out as well. They'd never have time to see each other, and if things didn't work out, or if one or other of them decided against staying in the bay then there was just too much potential fallout. His folks . . . Eliza, their lives were too intertwined.

Sam rapped his knuckles on the door frame. 'I'm going to head home, I left Mum on her own behind the bar.'

Drying her hands on a tea towel, she crossed the kitchen to face him. 'Hey, are we okay?'

He reached out to hook a strand of hair behind her ear. 'Absolutely.' His fingers lingered on her cheek. 'It's terrible timing—'

Beth pressed a finger against his lips to cut him off. 'The worst.'

Capturing her hand, he pressed a kiss to her palm. 'If things were different . . .'

'But they're not.'

'No, they're not.'

He was still holding her hand, his thumb tracing distracting circles in her palm. She tugged it free, before she did something stupid. They were doing the right thing, the sensible thing. If she kept telling herself that, she might even believe it. 'So, are you going to talk to your dad about the skittle alley?'

'Definitely. Once I've had a chance to think it through. I don't want to rush into it and screw it up. I need to do some costings, maybe give my old boss a call and see what he thinks about it, talk to the bank.' He sounded hopefully, and whatever regrets she might have about this afternoon, she was thrilled to have been able to give him something to aim for.

'I don't have any expertise to offer, but I'm happy to act as a sounding board any time you want.'

Sam tucked his hands into the front pockets of his jeans and took a step back into the hallway. 'You'll be bored to death by the time I'm finished.'

'Never, and besides, I'll get my own back by talking to you about the qualities of souvenir tea towels.' They both laughed, and she was relieved to find it was easy between them again. This was what she needed, a shoulder to lean on, a friend to support her who she could support in return. And if she found herself feeling lonely, she could take her old teddy bear to bed.

Chapter Nine

Sam spent every night for the next week tossing and turning. When he wasn't thinking about ideas for the skittle alley, he was haunted by images of Beth blinking up at him, her brown eyes blurred with passion, her lips plump from the force of his kisses. *Stop it.* He'd deliberately avoiding going anywhere near the emporium, a few more days of distance and he'd have everything back under control.

The more he thought about creating a restaurant in the skittle alley beneath the pub, the more excited he was about it. He'd always wanted a place of his own, initially in London, because that's where most of the top-flight chefs made their mark. Working for Tim Bray had shown him there were other options. Tim's restaurant had turned the small town of Alderstone into one of the most popular places in Suffolk. What if Sam could do the same for Lavender Bay?

At first glance, the alley wasn't the most inviting of spaces, but he could turn that to his advantage. The lack of windows would allow him to design the perfect lighting system, which together with the right décor would create an other-worldly atmosphere. He wasn't in the market for a run-of-the-mill eatery, he wanted it to be a totally immersive experience, something people would talk about for days afterwards.

And it wouldn't be all style and no substance. The food itself would have to be exquisite. The very best of local ingredients, including lavender straight from Gilbert's Farm. A lavender and lemon sorbet to refresh and cleanse the palate between courses, or some delicate lavender shortbread bites served with coffee at the end of the meal. Though he loved all types of cooking, desserts were what truly made his heart sing. His training in Paris had included a placement at one of the top patisseries where he'd been taught to craft tiny morsels of perfection. The rest of the menu would be traditional dishes with a unique twist.

With hard work, and a dollop of good luck, he might even create a venue to catch the eye of the Michelin judges.

Dragging himself out of bed, he made a quick pass through the bathroom to brush his teeth, and his hair before dragging on his gym kit. Contrary to his best efforts, his mind was still fixated on Beth as he jogged downstairs ready to start his morning run. It was early, so she'd probably still be in bed. He bet she was a pillow-drooler, or a quilt-hog, or even worst of the worst, one of those women with permanently cold feet who insisted on sticking them against a man's back. He'd never been in the market for a serious relationship; after long hours at work the last thing he'd wanted was to go out to dinner or make a fancy meal, which too many girls expected when dating a chef. He definitely wasn't going to start now.

'What are you smirking at?' His mum asked as she met him at the bottom of the stairs. Something had obviously woken her up because her hair was completely flat on one side and sticking up on the other. She tugged the belt of her dressing gown more firmly around her and he couldn't help but grin more.

'Why are you up?' She'd still been in the kitchen prepping lunches for today when he'd staggered upstairs after closing the bar the previous night.

She glanced towards the door, then swallowed hard. 'Your dad's in the yard.'

93

His good humour vanished. 'Doing what?'

'He said he wanted to tidy up, was fed up of it being a mess out there.'

'For God's sake, why didn't you stop him?'

'Watch your tone, young man, he's still your father.' Annie tugged on her belt like she was considering removing it and throttling him with it. He'd seen her quell more than one potential fight with a steely-eyed glare and a strategically twisted ear, but he couldn't help his frustration.

He leaned down to brush a kiss on her cheek. 'I'm sorry. I'll go and see what he's up to and see if he'll let me help him.'

His mum nibbled her bottom lip, worry written large on her face. 'Be gentle, darling.'

'I promise.'

Taking a deep, calming breath, Sam swung open the back door and stepped out into the yard. A stack of empty barrels stood against one wall, waiting to be returned to the brewery. There were some wooden pallets nearby, scavenged by Sam because his mum had talked about adding some planters to the front of the pub and he'd had some idea he might be able to make them himself. A couple of broken chairs waited a trip to the local dump along with some other bits and pieces of rubbish. Not spotless, but nothing that anyone needed to worry about on a chilly morning.

Sam zipped up the neck of his tracksuit top and wandered over to where his dad was poking around in the junk pile. 'You're up early, Dad,' he said with his best smile.

Straightening up, Paul eyed him as though waiting for him to start fussing, but when Sam remained silent, he nudged the pile with his foot. 'Got fed up of looking at this crap and waiting for you to do something about it.'

Okay then. Propping one heel against the wall behind him, Sam folded his arms across his chest. 'This has to stop, Dad. You can't bitch at me for doing stuff without running every tiny detail past you then blame me if something doesn't get done on my own initiative.'

His dad snorted in disgust. 'You don't have to ask me if it's okay to make a trip to the dump.'

'Are you sure about that?' Sam closed his eyes for a second and reined in his flash of temper. 'I want to help you, Dad, that's the only reason I came back home—to help you.'

'I didn't ask you to do that! I didn't ask you to walk away from everything you've worked so hard for to end up behind the bar of some no-mark, backwater pub . . .' His dad trailed off into a fit of coughing, and Sam hurried over to offer him his arm to lean on.

When he was waved off, he reached instead for the pocket in his dad's sweatshirt and pulled out his inhaler. 'Here, use this.'

He backed off again, turning his attention to the pile of rubbish so his dad couldn't see him wincing at every harsh rack and sputter. The tension in his shoulders eased at the familiar puff of the inhaler and the ragged indrawn breath behind him. As he waited for his dad's breathing to settle down, he mulled over those angry, bitter words. Dad had always loved The Siren, had taken over the place from Pops with the delight of a man who was exactly where he wanted to be. To hear him denigrate the place broke Sam's heart and gave him a fresh insight into the problem between them.

Keeping his back turned, he traced the rough surface of the red-brick wall. 'I came home because I wanted to, Dad. Because I love you and Mum, and you needed some help.'

'You shouldn't have had to, though.' A familiar weight settled on his shoulder, and he reached up to pat the hand his dad placed on his shoulder.

Unable to bear the guilt in those words, Sam turned to face his dad. 'Shit happens. Life happens, and it's beyond our control. The only thing we can control, is how we deal with it.'

His dad shook his head. 'You put me to shame, lad.'

'Not really. I should have talked to you about this before instead of letting things fester like a prat.'

'I hear it runs in the family.' They both looked over to find Sam's mum standing on the back step shaking her head. 'If you've finished making a fool of yourself, Paul Barnes, perhaps you can apologise to our son and the two of you can come inside and talk things through properly.'

His dad laughed, not in the least bit offended, and slung his arm around Sam's shoulders. 'The boss has spoken, best we obey.'

They followed Annie back inside, but when his dad would have turned left to go upstairs, Sam stopped him. 'Can I show you something?'

'Of course.'

Sam led them through the bar to the side door leading down to the skittle alley. Flipping the lights on as he descended, he tried to keep a lid on the excitement bubbling inside him. After making his way to the centre of the narrow room, he turned in a circle arms raised to his sides. 'Welcome to Subterranean.'

The discussion with his dad about the restaurant couldn't have gone much better and he ran it over and over in his mind as his feet pounded out the regular route of his morning run. In his excitement over the potential new venture, Sam had forgotten all about his early morning thoughts of Beth until he was almost back at his doorstep and found her leaning against the shop doorway with a steaming cup in her hands. She looked better than the last time he'd seen her—the dark circles under her eyes had faded to soft smudges, and although her hair was pulled back, it was glossy in the morning sunlight. Full of exhilaration, he couldn't help but tease her. 'Waiting for me?'

She laughed. 'Only if you're in the mood for stock taking.'

Sam lifted his heel back to stretch his calf before his muscles cooled too much, 'Are you trying to lure me into the back room with you, Miss Reynolds?' God, he shouldn't be flirting with her, but it was too much fun watching the colour rise in her cheeks.

'I only want you for your body, Mr Barnes.' Losing grip on his raised leg, he almost toppled over in shock. Beth shook her head. 'Don't get excited, there are some boxes on the top shelves which I can't lift down. Goodness only knows how Eleanor got them up there in the first place.'

'So, I'm to be a beast of burden, is that it?' Sam grimaced, pretending to be disappointed. Or maybe he was only pretending to be pretending, he didn't know anymore.

Beth nodded. 'Pretty much.' She raised her mug and drained the contents. 'Oh, and bring me something tasty, whilst you're at it, those macarons are long gone. Don't take long, there's a lot to get through.' On that imperious instruction, she turned on her heel and marched back into the emporium without a backwards glance.

'Cheeky cow,' Sam said to the empty spot in the doorway, a grin splitting his face from ear to ear. Feeling incredibly buoyant after such a great start to his day, he headed back to the pub for a quick shower. Her timing was perfect, he'd be able to lend her a hand and tell her all about his latest plans.

Showered, changed and bearing a new Tupperware box containing half a dozen chocolate truffles and the same amount of peppermint fudge bites he'd made as sample ideas for petit fours, Sam cupped his hand to his eyes to peer inside the emporium window. Spotting Beth behind the counter, he tapped on the glass and she hurried over to let him in with a smile. 'I've been trying to make sense of the order books. I didn't get involved with a lot of that side of things when I worked for Eleanor, and her system is best described as unique.'

She locked the door behind him, then led the way back to the counter which was covered in a variety of ledgers, supplier catalogues and a couple of ring-binders. 'I want to convert everything to an electronic database, so I think I'm going to have to start from scratch and do a full stock count. I've started a spreadsheet so I can link everything to a supplier and make sure I have their correct stock reference codes.'

Sam pointed at the laptop, and when she nodded he pulled it closer to study the rows and columns she'd set up. 'Dad uses a software package the accountant recommended. It's probably geared up more towards the licensing trade, but she can probably point you in the direction of an off-the-shelf system that could work for you.'

'Thanks. It's on my list of things to look into, but I need to gather the raw data together in a way that makes sense to me.' Her hand waved over the open books and folders. 'I definitely need to get some professional advice on where things stand with the business though.' She sighed. 'I assumed I would be able to walk in and figure it out, told myself it couldn't possibly be more complicated than what I've been used to doing. Running a place like this single-handed is a lot tougher than I realised. I feel like I owe Eleanor an apology.'

'I know what you mean. It was a real eye-opener when I understood everything that went into running the pub. My folks always made it look so easy.' He chucked her under the chin. 'Don't be so hard on yourself, Beth. It's a steep learning curve, but nothing you won't be able to handle.'

'There you go again, finding exactly the right thing to say.'

Sam grinned. 'Let me try to go two-for-two; where're these boxes you want shifting?'

When they trooped into the stock room, it was clear she'd been hard at work already. Boxes were stacked in neat piles with an A4 sheet detailing the contents of those she'd checked and counted stuck to the top of each one. She pointed out those she wanted help with, and Sam could only be relieved she hadn't tried to move them herself when she carried over a rickety looking stepladder. 'Is that all you've got?'

She nodded. 'It's the only thing I could find. There used to be a little set of steps we could wheel around, but I can't find them anywhere.'

Testing the ladder, he found it more stable than appearances might suggest and risked climbing up another couple of steps. The shelves weren't too high for his six-foot frame, and he could reach the boxes with a rung to spare. He glanced down into Beth's anxious eyes. 'Just brace the bottom for me, will you? I want to see if any of these are heavy before we try and do anything with them.'

Beth leaned her weight into the bottom of the ladder, pressing against the back of his legs. 'Like this?'

'That'll work, thanks.' He checked each carton, found them light enough to move without straining and began to transfer those in easy reach to the shelf directly below. It might take a little longer, but would save him climbing up and down. Some still bore the label from the supplier so were easily identifiable as T-shirts, fridge magnets, that kind of thing, but a handful were unmarked.

They worked steadily for about half an hour until everything had been cleared down to a height at which Beth could access them for herself. Ignoring the labelled boxes, she settled cross-legged on the floor beside an array of mystery cartons, including one with just the word 'inflatables' scrawled across it. 'With any luck I'll be able to find something to replace that sorry-looking crocodile in here,' she said as she slit the seal with a safety knife.

Sam folded the ladder and set it away in the far corner to give them a bit more room, then hunkered down opposite her. The first box he opened was full of tea towels folded inside clear plastic bags which had been sealed with a supplier's sticky label. Following the system Beth had started, he counted the contents and wrote a detailed description on a sheet of paper which he then stuck to the top of the box. 'Like this?' He showed her, and she glanced up from the packages in her lap.

'Yes, perfect. Themed souvenirs are on the bottom shelf behind you, can you add it them?' She held up one of the sealed packages. 'I can't work out what these are, I suppose I'll have to open them.'

Sam moved his checked box then started on a second one, not paying close attention to Beth until she spoke again. 'What the hell is this?' She smoothed the plastic shape flat on the floor in front of her, then stared up at him with a puzzled frown. 'A sheep? What on earth does a sheep have to do with the seaside?'

Staring at the bright-blue make-up around the sheep's eye and the glossy red mouth, Sam started to get a bad feeling. An old schoolmate had invited him on his stag-do the previous year and had been given a blow-up sheep, complete with accessible orifices as a gag. They'd carried Flossy around all bloody night, and, if he wasn't mistaken, he was currently eye-to-eye with one of her flock mates.

'What's this pink one, do you think it's a pig?' Beth undid another package and shook out the crinkled pink plastic before he could stop her. 'Is that . . .? Oh my God, it is! It's a bloody blow-up doll!' She shrieked and threw the thing on the floor as though she'd been touching something contaminated.

The doll stared up at him with wide blank eyes making him want to look away, but it was hard to know which direction. Certainly not to his side where he could feel one of her flat, plastic legs draping over his hand, or downwards at the wrinkled circles of extra plastic which could be inflated to an impressive bosom. His shoulders started to shake with the force of holding in his laughter. What on earth had Eleanor been thinking?

There'd been some talk over the winter about whether the town should try and market itself towards the ever-growing trend for hen and stag weekends. The consensus had been against it, fearing the increase in noise, rubbish and potential for trouble would drive away their loyal patrons, some of whom were now bringing their own grandchildren for a traditional seaside getaway. The debate had raged for several weeks, and he'd gone as far as sitting down with his mum to discuss accommodation packages they might offer if the mood swung in that direction. Maybe Eleanor had done her own research . . . Oh, no, no, no! He was not going to think about his erstwhile neighbour with her penchant for florals and flannel contemplating the purchase of novelty sex toys.

Sliding the cold, clammy material off his fingers, he risked a peek up, worried he might burst out laughing. He found Beth studying the back of another package, reading what appeared to be a label. 'Somehow, I don't think this has anything to do with chickens, do you?'

She tossed the package into his lap and he stared down at the description. 'Fighting co—' he swallowed the last word with a snort. A hazy image from the stag night, one he'd long since banished, surfaced and he scrubbed a hand over his face to try and dispel the sudden blush heating his cheeks. 'Ah, no. Definitely not chickens.' He bit the inside of his cheek but there was no way to hold back the laughter. A strange wheezing noise escaped his throat, echoed by a squeak from Beth and the two of them collapsed.

'I . . . jus . . . where . . . oh, God.' Beth's failed attempt to form a sentence set them both off again.

Gasping for breath, Sam grabbed the deflated doll and posed it in front of him. Waving one floppy arm he held the limp head in front of his face and put on an affected falsetto. 'This is not in keeping with the Lavender Bay Improvement Society regulations. Just wait until the Major hears about this!'

'Don't, oh don't, please!' Beth covered her face with her hands, almost crying now.

Their mirth subsided eventually, and Sam made a vague attempt to fold up the doll, nose wrinkling at the stale, plasticky smell coming from it. He stuffed it out of the way then rubbed the tips of his fingers together to try and dispel the lingering feel of the cold material from his skin. 'Ugh, these things are gross.' He leaned back, bracing his weight on his hands behind him and folded his legs at the ankles. 'Want to hear something interesting?'

Beth snorted. 'Not if it has anything to do with a box of unmentionable inflatables!'

'Ha! Definitely nothing along those lines.' He explained to her about how his day had started and the subsequent discussion with his dad.

'Subterranean?' Beth's eyes were wide as saucers and he could see it had captured her imagination.

'I was trying to find something to fit the location, what with it being down in the basement. I want it to be more than a dining experience, I want it to be something that stimulates all the senses.' Grabbing a sheet of paper and the marker pen, he drew a rough sketch as he continued to talk. 'I want to cover the walls in some kind of simulated rock effect, stud them with crystals and mineral samples which will catch and refract the light from some uplighters studded in the floor.'

She edged closer, their heads almost touching as they peered at the piece of paper between them. 'Go on, what else?'

Sketching a long rectangle down the centre of the page, he added a dozen circles on either side. 'I want to divide the room with a fish tank. It'll provide additional ambient lighting as well as a beautiful visual display. I heard about an artist who creates these little boxes that are covered in curtains. The idea is you put a hand through and touch what's inside. Nothing gross, but it's still an adventure into the unknown.'

Beth shivered. 'I'm not sure I'd be brave enough to put my hand in.'

'Not everyone will, that's part of the experience though.'

'I get it. And the food will provide the biggest stimulation, right?'

She got it. Sam sighed in relief. 'Exactly. A combination of taste, smell, texture and visual delights. Speaking of which . . .' He looked around, seeking the box he'd brought with him. When he spotted it on the shelf above her head, he had an idea. 'Close your eyes a minute.'

'Why? What are you doing?' She did as he asked though.

Getting up, he fetched the box of petit fours then squatted next to here. 'Keep them closed now.'

'Sam . . .' A smile teased her lips, plumping her perfect cupid's bow. He dragged his eyes away, forcing himself to focus on the task at hand. Prying open a corner of the lid, he positioned the box beneath her nose. 'Breathe in.'

'Oh, oh wow.' Her voice was dreamy. 'That smells heavenly.' She licked her lips, as though anticipating the flavours to come, causing things inside him to tighten. *Get it together, Sam*, he told himself. He had to remember all the reasons why this would be a phenomenally bad idea, but the voice of reason was really starting to get on his nerves.

Setting the box down, he selected a square of fudge then raised it to press against her mouth. 'Open up.' He slipped the treat inside when she obeyed, watching intently as she chewed.

A line appeared on her forehead then smoothed out and her lashes fluttered. She took her time, long enough to set his nerves jangling, then opened her eyes. 'That might be the best thing I've ever had in my mouth.'

Her words sounded all kinds of dirty, and Sam surrendered to the need twisting inside him. A man could only resist so much. Ducking down, he captured her mouth beneath his own, savouring the lingering peppermint sweetness on her tongue when it curled around his. She withdrew on a sigh. 'If you serve all your female guests that way, Subterranean will be a surefire hit.'

Laughing, he rested his temple against hers. 'Tell me again this is a bad idea.'

'It's a bad idea.' She didn't sound any more certain about it than he felt though. Kissing Beth was becoming a habit he wasn't sure he knew how to break.

Chapter Ten

Beth opened the fridge to fetch the milk, and her eyes fixed on the plastic box on the shelf. Sam had left the rest of the petit fours for her to enjoy and she'd been rationing herself to one every day. There were only two left—one each of the fudge and the truffles. Every time she saw them, she was transported back to the dusty stock room floor and that kiss.

In spite of their mutual agreement to keep things on a friendly basis only, she'd found herself conjuring up ever-more ridiculous excuses to drop into the pub. So far she'd resisted the temptation. For nine whole days she'd pushed her tangle of feelings for him to the back of her mind, but her resolve weakened a little more each time she savoured one of the treats. 'Get it together, Beth,' she muttered, slamming the fridge closed with more force than strictly necessary.

She'd just finished her coffee and was perusing that morning's to-do list when the bell attached to the back gate buzzed. Hoping Sam's determination had cracked, she scampered down the stairs and unlocked the gate. 'Oh, it's you.' There was no hiding her disappointment.

'Gee, is that anyway to greet your best friend?' Libby smacked a quick kiss on her cheek. 'Annie should be right behind me.'

'Annie?'

'I'm here, darling.' Sam's mum appeared with a roll of black bin bags under her arm and a spotted scarf tying her hair back off her face. 'Well, let us in then, Beth, there's a good girl. We've a lot to get on with.'

Thoroughly confused, Beth stepped back, and the two women bustled past her and straight up the stairs. She hurried on their heels. 'Umm, not to seem rude or anything, but what are you doing here, exactly?'

It was Libby who answered her. 'We're staging an intervention, B. Sam mentioned to Annie about you sleeping in your old room, and she called me. I had to wait until my day off came around, but we're here to help you sort through Eleanor's things.'

'But . . .' Beth paused just outside the door to Eleanor's bedroom watching her friends survey the room with sad shakes of their heads.

'But what? I could brain you for being so daft. You're clearly finding it too tough to do this on your own, and you're too bloody pig-headed to ask us for help, so we're left with no choice.' Libby folded her arms, giving Beth a challenging look she remembered all too well. Libs was braced for a fight, and she wasn't sure she had the energy, or the will, to go toe-to-toe with her.

Ducking away from the confrontation, she crossed the room to fiddle with one of the Wedgwood figurines scattered across the dressing table. A thin layer of dust coated the little shepherdess, but other than that it was in flawless condition, without even a trace of wear on the gold edging around her crook.

They weren't at all to her taste, but Eleanor had collected them for years and they were too good to throw away. Selling them seemed a bit mercenary, so it had been easier to ignore them, along with everything else in the room. She carefully replaced the statue. There were just too many decisions to be made and she didn't feel equipped to tackle any of them. 'There didn't seem to be a lot of point doing anything in here when I haven't decided if I'm staying or not.'

The excuse sounded pathetic to her own ears, and Libby's snort told her exactly what she thought about it. Annie had apparently appointed herself 'good cop' because she curled an arm around Beth's shoulder to give her a hug. 'Come on now, lovey. You'll have to go through everything whatever you decide. Might as well be able to rest in comfort until you make up your mind. You should have a painting party, get some prosecco in and invite Eliza down for the weekend. She could probably do with an excuse to get away.'

Beth raised her eyebrows as she and Libby exchanged a look. They'd had a chat with their friend last week and she'd sounded her usual chirpy self. Or maybe Beth had been too caught up with everything to pay enough attention. Eliza had made a few passing comments, but she'd dismissed them as the usual ups and downs all couples went through. She ran a quick calculation in her head; Eliza was ripe for a dose of the seven-year itch. Still, if Annie was worried enough to mention it, then perhaps it was time to get her down, so they could have a proper conversation. 'What do you reckon, Libs?'

'I'll have to cover the early evening rush on Friday and Saturday, but Dad will pick up the slack for me.' A twinge of guilt hit Beth square in the gut. Running the fish and chip shop took a lot of work, and she didn't want to take advantage of her friend, or her father.

'I can get someone in. The guys who did the windows were brilliant.' It had become abundantly clear to Beth she had neither the experience or a steady enough hand to paint the exterior woodwork to a professional finish, so she'd recruited a local father-and-son team of decorators, whilst she'd confined herself to touching up a few faded spots around the shop floor itself. 'I'm sure they'd be able to knock this place into shape in no time.' She stared at the floral papered walls. Something neutral so potential buyers wouldn't be put off . . .

Libby gave her the evilest of eyes. 'Call me Madame Zelda and set me up a booth on the beach, 'cos I can read your mind. A splash of taupe, a dash of cream, nothing to tie you to the place. Well, bollocks to that.' She pulled a fistful of colour sample strips from her handbag and thrust them at Beth. 'We're going to make you feel at home, whether you like it or not.'

Annie laughed. 'Well, I might not have put it quite like that, but I agree. You need a space to call your own, lovey. And you certainly deserve it after everything you've been through.' She squeezed Beth's shoulders again. 'Oh, don't look so aggrieved. Eliza might be your best friend, but she's my little girl first. Whatever she tells me goes no further, but I worry about you.' She held out her hand to Libby. 'I worry about both of you, but at least our Libs is close enough to keep an eye on. With Eleanor gone you need a bit of cossetting, and that's what I'm here for.'

A warm glow spread through Beth at the sincerity in Annie's words. She was loved, and cared for and needed, so why keep fighting it? As the three of them settled into a slightly tearful group hug, Beth's thoughts drifted to Sam.

He'd arranged all of this—somehow understood exactly what she'd needed when she had no clue for herself. Even with everything on his plate, he'd taken the time to rally the troops. She could get used to having him take care of her if she wasn't careful.

Turning her thoughts away before they strayed too far back towards the kiss again, she began to clear the dressing table, wrapping each of the figurines carefully in some old packing paper Libby had produced from the store room and stowing them safely in a cardboard box. She could decide what to do about them—and Sam—another day.

Beth hefted the final box from the bedroom, hooking the door closed behind her with her foot before she made her way down the back stairs. The airy room had been emptied of everything but the largest furniture which she, Annie and Libby had shifted away from the walls between them. Old sheets had been draped over them and the bedframe to protect them.

Everything she wanted to keep was stored safely in the larger of the spare bedrooms, and the last of Eleanor's things had been delivered to the RNLI charity shop. There'd been a lot of tears over the past couple of days, but plenty of laughter and fond memories too. All that remained was an old, red suitcase containing what looked to be personal papers, an intricately carved jewellery box, and the Wedgwood figurines wrapped up in the box under her arm.

Entering the shop floor, she placed the carton on the counter and turned her attention to the empty mirror-backed cabinet which held pride of place behind it. A smiling woman reflected back at her, a woman who was looking towards the future at last.

Once she'd stopped getting in her own way, organising the emporium became a challenge, rather than a chore. Getting to grips with the stock had made things so much clearer and had spurred her into clearing the junk and damaged items from the shelves and re-organising the layout of things. She wanted to keep the flavour and charm which Eleanor had worked so hard to create, but needed to put her own stamp on things.

Banana monkey still held court beside the front door, in all his ugly, kitsch glory. His outstretched arm held a circular, revolving hanger draped with diaphanous scarves covered in pretty florals and bolder seashell designs.

The joiners had finished and erected the new signage above the main window, but she'd asked them to keep it covered for now. She'd also cleared the window displays and lowered the internal blinds so interested neighbours (read: busybodies and nosy parkers) couldn't see the changes being made. She had enough doubts of her own without a chorus of tart observations and helpful 'hints' from Hester Bradshaw and her cohorts. Smiling enigmatically and murmuring, 'Wait and see,' seemed to be working to hold most people at bay, but she'd have to make a start on dressing the windows soon.

She still didn't feel quite at home, although her back was

looking forward to sleeping in the big brass-framed bed rather than cramped onto the single in her old room. She needed to get in touch with her landlord in London and make arrangements for the rest of her things to be shipped, but that could wait. Giving up her bedsit still felt like a commitment too far. Finding somewhere within her budget had been a nightmare, and she'd need somewhere to go back to if things didn't work out as she hoped with the emporium.

The colours for the walls had been picked; a white with the palest hint of lilac for the three larger walls, and a dusky mauve-grey for the solid end wall. Her budget wouldn't stretch to new furniture, but Eliza was the queen of crafty things and after screaming 'Project!' with an alarming amount of enthusiasm during a Skype chat had promised to transform the dark wood chest of drawers, wardrobe and matching dresser. There was also a trip planned to the local household superstore to hunt for complementary accessories and accent pieces for the walls.

Beth knew when to fight and when to surrender to the superior knowledge of others, and when it came to anything creative, Eliza was the expert of the three of them. Whilst she'd still been struggling to get to grips with threading a sewing machine properly, Eliza had been turning out her own clothes. Knowing her friend would be insulted if Beth tried to pay her, she'd set aside some vintage pieces from Eleanor's wardrobe in the hopes Eliza would like them.

Humming to herself, she began to unwrap the figurines and position them on the cabinet shelves. The quirky little figures were perfect for the revamped design of the shop—a graceful hark back to a bygone age with a touch of artistry. She hadn't decided whether she would sell them or not, and the locked cabinet would be both the safest place and provide a daily reminder of Eleanor. Beth had nosed around a bit on eBay, and had been stunned at some of the asking prices. She adjusted the angle of the little shepherdess and smiled to herself. If Henry the Eighth and his six wives had been part of Eleanor's collection, she'd have been straight online trying to sell them! No, she'd wait and see if anyone showed an interest and then decide.

Closing the cabinet, she turned the key and tucked it away in the cash register then checked her watch. There would just be time for her to grab some lunch and double-check everything was ready for the weekend. Mick had arranged for cover for his daughter at the chip shop, so they would have two whole days to spend together. A quick glance around the shop assured her everything was in order and she headed back upstairs.

Without Annie's near-constant supply of meals, Beth might not have got through the past few weeks, and although she was grateful, it was past time to stand on her own two feet. Heating up a can of soup wasn't beyond her, and she'd started book-marking videos on YouTube with basic recipes she was pretty sure she could follow.

If she was going to start taking care of herself properly, she needed to get into a regular exercise routine too. Especially if she was going to be on her feet all day in the shop. In London, she'd had to walk past the gym on her route from the tube to her front door, so it had been simple enough to call in and slog on the cross-trainer a few times a week. Perhaps she should start joining Sam on his morning run. Once he'd seen her sweaty and red-faced a few times, he'd soon lose his enthusiasm for kissing her.

'It's so good to see you!' Eliza swept Beth into a warm, richly scented embrace then stepped back to look around the room. 'Wow! Look at this place. It's the same and yet, so different.' Her words were the exact ones Beth needed to hear and a knot loosened in her tummy. Trust her sweet, sensitive friend to see exactly what she was trying to achieve. Eliza shoved up the floppy sleeves of her sweater—a pointless act as they fell straight back down again—and grinned. 'And look at you! You're looking so much better.'

Beth snagged an arm around Eliza's waist and hugged her close again. 'It's all the fresh air. Honestly, I feel like I've been shedding layers of city grime.' She stroked the end of the ponytail curling over her shoulder. 'Everything was dull, you know? Not just my hair, or my skin, but my brain too.'

Her friend nodded. 'I get it. The air up north doesn't taste the same either.' She breathed deeply. 'I don't know how I let Martin talk me into moving away in the first place.' A troubled look clouded her brow. 'And now he wants to drag me halfway around the world.'

'What?'

Pushing her cloud of curly hair back from her forehead, Beth sighed. 'Oh, nothing. I'm just being a drama queen. Martin's been invited to apply for a fantastic promotion, but if he gets it, it would mean relocating to Abu Dhabi.'

Clad in an emerald-green flowing wool dress, cinched at the waist with a bright red belt that matched her tights and the huge scarf wrapped around her neck, Eliza was a vision of jewel shades. The colours perfectly complimented her pale, freckled skin. Pale skin that turned bright red at the first hint of the sun. Her friend had spent every summer in Lavender Bay smothered in high-factor sun cream and sheltered under an umbrella. How on earth would she cope with the extreme climate of the Middle East? How on earth would Beth cope with her friend so far away? 'Eliza, you'll burn to a crisp! How will you cope with the heat?'

'It won't be so bad. The company has a lovely compound there. There's a swimming pool surrounded by palms and cabanas. The apartments all have wall-to-wall aircon. Martin's showed me the pictures.' The wavering in her voice belied the reassurance in her words. 'Oh, these are new!'

Still stunned at the prospect of them being separated by so many miles, Beth watched Eliza hurry across the room to examine the central display she'd created to exhibit local craftsmen and women. Eliza pressed her nose practically against the glass—making it clear the topic of Martin's potential promotion was off limits.

For now, Beth conceded silently.

Eleanor's notebook had proven to be a goldmine of information. Sylvia, the creator of the jewellery Libby had been so taken with, had invited Beth to join a Facebook group which was part chatroom, part artisans' guild. The post she'd put up offering display space on a sale-or-return basis had been inundated with responses. From hand-thrown pots to delicate watercolours, the local artists had provided her with a beautiful collection of unique pieces. A card stood beside each item providing details of the artist and a couple of lines about the inspiration behind it. 'What do you think?'

Eliza turned to her, eyes glowing. 'I think it's wonderful. Who knew Lavender Bay was such a creative hotbed?' It wasn't difficult to sense the longing in those words.

'You should think about making something for me to sell.' An impulsive suggestion, but the words tasted right on her tongue.

'Me?' Eliza scoffed. 'My silly little dabblings aren't a patch on these.'

If Martin had been standing there at that precise moment, Beth feared she would have done him violence, so great was the wash of anger filling her veins. She could picture him saying those exact words, his face fixed in a patronising smile as he hugged his wife around the shoulders. Passive-aggressive wanker. He'd never taken Eliza's interest in art seriously. Oh, it was fine for a hobby, but he couldn't see the value in it so therefore assumed no one else would either. He'd been the one to steer her away from an arts foundation degree, arguing in that perfectly reasonable tone of his she'd be better off doing something more appealing to prospective employers.

With the grades he'd achieved at school, Martin could have attended the university of his choice, but he'd chosen the same one Eliza and Beth had opted for. It had a decent enough computer science course, but there were others with a better reputation. The important thing for both he and Eliza had been to be together. Still deep in the throes of first love, nothing and nobody had been able to dissuade them otherwise. Beth had thought them too young, Martin too controlling in his need to be with Eliza all the time, and had tried to say so. It was one of the few serious fights the two of them had had, and in the end Beth had swallowed her doubts rather than risk destroying their friendship. Beth sighed. If anyone had tried to criticise Charlie to her, she'd likely have done the same thing. Tender hearts rarely listened to anything which didn't fit their ideal.

'Earth to Beth.'

Eliza waved a hand in front of her face, and she blinked back into the present. 'Sorry, I was woolgathering.'

Her friend wrinkled her nose. 'By the expression on your face, you were thinking about he-who-shall-remain-nameless.'

Beth held up her hands. 'Guilty as charged. Bloody hell, did you always know he was a total arse?'

'Always.' She softened the blow with a kiss and another fragrant hug. 'But then I know what you and Libby both think of Martin, so it's swings and roundabouts.'

She thought about arguing the point. Whilst she and Charlie were history, Eliza was still very much married. In the end, she copped out. 'As long as you're happy, that's all that matters.' They looked at each for a long moment, then burst out laughing.

'God, but you're a terrible liar, B, always have been,' Eliza said between giggles.

A knock on the front door startled them both and they turned to see Libby with her mouth pressed against the glass. She'd blown out her cheeks, the way they used to do as kids, pulling a hideous face which set them off again. 'Look at the bloody mess you've made on my nice clean window!' Beth wagged a finger at Libby as she pulled open the door.

Libby tugged the sleeve of her jumper down and rubbed it

vigorously over the wet mark, smearing it further. 'Look, see, all fixed.' She raised the arm she'd been holding behind her back to show a bottle of pink Lambrini. 'So, are we having a party, or what?'

An eternal goth, she'd paired thick-soled boots with the skinniest black jeans, a black and red striped jumper and ears full of studs. The rainbow hair had been covered in jet-black dye and stood up in all directions. She reminded Beth of a miniature Dennis the Menace, and she said so.

Libby gave a graceful twirl, which shouldn't have been possible in a pair of thick-soled Doc Martin's. 'You're just jealous of my style, B.'

Eliza grabbed the bottle from her with a hoot. 'Where the hell did you find this?' She shuddered. 'Just looking at it makes my head ache.'

Libby snatched it back. 'Hey! I don't care what kind of swill you drink these days, but I'm loyal to our past. It was this or a six-pack of Babycham.'

Beth shut and locked the door. 'Come on upstairs, the pair of you. You're supposed to be here to help me, not just get drunk.'

Libby's heavy boots thudded on the steps behind her. 'I vote we do both.'

'Me too,' Eliza piped up from behind her. 'Two to one, you're outvoted, Beth. Get the glasses out.'

Chapter Eleven

By the time the Lambrini bottle was empty, they'd managed a layer of undercoat on the two biggest walls. Libby dropped her roller into the tray, knuckling the base of her back to stretch it. 'Right,' she declared. 'I'm on strike until you feed me!'

Happy for an excuse to stop herself, Beth placed the brush she'd been using to edge along the skirting into a jar of cloudy water and stripped off the bandana she'd used to tie back her hair. 'I thought we might get a takeaway, if that's all right with you two?'

'Perfect!'

'Ooh, can we have pizza? I haven't had pizza in ages.'

Libby and Eliza almost tripped over each other in their eagerness to respond. Knowing only too well her own shortcomings in the kitchen, Beth tapped her chin, pretending to consider the point further. 'Or, I could make us something. It's the least I should do to thank you both for helping me out like this.'

Their responses were even quicker this time:

'Oh, no. Don't put yourself to any trouble!'

'It's our pleasure to help you, B, that's what best friends are for.'

She looked between the two of them; she could tell by the way Libby's eyebrow was twitching she was trying not to wince, and burst out laughing. 'God, you two are so easy to wind up! The menu's on the pinboard in the kitchen. Come on.'

Bypassing the board, Libby went straight for the fridge and grabbed a fresh bottle of wine. 'Who needs a menu? You and Eliza will split a large Hawaiian, because you're freaks who think hot fruit is an acceptable topping, and I'll have a regular spicy sausage.'

It had been their staple order whenever they were together, and Beth couldn't help but smile when she gave the details to Gina over the phone and the woman added, 'And two garlic breads, right, Beth? I heard Eliza was home for the weekend so I've been expecting your call. It'll be about twenty minutes. Shall I send Davey to the back gate?'

'Yes, please. We'll keep an eye out for him.'

'All right, love. How are things, by the way? I can't tell you how thrilled we both were that you're going to keep the emporium going. It's been such a feature of the prom for so many years, the town just wouldn't be the same without it.'

Beth knocked her head against the wall. She knew Gina meant well, and of course her return would be the talk of the town, but the weight of expectation didn't help the butterflies in her tummy. The moment she opened the doors, everyone would be in to have a good snoop around and offer their opinions on what she'd done with the place.

She sighed. 'It's a lot of work, Gina. A bit more than I expected, if I'm honest.' She felt a nudge at her elbow and smiled gratefully to Libby when she handed her a brimming glass of wine. 'But I've got plenty of helping hands, I just hope people like what I've done with the place.'

'You'll be grand, sweetie. Don't let those busybodies from the improvement society intimidate you. That leader of theirs is a nosy baggage. You know she came in here and told Davey we should consider upgrading our menu. Like this town hasn't run on our pizzas and kebabs for the past twenty-five years. Bloody cheek!'

Beth sipped her wine, and made appropriate 'uh-hum' noises,

letting Gina's diatribe wash over her. Hester had clearly ruffled the woman's feathers, and there was a real sense of hurt beneath the angry words filling Beth's ear. It would be easy for a stranger to make assumptions about the type of establishment Gina and Davey ran, but the food was all freshly prepared with ingredients of the highest quality. Yes, it was a takeaway, but not the kind that had drunks spilling out onto the pavement after the pubs closed. Gina finally ran out of steam and let Beth go with a promise to call them if she needed anything.

'Wow, who stuck a bee in Gina's bonnet?' Eliza asked with a smile as Beth hung up.

'Mrs Bradshaw, on behalf of the improvement society. Suggested they should upgrade from pizza and kebabs to stuffed ravioli and mezze.'

Libby snorted into her wine, choking so hard Eliza had to give her a thump on the back. 'Oh, to have been a fly on the wall for that conversation!'

Beth giggled. 'I know! I bet it wasn't the ravioli that ended up stuffed.'

Libby choked again. 'That woman desperately needs to find a hobby before she turns the whole bloody town against her.'

'Oh, I'm sure she means well.' Typical Eliza, keen to see the best in everyone.

'Sam told me she'd been hinting about the pub needing a facelift too . . . and he kissed me.' Beth had no idea what possessed her to blurt out her confession.

'The pub? Our pub? Cheeky mare! Wait . . . what?'

Blushing, Beth glanced from Libby's knowing grin to Eliza's open-mouthed expression of shock. 'Twice, actually.'

'Where? When? Come on I need details! And shut your mouth, Eliza, it's not like this hasn't been brewing for years.'

Eliza glugged a mouthful of her wine. 'Yes, you're right, but still the thought of anyone kissing my brother is a bit . . .' She shuddered, though her eyes were full of humour.

Taking her own fortifying drink, Beth held up her hand. 'Before you get too excited, we've decided to stick to just being friends.'

'What? Why?' Libby demanded. 'You two are a match if ever I saw one, I think you'd be great together.'

Beth shook her head. 'It's too complicated, and not the right time for either of us.' She waved her arm to indicate the space around her, almost spilling her wine in the process. 'I need to put all of my focus into this place, and Sam's got his hands full with the pub, and . . .' It was on the tip of her tongue to tell them about the restaurant idea, but it wasn't her news to share. ' . . . And everything. It's bad timing.' She was starting to hate those two words.

A familiar toot-toot sounded from the street below, and Beth grabbed her purse. 'Saved by the bell!' She hurried out of the flat and down the stairs.

Libby followed her out to lean over the top bannister rail. 'It'll take more than a pizza to save you, B. We want all the gory details!'

Beth took her time collecting the pizzas, trying to concentrate on the friendly conversation with Davey as he refused her offer of a tip and carefully counted out the change she was owed. She pocketed the coins and had just balanced the pizza boxes on one hand when he reached into his car to produce a plastic carrier bag. 'Here, Gina sent you each a slice of tiramisu, on the house.'

'Oh, Davey, that's very kind, but you should let me pay for them.' Beth had her hand halfway to her pocket before he waved her off.

'Don't you dare! You know she likes to spoil you girls when she can. Just make sure she has an invitation to your grand opening, and that'll be payment enough. She hasn't stopped talking about how pleased she is to see you picking up where Eleanor left off.'

Grand opening? Beth swallowed hard. She'd hoped everyone would be busy enough with their own businesses that she'd be able to open the doors to the emporium quietly in the run up to Easter. From what Davey was saying, that didn't sound like the case. 'I . . . I'll make sure to let her know the date.'

'Splendid.' He handed over the bag with a broad smile. 'I know you'll do Eleanor proud, Beth.'

It was hard to talk around the sudden lump in her throat, so she settled for a nod and a slightly watery smile. Hands full, she pushed the gate closed behind him; locking it seemed like overkill, it wasn't as though she was living in a high-crime area of London anymore. The only people who came to the back door were delivery men, and her friends. Entering the house, she kicked the back door shut with her heel. The Yale lock clicked into place and she used her elbow to push the deadlock button up. More than enough security.

She carried the food into the living room, to find Libby had opened another bottle of wine and laid out sheets of kitchen paper to use as napkins. Eliza took the pizza boxes from her hand, then noticed the carrier bag swinging from Beth's fingers. 'What's that? Garlic bread?'

Beth shook her head. 'That should be in the top box, I think. This is Gina's homemade tiramisu—her treat. I'll just pop it in the fridge for later.'

By the time she returned, Eliza had ripped the lid off one of the boxes and shovelled half the Hawaiian pizza together with several slices of garlic bread on to it. She slid it across the coffee table towards Beth and she sank into an armchair with a sigh. 'Gina's expecting a grand opening for the emporium.'

Libby paused with a slice of pizza just inches from her lips. 'The whole town is, B, I assumed you'd realise that.'

Groaning, Beth snatched up her wine glass and took a swig. 'Tell me you're kidding? I was hoping for something quiet.' She still had serious doubts about whether she could make a go of things, and hosting a big party felt like a commitment she wasn't sure she was ready to make. Easter would be the real test, so she'd give herself until the end of April and then sit down to evaluate her options. She'd keep that to herself for now; as much as she loved her friends, it had to be a decision for her and her alone.

'Fat chance of that around here. This is the most exciting thing that's happened since the newsagent's rearranged their shelves last summer. Face it, you're the talk of the town.' Libby stuffed half the slice in her mouth and began to chew, which must have been tough given the huge bloody smirk on her face.

'Just imagine what they'll be saying once they find out you've been smooching the boy next door,' Eliza added, tartly.

'What? Oh, God, don't even go there. It was two kisses.' Two of the best kisses she'd ever experienced, but that wasn't the point. 'I shouldn't have bloody said anything.' She grabbed for the remote control. 'Shall we watch a film?'

Eliza leaned forward to snatch the remote from her hand. 'Nice try, but you're not getting out of this. I want to know what's been going on between you two.' She didn't sound cross, much to Beth's relief, more concerned.

Libby on the other hand, was full of nothing but mischief. 'Yes, tell us everything. How was it?'

'It was okay.' Beth helped herself to some pizza, stuffing it into her mouth before she could say anymore.

'Okay?' Libby snorted. 'You don't blurt it out and then blush the way you are over an okay kiss. Details, B, come on now. Let me live vicariously through you.'

Beth couldn't help but laugh. The way Libby made things out to be, you'd think she'd never had a boyfriend. Sure, her choices might be limited by being in a small town, but things couldn't be as bad as she kept making out. 'It was nice.' Heat rose in prickling spots across her chest and throat. 'Very nice.'

Eliza shuddered. 'That's enough detail for me, thanks. When did this all happen?'

'The first time was when he helped me fix the sink.' She winced almost as soon as she said it, knowing she'd given the game away.

Eliza arched an eyebrow. 'And the second?'

'In the stock room,' Beth mumbled. 'When we had the mix up with the inflatable dolls.'

Libby choked on a mouthful of wine and kept spluttering until Eliza thumped her on the back to help clear her airway. 'Okay,' she said, when she finally managed to speak. 'I don't care what Eliza says, now I definitely want details.'

They stayed up late; Beth's anecdote about the dodgy sex toys had led onto Eliza telling them about a terrible Ann Summers party she'd been talked into attending by a member of her book group, and Martin's horrified reaction when she'd shown him the catalogue afterwards. They'd laughed until their sides ached, their noise level increasing as the contents of the wine bottle disappeared.

Full of pizza, feeling slightly dizzy and with a combination of minty toothpaste and garlic confusing her taste buds, Beth crawled under the cover of the double bed in the spare room. Eliza was already snuggled in against the wall, and Libby looked cosy enough in a kind of nest she'd made on the floor using the mattress they'd dragged in from Beth's old bed and a pile of quilts and pillows.

Stretching out, she clicked off the bedside light, leaving the room dark except for a sliver of moonlight peeping through a gap in the top of the curtains. She felt a hand brush against her side and slid her hand out to grasp Libby's fingers.

'I'm glad you're home, B,' she whispered sleepily.

'Me too, Libs. I missed you both so much.' A soft snore came back in reply.

Recalling the brief conversation with Eliza that morning, she stretched out her other hand to grasp her friend's arm. 'And now you might be moving even further away. What will we do without you?'

Eliza rolled towards her and shifted closer until her head rested on the edge of Beth's pillow. 'I don't want to go,' she murmured. 'Is it awful of me to say that? It feels awful, like I'm being disloyal to Martin. His career is important, and I know I should be more supportive.'

The wine had softened her inhibitions, and it was on the tip of Beth's tongue to tell Eliza exactly what she thought about Martin and his passive-aggressive bullshit, but she clamped her jaw tight until the urge passed. Whatever she thought about the situation, he was Eliza's husband and she didn't want to put a strain on their friendship.

Trying to feel her way towards the right thing to say, she settled eventually for, 'You've put him and his work first for a long time. I remember how hard it was for you when you first moved up north.'

'It's silly. I'm being silly. It's not like I've seen you every five minutes, but at least I knew you were only a train ride, or a couple of hours drive away. An eight-hour flight is something different all together.'

Beth squeezed her arm. 'You don't have to go if you don't want to.'

Eliza's sigh tickled the hair on her shoulder. 'It's not even certain he's going to get it, so I might be worrying over nothing. It won't be the end of the world, and it would be the ideal time for us to start a family as I won't be working over there.'

The lack of enthusiasm in her voice set alarm bells ringing in Beth's head. Planning a baby should be something joyful, a time for celebration and excitement. Eliza made it sound anything but. 'The last time we talked about it, you weren't ready to have children.'

Her friend rolled over onto her back, and Beth could sense her drawing away. 'I'm not getting any younger. If we're going to have kids, now's as good a time as any.'

Bloody hell, she was too drunk, and nowhere near drunk enough to have this conversation right now. 'There's plenty of time, Eliza. No need to rush into any big decisions just yet.'

'You're right. There's no need to worry yet, he hasn't even got an interview.' Eliza yawned. 'I think the wine's gone to my head and got me talking nonsense. G'night, B.'

Feeling like she'd failed her friend, Beth gave her arm a final squeeze. 'Night, darling. Sleep tight.' From the way Eliza tossed and turned beside her, it seemed a fruitless wish—for both of them.

Chapter Twelve

'Shoulda brought the spare key.' Sam muttered to himself as he knocked on the back door of the emporium for the third time to no answer. Having seen Eliza take a couple of bottles out of the pub fridge, he'd assumed they'd be a bit worse for wear that morning and decided to make them breakfast. Beth had left a spare key at the pub, for emergencies, and he'd briefly considered using it so he could set everything out properly, before worrying she might see it as a violation of trust.

He took a couple of steps back and looked up at the closed curtains over the windows of the flat above. Surprises always seemed great during the planning, but relied on other people to play their part—which was never guaranteed when they didn't know they even had a part to play. Balancing the cardboard tray in his left hand, he fumbled in his pocket for his phone and scrolled through to find Beth's number.

Buzz. Buzz. Buzz. 'Ungh?'

'Hey, Beth, you wanna come down and answer the door?' A loud groan echoed in his ear, and he stifled a grin. 'Beth, you okay?'

'Beth's dead. This is her ghost.'

Sam laughed. 'Can ghosts open doors? I brought you guys breakfast.'

'Ghosts don't eat. I'm never eating or drinking again.' She whimpered. 'You made me think about drinking, why did you do that? Do you hate me?'

'No, I don't hate you. I like you very much, that's why I made you bacon sandwiches and a Mr Barnes' Secret Hangover Cure shake.'

'Chocolate?' She sounded almost perky and Sam knew his instinct had been right.

'Yes, chocolate for you, strawberry for Eliza, and caramel for Libs.' There was no big secret to the milkshakes—the milk helped to hydrate and neutralise an acidic stomach, and the oats and a raw egg provided energy. He added their favourite flavouring to mask any bitterness from the soluble painkillers. The bacon in the sandwiches was grilled rather than fried because, contrary to popular opinion, greasy food was the worst thing going for a hangover.

'What are you waiting for? Bring them up.'

Sam rested his head against the back door. 'You need to unlock the door first.'

'But I'm dead and a ghost so I can't get up. Hold on . . .' Sam listened to her as she woke up the others, smiling so hard it made his face ache. God, she was adorable when she was like this—funny, sleepy, with just a little dash of vulnerability.

The dull sound of footsteps on the stairs sounded from inside and he straightened up in time to catch the full force of Libby's scowl as she yanked open the door. With her hair stuck up at all angles and the smudges of make-up under her eyes it was like being snarled at by an angry panda. Grabbing one of the tall plastic cups from the cardboard tray he thrust it at her. 'Caramel.'

Libby snatched the drink and took a deep slurp from the straw. 'God, that's good. I love you.' She sucked down another mouthful. 'Not feed-me-amazing-things-then-kiss-my-face-off love you, I'll leave that to Beth.'

'Excuse me?' He tried to ignore the heat rising on his face. What the hell had Beth been telling them?

The cheeky minx grinned at him, then clutched her head with a groan. 'Damn, it's hard to be smug when you're full of Lambrini regrets.' She pointed at the padded bag in his hand. 'What's that?'

'Bacon sandwiches.'

'Forget what I said before. I do feed-me-amazing-things-then-kiss-my-face-off love you.' She grabbed his hand and Sam found himself being dragged up the stairs. Halfway up, Libby called out, 'Beth, I'm stealing your boyfriend, all right?'

Beth shuffled out of the bedroom, tugging down the rumpled leg of her pyjama shorts. Her normally sleek hair straggled around her face which was so pale her dark eyes dominated her elfin features. 'I don't have a boyfriend, but if you're referring to Sam, you can do what you want with him if you stop shouting.' She held out her hand and Sam gave her the chocolate shake.

He'd never seen her grumpy before, and he had to admit he kind of liked it. 'I'll take these into the kitchen and plate up. Did you two break my sister?'

The bathroom door opened. 'I'm alive . . . I think.' Eliza pushed her wild curls off her forehead and frowned at him. 'I'm not talking to you.' She made to push past him, then stopped to grab the final milkshake from the holder. 'Traitor.' She stomped towards the kitchen.

Sam followed hot on her heels. 'What? What the hell did I do?'

His sister spun around to raise a shaky finger in his face. 'You kissed her!' She hissed through her teeth. 'She's my best friend, Sam, and she's been through a lot in the past few months. The last thing she needs is you fooling around with her. What were you thinking?'

Dodging the finger she was jabbing at his face, Sam crowded close to his sister. 'Woah! Back up there a little, missy.' He glanced over his shoulder to check they were alone, then lowered his voice. 'I'm not fooling around with Beth. It was something and nothing, it happened on the spur of the moment and we've both agreed to forget about it. Get your facts straight before you start throwing accusations around.' So why had she told them?

126

Clutching her head, Eliza slumped into the chair he'd hung his jacket on. 'Shh. I'm sorry, all right? I'm just worried about you, that's all.'

Sam abandoned his search for the plates and took the chair next to her. Looking past the pale face, the messy hair and smudged remains of her make-up, he could see the concern in her eyes. 'Hey, kiddo, what's got your knickers in a twist?'

'Don't tease me, this is serious.' Her hand closed over his forearm. 'I don't want her getting hurt.'

'No one's getting hurt. We're friends. Nothing more.' He paused, then frowned. 'Why aren't you worried about me getting hurt?'

Eliza made a rude noise. 'You're my brother, and I love you, but you're a bit of a player. When was the last time you were involved with any woman for more than a couple of dates?' Without giving him a chance, she answered her own question. 'I'll tell you when—never. Beth's not like that, she's had one serious boyfriend and he broke her heart.'

Damn. Eliza might look all sweetness and light, but she knew how to strike a low blow. Sure, he'd played the field, but it had never been malicious on his part, he'd just never found someone he felt truly comfortable around. There were women who he was friends with, and women he dated, but he'd never found anyone who managed to meet both criteria. Until now. The realisation hit him like a tonne of bricks. Mouth dry, Sam cast a quick glance at his sister, relieved to see she was rubbing her hands over her face in an attempt to wake herself up.

He dropped a quick kiss on head, then pushed himself to his feet. 'No one's getting their heart broken, least of all Beth. I promise you.'

The warming bag had done its job in keeping the bacon at a palatable temperature, so Sam made himself busy slicing the fresh rolls he'd brought with him and layering them with crispy rashers of meat. Whilst his fingers carried out the task almost by rote, his mind whirled. Before Beth had returned to the bay, he'd been restless and miserable, his relationship with his father under threat. Talking to her about everything had been easy, partly he supposed because she knew him so well already.

The attraction he felt for her was understandable. Sam had always had an affinity for leggy brunettes with eyes like melted chocolate; anyone looking at his previous girlfriends could have worked that out. Oh. Oh. He wanted to smack himself in the head for being so blind. He wasn't attracted to Beth because she resembled the kind of woman he liked. She was the original. The one he'd imprinted upon that blustery night on the promenade.

Voices sounded in the hallway, and he turned his back to busy himself with breakfast as Libby and Beth wandered in to join his sister at the table. The three of them were busy alternating between bemoaning their hangovers and slurping their milkshakes and didn't seem to notice his sudden silence.

They fell on the rolls like a pack of ravenous wolves the moment he placed them on the table. Sam braced his palms on the kitchen counter and took a deep breath. If he didn't pull himself together, they'd realise something was wrong. He'd grilled enough bacon for his own roll so claimed the last chair and looked back and forth between them. Nice and casual, easy does it. 'Just how much did you drink last night?'

It was Libby who answered. 'Only three bottles, and one of those was Lambrini.' She shook her head sadly, then clutched it with a whimper. 'When did we become such lightweights?'

Stifling a smile, Sam patted her hand. 'It's your age, Libs.' He stood up, crossed to the window and rolled up the blind. Shrieks greeted the bright steam of sunlight, and he shook his head. 'You guys are kind of pathetic, you know that, right?'

Feeling a bit steadier, Sam decided to stick with his original plan. He grabbed the kettle, filled it and flipped it on. 'Okay, I'll give you ten more minutes to feel sorry for yourselves and then you need to get dressed because we're going for a walk on the beach.'

A chorus of groans greeted him, then Beth muttered, 'You're not the boss of me.'

The little bite of sassiness was something new. She'd been a lot shier when she'd been a little girl. He liked this new side to her, it spoke of a growing confidence he wanted to encourage and nurture in her, and that meant giving her something to push back against. He turned to rest against the counter and folded his hands over his chest. 'Do you, or do you not want to get that bedroom decorated this weekend?'

She scowled and mumbled something. He cupped a hand to his ear, knowing he was being an annoying ass, but it didn't matter because she thought they were just friends and friends teased each other. 'What was that?'

Beth raised her hand to her face, pretending to scratch the side of her nose whilst giving him the finger and he laughed, utterly charmed. 'Nine minutes. Get dressed and I'll make some tea.' He dug inside the bag and produced four insulated mugs. 'Eight and a half minutes.'

For all their grumbling, the fresh air seemed to do the trick and Beth and the others began to look better. He watched as the wind blew his sister's unruly curls across her face for the third time in less than a minute and she dragged them free again before digging in her pockets. 'Damn, I'm sure I had an elastic band somewhere.'

'Here.' Sam yanked a black knit hat from his own coat pocket and tugged it down over her head. He smoothed the stray ends of hair behind her ears then tweaked her little snub nose the way he used to do when she was just this little bit tagging at his heels. 'Better?'

She nodded, then hooked her arm through his when he would have turned away. 'Hold up a minute, I want to talk to you.'

Until he'd worked out what he was going to do about him and Beth, he wanted to maintain the façade of indifference. 'Let it go, already. Beth and I kissed a couple of times, it's no big deal.' He tried to shake her off, but she clamped on, dragging him around until he faced her.

'I believe you, okay? That's not what I wanted to talk to you about.'

Sam tipped up her chin. The dark circles beneath her eyes were from more than one too many glasses of wine. His grip on her face softened. 'What's the matter, Sis?'

To his horror, tears pooled in her eyes. 'I'm so worried about Daddy.'

'Hey, hey, it's okay.' Sam gathered her into his arms and hugged her tight. 'Dad's a tough old sod, he's not finished yet.'

'I heard him coughing yesterday, it sounds so painful. I . . . I thought it would be better by now, but it sounds just as bad as ever.' Her voice sounded muffled against his thick jacket, but there was no mistaking the hitch in it.

Sam eased back so he could meet her eyes. 'I had a long talk with him, because I didn't really understand what was going on with him. His condition is chronic, I don't think I fully grasped what that meant until I'd seen him struggling every day.'

Eliza sniffed, then nodded. 'He's not going to get better, is he?'

'No.' The admission cut his soul to the quick. Their big vital father would never be the same again. Using his thumb, he wiped a tear off her cheek. 'But, with proper management and care, he won't get any worse and there's some room for improvement. He's promised me he'll follow the doc's guidance more closely, and as the weather warms up a bit that'll help him as well.' He had to believe that. He had to believe there was still hope.

Her hand came up to cover his. 'You would tell me if there was a problem?'

'I swear.' He crossed his heart, just like he'd done when she was little and made him promise something. Her warm laughter eased the knot in his chest. Slinging an arm around her shoulders, he steered her towards the ebbing tide to where Beth and Libby were strolling arm-in-arm just out of reach of the foam rolling over the wet sand.

Bending to pick up a stone, he skipped it out across the water, groaning when it sank into the waves after only three jumps. Eliza gave him a playful shove, then found her own stone. 'That was rubbish, watch the expert at work.' She twisted her body ninety degrees, flicked her wrist and sent the small projectile flying over the surf.

'Five?' Sam held his hands up in disbelief. 'You cheated.'

Eliza blew on her fingernails. 'Face it, Sammy, I've got skills.'

Laughing, he tugged her hat down over her eyes. 'You've got something all right.' The familiar pattern of their teasing warmed him through. He studied her, as she tugged the hat off with an exasperated sigh, then re-settled it on her hair. A flush of colour painted her pale cheeks, and her green eyes sparkled with laughter. She looked good, better than when he'd first seen her that morning. 'The fresh air suits you.'

His sister spread her arms wide as she turned in a slow circle. 'I love it here. I never feel quite myself anywhere else.' There was a wistfulness to her voice.

'Why don't you come back? Martin must be able to find a decent job within a reasonable commuting distance. Heck, these days the kind of stuff he does can be done remotely.'

Her nose wrinkled in a little frown. 'He's doing really well at work, I don't think he'd be keen to leave. Especially not when he's being considered for a promotion.'

She didn't look thrilled about the prospect, and he wondered why. A promotion would normally mean a pay rise . . . Before he could ask her about it, she spoke again. 'Besides, what would I do here? There's nothing for me locally.'

'You could help me with the pub.' It had been an instinctive response—The Siren was a part of her heritage as much as it was his. And she'd always loved the place. He could still recall her pride the first time their dad had let her work behind the bar. With her warm and welcoming personality, she'd be a huge asset to the place. It would also free him up to concentrate more on the restaurant. He'd been to see a local architect and plans were being drawn up ready for submission to the local council. Planning permission would take time, and he'd need it before he could approach potential investors for support.

'You're kidding, right?' Eliza's incredulous tone dragged him back from his daydreams.

'Nope. I'm deadly serious.' He put his arm around her shoulders. 'I'm not suggesting you drop everything and move back tomorrow, all I'm saying is that there are options here for you if you want them.' She tucked her head against his shoulder and they began walking again. 'I've been talking to Mum and Dad about converting the old skittle alley into a restaurant.'

Eliza stopped in her tracks to stare up at him, eyes wide with wonder. 'Oh, Sam! Your own place at last?'

He nodded, knowing she understood what it meant to him.

'What made you think of the skittle alley?'

'It was Beth's idea, actually. So, what do you reckon?'

Eliza's face was wreathed in smiles. 'I think it's perfect. The best of both worlds. Will you show me?'

'Show you what?' They'd been so busy talking, Sam hadn't noticed Beth and Libby approaching.

'Sam was just telling me about the restaurant he's going to open right here in the bay!' Eliza clapped her hands together.

Libby's brows rose in surprise. 'Here? Where?'

'In the skittle alley beneath the pub.' It was Beth who chipped in this time. 'Isn't it exciting?'

'Can we see it? When are you planning on opening?'

Their enthusiasm was gratifying, if a little overwhelming. 'Hold on a second! I haven't even submitted the plans to the council yet.'

'You have plans?' Beth grabbed his arm. 'Show us!'

Sam laughed. 'All right, all right! I have some draft plans, there's still some stuff to be finalised, but they should give you an idea.' He herded the chattering trio towards the pub, the smile on his face growing by the moment. There was no hesitation from any of them that the restaurant would happen, and it strengthened his own belief.

His own place. There was still a long way to go, but he could do it. He would do it.

Chapter Thirteen

The walk on the beach, followed by an amazing hour poring over Sam's plans for Subterranean had done them all the power of good. Filled with renewed enthusiasm for their own little makeover, they continued to make good progress with the painting.

Rolling another stripe of pale lilac onto the wall, Beth continued to turn over the issue sticking in her mind. From the conversation with Gina the previous night when she'd been ordering their pizza, and Libby and Eliza's subsequent agreement, she would have to face up to the fact she wasn't going to be able to just turn the sign on the front door and consider the emporium open.

The town was expecting a grand launch. Easter Sunday was just a few weeks away. Which meant she had a fortnight to plan everything if she intended to stick with the idea of being open in time for the first day of the school holidays. What could she do though? There'd have to be drinks of some description . . . Putting down the roller, she wiped her hands on the old T-shirt she was wearing and dug her phone out of her pocket. Maybe one of the big supermarket chains was having a deal on fizz. She said as much as she clicked open her internet browser.

'That's a good idea,' Eliza agreed. 'I can whip you up some canapes tomorrow—sausage rolls, a few vol-au-vents. Stuff you can stick in the freezer.'

Libby nodded. 'I'll make you a couple of sheet cakes. We can cut them up into bit sized pieces. I've got a couple of new recipes I want to try out, so your guests can be guinea pigs.'

Beth paused mid-scroll. 'When did you become the new Mary Berry?'

Her friend blushed. 'I don't want to sell fish and bloody chips forever, you know. I've got plans.'

This was news. Beth squatted on her haunches and ducked her head to catch Libby's eyes under the shield of her heavy fringe. 'I'm listening, Libs. What plans?'

A shy grin crossed Libby's face. 'I want to turn the chippy into a tea-shop. Not now, of course, but once Dad retires.'

She tried to picture Libby with her ever-changing hair and grungy clothes standing behind a pristine white counter serving up delicate desserts and fancy pots of tea and coffee. It shouldn't work, but somehow it did. 'I think that sounds fab, really wonderful. You know I'll help you in any way that I can.'

Eliza crouched down next to her. 'Me too, but let's get one grand opening sorted out before we start planning the next one.'

Libby reached out to squeeze both their hands, the little grin bursting into a huge smile. 'Thanks, both, and Eliza's right.' She turned to Beth. 'Didn't you say something about a Facebook group where you got in touch with those local artists? Why don't you post something in there and see if a few of them will come along? They can talk about the stuff they're selling through you. I'd love to meet the woman who makes that jewellery.'

'What a great idea, I'll do it now.' Beth clicked open the app on her phone. A slew of notifications hit her, and she began to browse through them on autopilot. She'd posted a picture of the empty wine bottles and pizza boxes earlier and there were lots of likes, smileys and joking replies. If she was honest, some of the responses were from practical strangers. Collecting friends on social media was like breathing, something you just did without thinking about it.

Libby knelt up to glance over her shoulder. 'Did you add a page on there for the emporium, yet? It'd be a great way to garner some interest in the place. And you'll need a Twitter account too.'

'And Instagram,' Eliza chipped in. 'You could take some really lovely mood shots of things in the shop—like those gorgeous scarves I saw hanging from banana monkey.'

'Oh, I know! We should make him his own account. That could be a right laugh, and people love a gimmick.' Libby clapped her hands. 'We could take him on a tour of the town, post photos of him on the beach with a bucket and spade, with a bag of chips in his hands, that kind of stuff.'

Their enthusiasm was catching, and Beth's mind started racing a mile a minute as the possibilities opened up before her. If she was really going to do this, then what better way to stamp her own personality on the place? If she had a page, then visitors could check-in when they came to browse, and she could run a few little contests . . .

As the ideas swirled in her head, she clicked on the little speech bubble which indicated someone had sent her a personal message. Still distracted, she frowned at the little sun-tanned profile picture of Charlie. Charlie?! Why would he be messaging her after all this time?

After the countless texts and messages he'd ignored, she was tempted to do the same. Curiosity got the better of her though, so she clicked on the message and began to read.

Hi, stranger!!! Long time no speak. I hope all is well with you. I'm fine, crazy busy at work though. I've just had a promotion at work so things are SUPER stressful, as I'm sure you can imagine ☺ *Look, I'm sorry for what happened before. You probably hate me (and I can't say I'd blame you) but everything got really complicated and it felt like a clean break would be the best for everyone.*

Anyway, I know you keep in contact with a few of the gang, and I didn't want you to hear the news from anyone else.

A lead weight formed in Beth's stomach. Had something happened to him? The rest of the message lay below the edge of the screen and for a second she was tempted to close the whole thing rather than use her thumb to scroll down. Whatever was going on with Charlie, it was no business of hers any longer. Hadn't he made that abundantly clear when he'd cut her out of his life? Oh, who was she trying to kid? If she didn't read on, it would prey on her mind. She scrolled down.

Kimberly and I have known each other forever. Our parents have been friends since university, you probably won't remember but her dad and mine set up the partnership together. There was always this expectation that she and I would end up together.

'B? Are you okay, you look really pale.' Libby's voice seemed to come to her from far away. The lead weight in her middle grew exponentially heavier, and Beth slumped down on the side of the cloth-covered bed. Swallowing against the bile burning in her throat, she continued to read the rest of the message.

We dated all through school, and it was all going swimmingly. Only, then I met you, and that put a spanner in the works.

Anyway, I don't want to rake up the past, I just wanted you to know that Kimberly and I are engaged and there's going to be a big announcement. I wanted to forewarn you, so it didn't take you by surprise if you saw anything on here.

I know I didn't treat you right, but I want you to know that I really did love you.

Let me know if you need to talk XOXO

'Let me know if you need to talk?' Libby snatched the phone away and started browsing.

'Give me that.' Beth made a grab, only to have her knuckles slapped by Libby who then turned away, eyes still locked on the phone.

'Who wants to talk, what's going on?' Eliza leaned across Beth's lap to try and see the screen. She tilted her head to one side and Libby turned the phone, so she could see better. 'Married? Charlie's getting married?'

'According to this message, he is.' Libby clicked into Charlie's profile and started scrolling through his photos. 'God, look at this lot. They look like those people you see in the back pages of *OK!* magazine—all trust funds and privilege.' She looked up at Beth, her nose wrinkling like she'd smelt something nasty. 'What did you ever see in him?'

Beth considered Libby's question. Charlie had been everything she'd wanted in a boyfriend. Charming, good-looking and attentive. She'd given him her heart without hesitation, and if his text was to be believed, he'd loved her too. But that sophistication, which had impressed her at first, had begun to grate. His attitude towards waitstaff in restaurants, his weary sigh if she asked a question he deemed naïve—he'd been just a touch too cynical, his humour a shade too cutting for her liking. She'd buried those doubts, put them down to the disparity in their backgrounds.

Now though she could see they had never really been suited. She'd been drawn to him because he was exactly the sort of man her mother had spent years telling her she should be with. The fact they'd fallen in love with each other didn't negate the underlying dishonesty at the heart of their relationship. If Charlie had used her to try and escape his parents' expectations, then she'd surely used him for the exact opposite.

The walls seemed to close in on her, and Beth stumbled to her feet. She needed to get some air, to get away from the concern in Eliza's eyes, and the furious anger in Libby's. They probably thought she was devastated by the news, but she didn't know how to explain the guilt churning inside her. Unwittingly or not, she'd been the other woman. She'd been responsible for the break-up of a relationship. No wonder the others in the group had been a bit frosty towards her. Poor Kimberly.

Heedless of her lack of coat, and the slippers on her feet, Beth ran down the stairs, through the shop and out the front door. The stone steps leading to the beach were a few doors down from the emporium and she ran for them like a woman possessed.

A disgruntled flock of seagulls scattered into the sky before settling back onto the sand behind her. The beach was mostly empty, just a couple strolling hand in hand near the water's edge and a familiar figure, just a few feet away, wearing a bright orange high-vis vest with the words 'Beach Patrol' inscribed in big white letters across the shoulders.

Not in the mood to talk, Beth turned away too quickly, losing one of her slippers in the process. Her toes sank into the sand and she bent over to brush them off and try to shake the worst out of her slipper. A pair of black Wellingtons loomed into her eyeline. 'Hello, lovey, everything all right?'

She closed her eyes and tried to rein in the tangle of emotions roiling inside her. Straightening up, she pasted on the best smile she could muster and greeted Libby's father. 'Hello, Mr Stone. How are you today?'

The big man grinned. 'I'm very good, thank you. Did you forget your shoes?'

Beth laughed in spite of herself. 'Looks like it.'

Mr Stone joined in for a moment, before his expression grew solemn. 'You look upset, lovey. Are you sure you're all right?'

'What? Oh, no, I'm fine.' Beth brushed a strand of hair off her cheek, surprised when her fingers came off wet. 'I'm fine.' Her shoulders heaved. 'I'm really fine.'

Before she knew it, she was snivelling into the front of his thick sweater whilst poor Mr Stone patted her back with a big, clumsy hand. 'Don't cry. Shh, don't cry.'

Get a grip, for goodness' sake, she told herself. After a few more sniffles, Beth forced herself to straighten up one more. She pressed the palms of her hands against her eyes to try and stop the flow of tears. 'So . . . sorry, about that. I'm just being silly.'

His hand patted her shoulder a couple more times before

disappearing into his pocket to produce a neatly folded pristine white handkerchief. He shook it out then pinched her nose between the folds. 'Blow.'

Beth couldn't help herself and started to giggle. The noise came out more of a squeak with her nostrils trapped between his thumb and forefinger, making the giggles worse.

With a tenderness that touched her deeply, Mr Stone wiped her nose, dabbed at her cheeks with more concern than finesse then tucked the dirty hanky back into his pocket. When he withdrew his hand, a shiny round grey pebble tumbled out and fell to the sand.

Bending to pick it up, Beth stared in wonder at the stone. A miniature boat had been painted on one side of it. There was a delicacy to the brush strokes which spoke to the artist's talent. She couldn't begin to fathom the patience and concentration it would take to render something so small in such detail. 'This is great, who gave it to you?'

Libby's dad shrugged, as though embarrassed. 'I made it, Beth. It gives me something to do in the evenings.'

Tears forgotten, the beginnings of an idea formed in her mind. Nurturing local talent was one of the things she most wanted to do with the emporium, and who better fit that than the gentle, kind man in front of her? 'This is brilliant, you're really talented. You should think about selling them.'

Mr Stone scoffed. 'It's a bit of something and nothing. Who'd buy it?'

'I would. In fact, I'll sell them via the emporium if you're interested.'

'Oh, I don't know about that . . .' He scrubbed a hand over the short stubble covering his scalp.

Beth smiled. 'Well, why don't you think about it?' She offered him back the pebble, but he shook his head.

'No. You keep it. It's made you smile, and that's enough payment for me.'

Her hand closed over the smooth stone. 'It certainly has. Thank you, Mr Stone.'

'You'd better go back inside before you catch a cold.' He ambled off with a wave.

As though breaking a spell, his words drew her attention to the thinness of her T-shirt and goose pimples ran up the length of her bare arms. Shivering, toes full of gritty sand, she began to slop her way back up the beach.

When she reached the bottom of the stairs, she saw her friends were waiting for her at the top. They'd at least had the sense to put on proper outerwear. Eliza's expression was one of pure concern as she held out her hand. 'Come back inside and we'll make you a cup of tea.'

Gripping the pebble like a talisman, Beth hurried up the steps. Running away didn't solve anything, and she needed these two more than ever. 'I'm sorry. It just took me by surprise, that's all.'

Libby hooked an arm around her shoulder and gave her a squeeze. 'Come on. Gosh, B, you're freezing! That git isn't worth catching pneumonia over, you're well shot of Charlie. I almost feel sorry for the poor cow who's getting lumbered with him.'

They were halfway up the stairs when it hit her like a freight train. Charlie was getting married. Beth collapsed to her knees, sobs wrenching from her chest so hard the pain burned like a brand. 'He . . . oh, God . . . he . . . married.' She choked on the words.

Eliza sank down beside her, enveloping her in a familiar sweet-smelling hug. 'It's all right. Shh, it's all right.' Beth turned her head into the thick curls of Eliza's hair and cried like the world was ending.

A hand settled on her back, rubbing in circles just the way her mum had done when she'd been sad or unwell as a child. 'Oh, B, I'm so sorry for upsetting you. It's just me and my big mouth, ignore me.'

The edge of one of the treads dug uncomfortably under her ribcage, and her eyes were starting to sting from the salty tears, but it didn't matter because her friends were there, as always. She cried herself numb, until there was nothing left inside but a dull ache, and they let her. Legs shaking like a newborn colt, she allowed the other two to help her up the stairs and onto the sofa. Libby disappeared for a few moments, returning with a soft blanket which she settled over Beth.

Eliza slipped out to make a cup of tea for them all and Libby assumed her perch on the arm of a nearby chair. 'How are you feeling?'

Beth stared down at where her hands were knotted together in her lap. 'I don't know. I thought I was over him, but I can't be, can I, if I'm this upset?'

Libby shrugged. 'It's bound to be a shock. You guys only broke up a few months ago and now he's getting hitched? Something seems a bit off about the whole thing.'

She knew Libby was trying to be supportive, but there was no getting around it—she must still be in love with Charlie, and that meant only one thing. She had no place thinking about Sam as anything other than a friend.

Chapter Fourteen

She was avoiding him. He tried to tell himself otherwise when he was summoned by Eliza to help shift the furniture back into Beth's bedroom and she was nowhere to be found. The changes they'd wrought in less than forty-eight hours blew him away, and there was no mistaking the space for anything other than Beth's room now. The muted lilac and mauve walls were complimented by new curtains and a large rug in silvery-grey tones. He hung around for a few moments, watching his sister place a couple of pewter vases on the previously cluttered dressing table and a group of pillar candles on one of the bedside cabinets.

Whilst his sister hung a new shade to replace the old-fashioned glass fixture, he crossed the room to where Libby was smoothing a dark grey fitted sheet over the mattress. 'Where's Beth?'

Libby handed him two corners of a pale silver duvet cover with a thick band of pewter scroll work decorating the top and muttered something about them running out of milk and an emergency trip to the corner shop for a pint.

Holding still whilst she fed the duvet inside the cover, Sam did his best to keep his tone nonchalant as he said, 'We've got tons of milk next door, you should have asked me to fetch some.'

Libby plumped the pillows before placing them at the head

of the bed. 'Look, she got a bit of bad news yesterday. Her ex is getting married, and she took it hard, so we're giving her a bit of space whilst she sorts things out in her head.'

'Oh. Oh, I see.' Well that put a kibosh on things. He'd been hoping to catch Beth alone for a few minutes, see if she fancied joining him for a run in the morning. Nice and casual, just two friends hanging out. If he played his cards right, he might have been able to coax her into a kiss or two along the way. So much for best laid plans.

His disappointment must have showed, because Eliza crossed the room to slip an arm around his waist. 'Hey, what's with the face?'

Giving himself a mental shake, Sam gave his sister a quick squeeze before letting her go. 'It's just my face, Eliza, nothing much I can do about it.' He crossed his eyes, and pulled his jaw off to one side, knowing it would make her giggle.

'Silly sod.'

He nodded in agreement. 'That's me. Are you planning to see Mum and Dad before you go in the morning?'

'My train's not until ten, so I'll come over first thing. Will you be around?'

'I'll make sure I am. See you later.' He ruffled her hair, then jumped out the way of the elbow she aimed at his ribs. 'Vicious! I'll see you later, Libs. Tell Beth I hope she feels better soon.'

Instead of going home, Sam wandered down the steps at the edge of the promenade and out onto the pale sand. Not thinking about where he was going, his feet took him towards the far end of the beach where the rocks spilled out into the water in a haphazard jumble. Climbing up to his favourite spot, he stripped off his jacket and folded it into a makeshift cushion. How many hours had he spent exploring the pools lurking in and around these rocks? His bedroom windowsill held a collection of pebbles, shells, odds and ends of driftwood, orange string and other detritus which had been fascinating to his eight-year-old self.

The sand beside the rocks had been the best for building. Some kids waited for the tide to go out, so they could draw pictures in the wet sand with sticks, others turned cartwheels and practised elaborate tumbles, heads filled with dreams of joining the circus that passed through the bay every year. He'd always been a builder, though.

He'd tried every location up and down the front, but had always gravitated back to this exact spot with his trusty bucket and spade to sculpt myriad castles, forts and fancy palaces. They'd stood proud and strong all day until the evening tide swept in and wiped them away. It had never stopped him though. When he'd woken up the next morning, he'd been excited to get back down to the beach to build something bigger, something better and even more beautiful than the day before.

His initial disappointment over Beth was wearing off. She'd been with Charlie for a couple of years, so it was bound to come as a shock to her if he was getting hitched so soon after they'd spilt up. Thinking back over the past few weeks, she'd never struck him as someone pining for a lost love. Her grief had all been for Eleanor, and though she'd still not decided for certain whether she'd keep the emporium in the long term, there had been no indication her plans hinged on the possibility of getting back together with Charlie. When they'd been looking for excuses as to why the two of them should remain just friends, he'd never come up.

As far as Sam could see it, he had two choices. Either forget about the burgeoning feelings he had for her or try to persuade her to give them a chance. It didn't need to be anything serious, a spring fling, maybe leading to a summer romance if they were both so inclined. They could focus on their separate businesses without guilt or expectation, and what free time they managed to eke out could be spent getting to know each other better. If it didn't work out, they'd part as friends, and if it did . . . well, there was plenty of time to think about that later.

He was a builder. Time to lay the foundations of what might be a promising future.

'All right, all right, I'm coming.' The bell above the door jangled as Beth yanked it open.

Her face was pale, her eyes bruised and puffy. She looked like hell and for a moment the idea he'd come up with whilst staring at the sea seemed at best foolish, at worst like he was taking advantage of her vulnerable state. Or maybe he was just scared of finding out her heart was still taken. He needed to act before he chickened out. 'Here. These are for you.' He thrust the huge bouquet of roses in shades of cream, lilac and pink at her.

She stared at the flowers. 'What are these for?'

'Read the card.' He pressed the stems against her fingers until she took them.

Balancing them in the crook of her arm, she tugged the little card from the envelope. Her eyebrows rose and she stared up at him. 'Is this some kind of joke?'

Sam leaned one shoulder against the doorway. 'Nope. I mean every single word.'

Colour spotted her cheeks. 'Let's have a spring fling?'

A strand of hair had escaped her ponytail and he reached out to tuck it behind her ear. Unable to resist the softness of her skin, he traced the delicate shell of her ear with the tip of his finger. 'We don't have to call it that. How do you feel about a little March hare-madness, followed by some April fool-about? I know we said we should stick to just being friends, but I can't stop thinking about you, Beth. We could have a great time together.'

Her arms tightened around the bouquet and her eyes narrowed. 'Your timing's lousy.'

She opened a metaphorical door with that comment, and Sam decided to shoulder his way through. 'Eliza told me about Charlie. Don't sulk, it's unbecoming.'

'Don't sulk? Who the hell do you think you are? The man I loved, the man I planned on spending the rest of my life with is

146

getting married, and you have the nerve to tell me not to sulk about it?' She slammed the flowers against his chest. 'Get lost, I never want to see you again.'

He straightened the crumpled cellophane around the flowers before handing them back to her. 'You don't mean that, you're just pissed off because you failed.'

Her jaw dropped and he decided to take the roses back before she beat him around the head with them. They'd cost a bomb, even with Emma, the florist, giving him mate's rates.

A sharp scowl distorted Beth's features. 'I hate you.'

'Nah, you don't, not really.' He set the flowers down on the wide windowsill of the emporium then cupped her shoulders. 'To be clear, I don't think you've failed, but I'm betting that's what you're thinking. I bet you lay in your bed all night soaking tissue after tissue in bitter tears, telling yourself your heart's broken and wracking your brains trying to figure out what you did wrong, why he wants to marry someone else and not you.'

She would've twisted away had he let her, but he tightened his grip on her arms, so she resorted to turning her face to the side to hide her tears. 'Stop it, stop it.'

Doubts wracked him and he questioned the wisdom of playing bad cop, but he'd come too far to stop now. Every tear that trickled down her cheek stabbed him in the gut, and it would be so easy to gather her close and let her cry on his shoulder.

No. No way. If he did that, she'd park him so far in the friend zone, he'd never get back out again. Beth needed someone who would stand up to her, as well as stand up for her. He gave her a gentle shake. 'Your pride is hurting, and that's understandable, but you haven't been acting like a woman with a broken heart for the past few weeks. You've been acting like a woman who's excited about making a fresh start. A woman who's open to new opportunities in both her professional and her private life. When we kiss, it doesn't feel like you're thinking about someone else.'

Releasing one shoulder to cup her cheek, he urged her to

turn back and face him. 'When we kiss, it feels like you are one hundred percent in the moment. That the butterflies dancing in my belly are fluttering around in yours too.'

Her lashes shuttered down, and he knew she wasn't thinking about Charlie anymore. 'And it would be just a fling? Nothing serious.'

He ducked low to whisper against her lips. 'Nothing serious, just two friends exploring an attraction. Nobody's business but ours. If you need someone to rebound into, why not me?' Turning his face to the left, he kissed his way across her cheek, seeking the tender skin beneath her ear.

'Oh, Sam.' She melted against him, the tension in her body easing until she fit perfectly against him. Her hands stole around his waist to grip his back. 'What if we're making a big mistake?' She didn't let him go though.

Sliding a hand up to stroke her nape beneath the length of her ponytail, he cuddled closer. 'We're going into this with our eyes wide open. We can lay down some ground rules if you like.'

Her shoulders hitched with a little laugh. 'You've been thinking about this a lot, haven't you?'

'Every day since we were in your stock room.' He kissed her temple. 'Speaking of which, I'd be quite amenable if you wanted to lure me back there.'

Her lips brushed the underside of his jaw. 'Can I have my flowers back?'

Releasing his hold, he gathered the slightly sorry-looking roses from the windowsill and held them out. Beth took them in her arms and lowered her head to breathe in the scent. 'They're really beautiful.'

Feeling like he could take a decent breath for the first time since she'd opened the door, he relaxed his shoulders. 'I thought they'd look good in one of those pewter vases in your bedroom.'

She shot him a glance through her lashes that set his heart racing faster. 'I know what else would look good in my bedroom.'

'Oh, really?'

Beth gave one of those one shoulder shrugs that every man knew spelled trouble. 'I saw this gorgeous antique mirror in one of the shops in the arcade yesterday. I could do with a hand to carry it.' She buried her nose back in the flowers, but couldn't disguise the amusement shaking in her shoulders.

He supposed he deserved it after accusing her of sulking, but raising a man's hopes—and other things—was just plain mean. 'Low blow, sweetheart.'

She flashed him a smile that showed not one ounce of repentance. 'Well, I've got a busy day ahead. Thanks for the flowers, and your very kind offer. I'll take it under consideration.' Stepping back inside, she closed the door in his face, the happy jangle of the bell adding insult to injury.

He knocked on the glass to catch her attention before she walked away. 'I'll meet you by your back gate at eight tomorrow morning. We can go for a run and work out some of those ground rules.'

She shook her head, but her eyes were bright with amusement. Taking that as acceptance, he tucked his hands in his pockets and sauntered off. Sam couldn't fight the grin spreading over his face. He was a builder and the foundations had been laid.

'I haven't been up here for ages,' Beth said when they paused at the top of the hill to catch their breath.

He shaded his eyes and followed her gaze out across the higgledy-piggledy warren of streets laid out below them. Like a lot of places which had started from a reliance on the sea, the town had grown outwards from the main beach area with no plan. Houses had been added as required, their mismatched styles reflecting whatever the trend had been at the time, or more often, whatever the budget of the new owner could afford.

Unhooking the small backpack he carried, he fished out his water bottle and went to take a drink then offered it to Beth first.

Her cheeks were rosy, from a combination of exertion and the chilly breeze. Sweat-dampened tendrils of hair clung to her forehead and curled around her neck where they'd escaped from the high ponytail. Having taken a good drink, she offered the bottle back to him and he took a swig before stowing it away once more.

'Have you had enough, or do you want to carry on?' He could manage another couple of miles easily, but he was conscious she might not be used to the same pace.

'I'm not in a hurry to get back, but maybe we could walk for a bit?'

That was more than fine with him. 'We could carry on over the rise and make our way towards the lavender farm.' There wouldn't be much to see this time of year, but the bridle path would be quiet, and they'd be protected from the worst of the wind once they got down the hill a bit. He held out his hand, and she stared at it for a few moments before slipping her fingers in between his.

They strolled in silence for a few minutes. From the little frown line between her brows, Sam got the feeling Beth was working something out in her mind so he was content to leave her to it. A few puddles lingered in the centre of the stony pathway carved out over generations by walkers and riders, so he steered her to the left, letting her walk in front of him, but keeping hold of her hand.

The scrubby trees on the banks bordering the path were bare at first glance, the grasses surrounding their trunks yellowed and limp. But to a discerning eye, the signs of spring were there in the tiny buds greening on the twigs, the hints of birdsong carried on the breeze. Sam loved this time of year when it was like the land was stirring from the deep sleep of winter, waiting for its cue from Mother Nature to burst into life once more.

As the trees thinned out again, the landscape opened to reveal the rolling fields of Gilbert's farm. Row upon neat row of closely pruned lavender plants marched across the surrounding hills. Even this early in the season, a heady scent drifted from the traditional grey slate and stone farm buildings clustered in the natural hollow formed by the surrounding hills. In the sea of muted colours below, the bright red sports car parked in front of the farmhouse was unmissable.

He stopped to inhale the rich fragrance mixed with the salty breeze coming in off the sea wondering if there was a way to capture it. It would be perfect for Subterranean. A couple of diffusers hidden discreetly in the entrance alcove would set the scene for an evening of sensual delights.

Beth glanced back at him. 'What's put that look on your face?' she asked, with a gentle squeeze of his fingers.

'Take a breath. Tell me what you smell.'

She closed her eyes and did as he bade, her lips curving up at the corners. 'Home. I smell home.'

Unable to resist the temptation of that smile, Sam closed the small distance between them and cupped the back of her head, beneath her ponytail. He waited for her eyes to open, watched as her pupils dilated in acknowledgement of his closeness to her body, and waited some more. Only when she began to move, to stretch on tiptoe, her fingers curling into the thick cotton of his tracksuit top did he lower his head to bring their mouths together.

Needing to know she was fully on-board, he ceded control of the moment to her, following her lead as she nibbled at his lower lip, letting her take her time. And then he was beyond conscious decision as she traced her tongue along the seam of his mouth and he lost himself in the sweet taste of her, in the delicious press of her body against his.

When she lowered her feet flat, he followed her down, straining his neck to catch every last moment until she turned her face away with a breathy laugh. 'I think we should talk about those ground rules, don't you?'

Tucking her beneath his arm, he started them moving back along the track. 'As long as kissing you as often as I can remains on the table, I'll be happy.'

Beth halted to tug his head back down for another kiss so hot it made him forget the chilly edge of the March breeze. 'I'm very amenable to that,' she whispered against his cheek once they finally came up for air. 'As for the other rules, there's only one that's really important to me . . .'

At the sudden seriousness in her tone, he moved back to put a little space between them, so he could focus on what she had to say without being distracted by the growing demands of his body. 'I'm listening.'

She snagged his hand, lacing their fingers together. 'Everyone's been so fantastic since Eleanor died. They've offered me support, a shoulder to cry on, but you're the only one who's stood up to me. I needed your honesty yesterday, about Charlie. Promise me that however this thing between us progresses, you won't stop delivering the hard truths if you think I need to hear them.'

Sam tightened his hand around hers. 'I promise, but only if you do the same. You were the one who helped me see past my own disappointment to better understand my dad's point of view. I don't know where we'd be right now without that.'

152

Chapter Fifteen

Beth set the tray of borrowed glasses down on the front counter and adjusted the handset under her ear. 'I'm not ready, it's going to be a disaster,' she wailed into the phone.

Deep laughter greeted her declaration sending little tendrils of warmth curling through her. 'Stop being a wimp, you've worked your arse off all week and everything is going to be fantastic.' Sam paused. 'And if it's a disaster at least your guests can enjoy all that delicious food Eliza and I made for you.'

It was her turn to laugh. 'Is that your idea of a pep talk? Why do I even bother with you?'

'Because I'm the best kisser in Lavender Bay.' The man had a point—not that she'd been getting any lately. Getting the emporium ready for opening was taking up every waking moment of her time and they hadn't had a chance to put any of their ground rules into practice. Her life was distinctly lacking in anything remotely resembling a fling.

Exaggerating a sigh, she swapped the phone to her other ear and started pulling sheets of cling film off the bowls of nibbles she'd set out on every available surface. 'Yeah, I vaguely remember you having some basic skills in that department.'

'Basic? Basic?'

153

Whatever he said next she missed because she was laughing so hard she dropped her phone. 'Damn!' She bent down to scoop it up and knocked her head on the corner of a shelf. 'Ouch.'

'What was that? Are you okay?'

She rubbed her head. 'I'm fine, just a little karmic rebound, that's all.' Closing her eyes, she sucked in a deep breath. 'Tell me I've got this.'

'You've got this. You do. The emporium looks great, especially the local art collection. I think it's inspired. Mum and Dad will be there to lend a hand, not that you'll need it. And you can tell me all about it later.'

'Thank you. You might be a basic kisser, but your pep talks are on the money.' She lowered her voice to a husky murmur. 'If you've got time to work on your skills, there's a couple of boxes I could do with a hand with in the stock room.'

'Temptress.' He heaved an exaggerated sigh. 'Much as I'd love to take you up on such a delightful invitation, this basic kisser has to go because we've got a walk-in looking for a room. I'll call you later, okay?'

They'd both agreed that work came first, but she couldn't hide her frustration. 'Okay.'

'Hey, no sulking, it'll be great.' He hung up and consequently missed her outraged squawk. She was seriously starting to regret asking him to be honest all the time. Checking her watch, she did a quick mental calculation. It would be early in Florida, but her mum had always been an early riser. She shouldn't have left it this long; dutiful daughters called their mothers every fortnight. It was another part of her mum's happy family charade. It was a miracle word hadn't already got back to Linda, although she'd cut ties pretty thoroughly after leaving the bay.

Bracing herself with one hand on the counter, Beth scrolled through her address book and pressed dial.

'Hello?'

'Mum? It's me, Beth.'

'Hello, stranger. So you haven't dropped off the edge of the earth then? I did wonder when I hadn't heard from you.'

Beth bit back a sigh at her mother's snippy tone. The amazing thing about phones was that they worked both ways. She might not have called, but neither had Linda—not that it would occur to her, of course. 'I wanted to make sure I caught you before you started your day, I know how busy you are.'

'Well actually, it's a good job you did call now because the girls from the bridge league are meeting for breakfast at the club this morning.' Girls might be stretching it a bit, even with the extensive amount of plastic surgery popular amongst them.

'I wanted to let you know that Eleanor left the emporium to me in her will, and I've decided to take over running it.' She took a deep breath, then hurried on. 'In fact, I'm hosting an opening party this evening.'

'But what about your job in London? You can't possibly hope to manage a shop and keep up with all your other work at the same time. What were you thinking?'

Realising her knuckles had turned white where she was gripping the counter so hard, Beth forced her fingers to unclench. 'I was thinking that my job wasn't making me very happy, that I was being taken for granted. Running the emporium is a real challenge, Mum, and I'm having fun being my own boss for a change. I thought you'd be happy for me.' She hadn't really, but it was worth a try.

'Happy?' Beth winced at her mum's shrill tone. 'You've thrown away all your prospects to run that smelly, shabby hovel. I knew I shouldn't have left you in that woman's care. She's brainwashed you!'

'Eleanor was a wonderful friend to me, and it was only through her kindness that you were free to start your new life with Reg. Please don't speak ill of her.' It took effort not to raise her voice, but getting into a full-blown fight with her mum wouldn't do any good. Linda hated Lavender Bay and she would never understand why not everyone else felt the same way.

'Oh, I might have known I'd end up being the bad guy in all this, when all I've ever wanted is what's best for you. You're throwing your life away, Beth. I hate to see you throwing away all that potential so you can play at being a shopkeeper.' A loud sniffle followed the outburst.

When Beth didn't jump in to placate her, her mum huffed, her crocodile tears abandoned almost as quickly as they'd started. 'Don't expect me to wish you good luck. If you have any sense at all you'll sell that place and use the money towards building a proper future.'

Beth closed her eyes and prayed for patience. Why had she honestly expected anything other than this? 'Nothing's set in stone, Mum, but if I do decide to sell it then surely it's better to be able to offer a going concern rather than an empty shell?'

Stony silence. She bit her lip, refusing to let herself get upset. Well, I just wanted to tell you about the opening tonight. I'll give you a call sometime and let you know how I'm getting on. Bye, Mum.'

She hung up before her mum had even finished saying goodbye, disappointment weighing her shoulders down. There was no time to brood as someone knocked on the front door. Flipping the lock, she fixed a big smile on her face and opened it. 'Welcome! Oh, it's you.'

'Jesus, B, that's the scariest expression I've ever seen. If you're not careful, you'll scare off all your potential customers.'

'I just got off the phone to Mum.'

'Oh, God, no wonder you look ready for a scrap.' Libby bustled in a large box under her arm. 'Wow, it looks great in here.' She grabbed a handful of peanuts and stuffed them in her mouth. 'I'm starving!'

Slapping her hand away from the bowl, Beth laughed, her friend's vibrant personality the perfect foil to her mother's coldness. 'You work in a chip shop, Libs, how can you possibly be starving?'

'Ugh! Are you kidding? If I never see another saveloy in my life, it'll be too soon.' She turned in a circle. 'Where can I put this?' She started pushing some of the carefully positioned bowls aside.

Beth leapt forward. 'Hey, it took me ages to get these in the right place.' Easing Libby aside, she shifted a plate back six inches to the left. 'What's in the box, anyway?'

'Be patient.' Libby pulled her tablet out from her shoulder bag and started fiddling with it. She clicked on an icon and Eliza's face filled the screen. 'Finally! Did she open it yet? Put me somewhere I can see what's going on.'

'Hold your horses,' Libby scolded. She held the tablet against her chest, pointing it at Beth. 'Can you see now?'

'I can see her belly button. Nice blouse, by the way, Beth. Very classy.' Libby lifted the tablet higher. 'That's it, hold it there!'

'God, you're bossy.' Libby nodded at Beth. 'Eliza and I wanted to say we both think what you're doing is amazing, and we couldn't be more proud of you.'

'And we know you're going to be a runaway success,' Eliza chipped in.

'I was getting to that bit.' Libby rolled her eyes. 'So, anyway, we wanted to get you something to celebrate your new venture.'

A familiar tingle started behind Beth's eyes and she blinked rapidly to chase away the impending tears. 'You didn't need to do that.'

'Oh, hush, of course we did. That's what best friends are for.' Libby said. 'Now open the box.'

The top of the box had been folded in on itself and she tugged one of the long flaps free. A pile of pink tissue paper greeted her. Lifting the other flap, she lifted out handfuls of the paper to reveal a bubble-wrapped rectangle. A gold label she recognised secured the wrapping in place. Pausing, Beth, glanced up. 'What did you do?'

Libby grinned. 'Open it.'

Fingers shaking, she peeled the label and folded back the bubble wrap. 'Oh. Oh my God.' Inside a white pine frame was a delicate watercolour rendering of a small section of the promenade from the perspective of someone on the beach. Sitting in the centre, slightly larger than the buildings to either side was a beautiful rendering of the emporium, complete with its brand-new stripy awning and a sign showing the new name.

No amount of blinking was going to hold back the tears this time. 'It's beautiful,' she snivelled. 'Just beautiful. Thank you.'

'Oh, B, not your make-up!' Libby dumped the tablet on the counter to fumble in her pocket for a tissue. 'Deep breaths, deep breaths, come on now.' She flapped her hands in front of Beth's face as she pressed the tissue hard against the corners of her eyes.

'I'm okay, I'm okay.' Beth took a deep breath and held it for a count of five. 'I'm okay.' She grabbed Libby's face between her hands to smack a kiss on her lips. 'Thank you. You're amazing' Picking up the tablet, she kissed the screen. 'You too, Eliza. You're both incredible and I couldn't have done this without you.'

'Nonsense.' Eliza grinned at her from the slightly smeared screen. 'You did all the hard work, not us. Take pride in what you've achieved, and this is only the beginning. I just wish I could be there with you.'

'Me too. Maybe you can come and see us again in a few weeks once the weather warms up? You'll need to work on your tan if you're going abroad.' Eliza's bright smile faded, making Beth wince. *Foot, meet mouth.*

A knock was swiftly followed by the jaunty ring of the bell over the front door. Beth glanced over her shoulder. 'Oh, hey, your folks are here. Do you want to say hi?'

Leaving Annie and Paul chatting to their daughter, Beth did a final circuit of the shop, double-checking—or more like quadruple-checking—everything was in place.

Libby came over to join her. 'What can I do?'

'There's a checklist over on the counter . . . what? Why are you laughing?'

'Of course, there's a checklist. I don't know why I didn't just look for it in the first place.' Still chuckling, Libby joined Annie and Paul at the counter where they divvied up the last couple of jobs.

Beth checked her watch. It was twenty minutes to the opening and the first of the artists should be there any moment. The bell over the door rang again, and Beth fixed her 'I'm confident and organised smile' in place as she headed over to greet them. She was keen to expand, using the emporium as a showcase for their work. If running the shop didn't work out for Beth in the long run, she had it in mind to ask whether they'd be interested in taking it on in some kind of collective capacity. It might mean a shift from the current eclectic stock the place carried, but Eleanor had been the one to bring them on board in the first place so a part of her legacy would live on.

Annie edged through the crowded shop towards Beth and handed her a glass of champagne. 'Everyone else has got a drink so I think it's time. If you're ready I can start herding people outside?'

Beth nodded. 'Thank you.' She touched Annie's arm when she would have turned away. 'It's going okay, isn't it? I mean, everyone's here. The place is packed, and they've said lots of nice things. It's just . . .'

'Everything's perfect.' Taking care not to knock either of their glasses, Annie swept Beth into a sweet-scented hug. Chanel No.5. Beth smiled to herself as the elegant perfume wafted around them. For as long as she could remember, Annie had kept a bottle of it on her dressing table. She and Eliza had snuck in there to play dress-up and had drenched themselves in the stuff. Instead of getting mad, Annie had sat them both down and showed them the secrets of her make-up bag.

Annie stepped back and clinked their glasses together. 'You've got a huge hit on your hands, especially with the artists. I've already talked Paul into arranging for that lovely jeweller to make me some earrings for our anniversary next month. It's pearl.'

Beth grinned. 'I get twenty percent commission on any orders placed here tonight so make sure he doesn't scrimp.'

'Good point, I'll talk him into a matching necklace. I pushed two of his babies out of my body so that man owes me.' She raised an eyebrow. 'Don't look at me like that, young lady. Thirty hours of labour for the first and over eighteen for the second. He's going to owe me for the rest of his life.'

Paul slid his arm around her waist, the other resting on a walking stick Beth hadn't seen him use before today. Another sign he was taking his health more seriously. 'And I enjoy paying back the debt, my dearest heart. Come on now, let's get this lot outside before they drink all the booze.'

Watching them go, a tingle of warmth spread through Beth easing her nerves. Most of the people there had been on their feet all day dealing with the worries and stresses of their own businesses, and yet they hadn't hesitated to give up their evening to welcome her back into their fold. It made her sad to think her mum had never been able to see this side of life in their small town.

Once everyone gathered on the pavement outside, Beth took her place next to the rope the joiners had attached to the tarp covering the sign above the front windows. Libby handed her a teaspoon which she tapped against her glass until the conversation died down. Staring out at her friends and neighbours, she felt the collective weight of their expectations and uttered a silent prayer she'd be up to the challenge.

'Ladies and gentlemen. I want to thank you all for coming here this evening to help me celebrate the official re-opening of the emporium. I know how much Eleanor meant to you all, and she meant the absolute world to me.' Beth had to pause for a moment and gather herself. 'I never expected such an incredible gift and I only hope I can do her faith in me justice. Yes, I've made some changes, but this will always be her place.'

She passed her glass to Libby and took the rope in both hands.

Please work. Please, please, please. Beth pulled hard and the tarpaulin tumbled down. A sigh rippled around the crowd and she knew she'd made the right choice. 'Welcome to Eleanor's Emporium.'

'Last load.' Beth promised herself as she yanked open the dishwasher door and wafted away the steam billowing out. Her feet were killing her—the heels had been a huge mistake, even if they'd been a perfect match for her blouse and pencil skirt. First thing tomorrow, she was going online to look for some pretty flats. She scrunched her aching toes inside her fluffy slippers and sighed in relief. Now if she could only find a full-body slipper to ease the stiffness in the rest of her. 'Last load,' she muttered and bent to empty the glasses from the dishwasher.

She'd just placed the last glass in the slotted box they'd come in when the bell at the back door buzzed. Grumbling about the strain in the back of her calf, she limped down the stairs. Common sense kicked in the second before she pulled open the door—she was alone in the place after all. Flipping on the exterior light, she squinted at the large shape on the other side of the frosted safety glass. She checked her watch; it was past eleven. A frisson of fear shivered through her and she took a reflexive step backwards. 'Who is it?'

'It's me.'

'Sam?' The security chain rattled as she slipped it off and opened the door. 'What are you doing here?'

He held up a bottle of champagne and a polystyrene box. 'I bought you dinner.' Her stomach rumbled reflexively and he smiled. 'All those sausage rolls, and I bet you didn't have a single mouthful all evening.'

Her hand settled on her noisy stomach and warmth flooded her cheeks. 'I was a bit busy. By the time I thought about it, the plates were empty.'

He lifted the box towards her. 'Tonight's special was chicken curry.' Her mouth watered at the thought of it. 'I didn't get around

161

to eating either. That drop-in guest turned out to be a pain in the arse. He hated everything about his room, even down to the brand of the freebie toiletries. I ended up giving him a bottle of fancy shower gel Mum gave me for Christmas and changing out the pillows. About the only thing he didn't complain about was the curry, so it must be good.'

Beth laughed and held open the door to let him in. 'You should have come to the party, I had nothing but happy customers.'

'Really? That's fantastic. We definitely need to toast that.'

Beth locked up and followed him up the stairs and into the kitchen. 'One more glass and I might fall over. What I missed out on with the nibbles, I more than made up for with drinks. Every time I turned around, someone was there to refill my glass.'

He paused in the act of pulling plates out of the cabinet. 'We can have a soft drink, it's no big deal, I just wanted to celebrate with you.'

Sliding her arms around his waist, she pressed against the broad, solid warmth of his back. 'Open the champagne. If that chicken curry is as good as you claim I might just take advantage of you.'

Sam turned in her arms. 'That sounds like the booze and the aftermath of the adrenalin talking.'

She pressed a row of kisses along his jaw. 'Maybe a little, does that matter?'

His arms dropped to press her tight against him for a moment, before he eased her gently away. 'It matters. I wish all the way down to the ache in my groin that it didn't, but it matters. We're going to eat this curry, drink a pint of water each, smooch a bit on the sofa and then I'm tucking you into bed—alone.'

'Do you know how annoying it is when you take charge all the time?' She stamped her foot, immediately regretting her show of petulance when her toes began throbbing again.

'You'll thank me in the morning when you don't have a hangover or any morning-after regrets.'

He had a point, although she doubted there would be anything to regret about letting him into her bed. Opening the cupboard next to him, she grabbed a couple of pint glasses and carried them over to the sink. 'You're probably right. After all, being such a mediocre kisser doesn't give me much hope for your prowess between the sheets.' She bit her lip to hold back a giggle as she filled the glasses.

'Mediocre? When did I get downgraded from basic to bloody mediocre? Your memory must be failing, woman. Here, let me remind you.' Beth found herself hauled around and swept into a tight embrace. Sam's lips slammed down onto hers, and then he was kissing her so deeply she didn't even mind the way it made her aching toes curl in her slippers. By the time he released her, she had to clutch the sink behind her so she didn't slide to the floor.

With a satisfied sniff, Sam wandered away to dish up the curry. Placing the plates on the table, he nodded at the seat in front of her. 'Are you sitting down? Your dinner's getting cold.'

'I'll be there in a minute, just as soon as my knees stop wobbling,' she admitted.

The expression on his face could only be described as gloating. 'Mediocre, huh?'

Gathering the shreds of her dignity, she slid into her seat. 'Did I say that, I think I meant to say adequate.' It might have been her turn to gloat as he choked on a mouthful of his curry. She offered him one of the glasses. 'Water?'

Chapter Sixteen

It had been the right thing to do. Sam attempted to console himself the next morning when he climbed out of his lonely bed and hit the shower. Beth had been buzzed, and not just on the champagne. Once he got her talking about the party she couldn't stop, her eyes shining with excitement as she recalled anecdote after anecdote about things that had happened, comments and compliments she'd received. When he heard about the reaction to the new sign, as well as what she'd chosen to call the place, he got a lump in his throat the size of a boiled egg. Speaking of which . . . he was on breakfast duty for their guests this morning so there had been a shred of practicality to his decision not to stay over as well.

Dragging on a clean T-shirt and jeans, he made his way to the small upstairs dining room where he'd set up three of the tables for breakfast the previous evening. One of the tables was already occupied, and he paused on the threshold to swallow a sigh when he recognised the awkward guest who'd arrived the previous day. 'Good morning, Mr Coburn. You're an early bird. Did you sleep well?'

'Once all the racket next door quietened down I had a reasonable night, thanks.' He looked at his watch. 'Your literature implied breakfast started at 7 a.m.' The timepiece on his wrist looked as expensive as the discreet logo above the breast pocket on his immaculately ironed shirt. The neck lay open, showing a thin gold chain with a St Christopher medal hanging from it. He'd seemed older when he'd arrived the night before in a smart pinstripe suit, but in the early morning sunlight, Sam judged him to be near-enough the same age as him.

Resisting the urge to check his own watch, Sam stuck his hands in his pockets and offered a friendly smile. He knew it was barely five past because he'd checked the clock before leaving his bedroom. 'There was a party to celebrate the reopening of the shop next door, I should have thought about that before I moved you to one of the front bedrooms. And I'm sorry you've been kept waiting for your breakfast. I set the coffee brewing before I had a shower, so it should be almost ready. Would you like some juice?'

'Orange, please. Do you have newspapers?' Mr Coburn gave a pointed glance around the room. There was a small cardboard rack filled with leaflets on the Welsh dresser in the corner detailing local attractions which was usually the only reading materials their guests were interested in.

'If you let me know your preferences, I'll nip down the road to the newsagent's as soon as I've fetched your drinks. We do the usual breakfast choices: a full English or any permutation thereof, grapefruit, cereals, porridge, pastries. Have a think about what you want, and I'll be straight back.' Sam escaped into the kitchen to fix both himself and Mr Coburn a large coffee before the man had the chance to voice any further complaints.

'Not your usual reading material, Sam.' Neil Tate observed from across the newsagent's counter as he took the ten-pound note Sam proffered him.

'Just trying to keep the guests happy, Neil. I don't know why we hadn't thought about this before. I might have a chat with you sometime soon about a regular order for the pub.' He patted the stack of papers under his arm. 'Not sure we'll have much call for the *FT* on a regular basis though.'

Neil smiled. 'Whatever you need, Sam. Mabel at the B&B asks guests when they book what their preferences are, maybe you could do the same.'

'Great idea. I'll add it to the website and get back to you.'

'No problem. Hey, I saw your folks at the party last night, I assumed that meant you were working.' Sam nodded the affirmative. 'You missed a great do. That girl's really outdone herself. Claire and I both said afterwards what a lovely tribute it was to Eleanor to rename the place after her. We have high hopes for Beth.'

His mum and dad had been full of praise when they'd got in, and he'd heard Beth's side of things, but it pleased him to know people like Neil were spreading the good word about the emporium. In a small town like Lavender Bay it was vital to have the support of the other local businesses and it sounded like Beth was off to a positive start. 'Me too. I'd better scoot, guests waiting and all that.'

Having settled his guest behind a plate of poached eggs, bacon and toast and the newspapers of his choice spread out over the table, Sam grabbed his own toast and took five minutes to scribble out a list of chores for the day. His plans for Subterranean had taken a bit of a backseat whilst they all adjusted to a new routine at the pub.

With his dad back in charge of the stock and helping out with a couple of the quieter shifts behind the bar, things were much easier between them all. There would likely be a few tweaks to be made now the first influx of tourists had arrived, but at least they were communicating properly. Now he knew he had something to work towards for himself, Sam was in much less of a hurry. Better to do it once, and do it right.

Hoping he'd given Mr Coburn enough time, Sam poked his

head around the dining room door. Spotting the empty plate pushed to one side, he entered the room. 'All finished? Can I get you anything else?'

Mr Coburn glanced up over the edge of his paper. 'Another coffee, please, and do you have a guide or directory of some kind for businesses in the area?'

Sam frowned. 'There's a local traders' association. I can give you the address for their website which details the members. Do you mind if I ask what you want it for?'

'I'm on the lookout for investment opportunities. I thought I had a line on something, but it fell through.' He stuck a hand in his shirt pocket and produced a business card. 'I'm a redeveloper.'

Alarm bells started ringing in Sam's head as he studied the card. Hadn't Beth told him a developer had been interested in the emporium before she'd decided to keep it? If this was the same guy, what was he doing sniffing around the place?

'The website?'

Sam started. 'Sorry, of course.' He fished a pen and the notepad he used for breakfast orders out of his pocket and scribbled down the address. 'Here you go.' At least Beth hadn't got around to joining the association, so her contact details wouldn't be on the site. 'I'll get you that coffee now.'

By the time the other guests had been fed, watered, and pointed in the direction of local attractions it was past nine-thirty and Sam was itching for some fresh air. Donning his running gear, he set out on his usual route.

The number of people already on the beach filled him with hope. An early Easter season was always touch and go with the weather. Some families chose to stick closer to home rather than risk spending hard-earned money and then sit in a rain-lashed caravan for a week. The temperature might still be on the fresh side, but the sun was up, and it was blue sky as far as the eye could see.

Continuing towards Baycrest, it cheered him to see the staff had pulled back the wide patio doors and were setting up a few loungers, chairs and tables outside. Spotting his grandad, Sam changed direction and jogged up onto the patio. 'Hey, Pops, how's it going?'

Pops doffed his cap to scrub at the thick curls on his head. 'Morning, Sammy. Looks like a good start to the season, eh?'

Sam smiled. Pops might be a little slower on his feet these days, but his mind was still sharp as a pin and Sam would encourage his interest for as long as he expressed it. 'Signs look hopeful. The beach is busy, and according to the traffic report I heard before I set out there's a long tailback on the motorway already.' Busy roads might be frustrating for drivers caught up on them, but they also meant extra visitors.

Pops rubbed his hands together. 'That's what we like to hear. It's a bit brisk, so make sure you get that specials board out early and make a double batch of soup. People like easy meals for lunch and soup will give them a chance to warm up ready for the afternoon.'

It was already on his to-do list, but Sam didn't mention that. 'Good idea, Pops, thanks.'

'So, how's that girl of yours getting on?' The twinkle in Pop's eye was nothing if not mischievous.

It would be easy enough to protest, to deflect and demure with some statement about them being friends, but Sam was tired of that. 'She's doing great. The party last night was a real hit and with so many early visitors to the bay, I'm hoping the rest of her opening week will be as successful.'

Pops gave him a speculative look. 'You've decided to give it a go with her then, boy? Well, it's about damn time.' Smoothing his hair, he tucked his cap back on his head. 'I had a chat with some of the ladies over breakfast, and seeing how it's such a nice day we thought we'd take our morning coffee on the patio and then have a bit of stroll along the prom, have a little look around, do a bit of shopping.'

Sam hugged his grandad tight. 'Thanks, Pops. That would

mean the world to her. Oh, and don't get carried away with the idea of me and Beth being together, it's just a bit of fun, nothing serious.' Ignoring his grandad's snort, Sam waved to the three ladies who'd just stepped out onto the patio to join Pops, and set off on his run again.

He'd made it almost all the way home when Emma stepped out of the florist's shop and called out to him. 'Oh, Sam. How did those flowers work out for you the other day?'

He thought about the sweet, sleepy kiss Beth had given him on the doorstep as he'd left the previous night. 'They did the trick, thanks.'

She touched his arm. 'That's lovely to hear, it's about time you found someone to appreciate you.'

Having already said more than he'd meant to to Pops, he drew a zip across his mouth. 'My lips are sealed.' He cast a quick glance down at himself, then gave Emma a rueful smile. 'I'd better hit the shower and get prepping for lunch. See you later.'

It wasn't worth jogging the hundred yards from the florist to the pub, so he set off an at easy stroll. If he walked slowly enough he could get a good gander through the window of the emporium and see how things were going. He wouldn't stop, he didn't want Beth to think he was checking up on her, but a casual glance was what any passer-by would do.

He was almost parallel with the business next door when he recognised the man walking towards him. He'd pulled a blazer on over his shirt, but there was no mistaking the imposing figure of Mr Coburn. Maybe he was just taking a look around, as he'd mentioned over breakfast . . .

Not looking left or right, Mr Coburn marched straight through the front door of the emporium. Or maybe not . . . It took all of Sam's willpower to walk past the front door.

Chapter Seventeen

The bell over the door hadn't stopped ringing since Beth had taken a deep breath and flipped the sign from 'closed' to 'open'. It had mostly been curious locals who hadn't made it to the opening party, but she'd also had a pleasing number of tourists coming for a nose around. The buckets and spades had proven popular, as had the jars of penny sweets. She wouldn't be buying a Rolls Royce any time soon, but there were coins and notes in her till other than the ones she'd put there herself for a float.

'Beth? Can you give me a hand, lovey?'

The smile on her face as she stepped out from behind the counter was not in the least bit forced as she responded to the request. 'Hello, Mr Stone, what can I do for you? Have you come to sell me some of those painted stones of yours?'

He gave her shoulder a nudge as she came to stand beside him. 'You're all grown up now, so I think it's past time you called me Mick, don't you? And no, it's not about the stones, I'm looking for some help with a gift.'

Although she'd been on first-name terms with Eliza and Sam's parents for years, she'd never relaxed the formality with Libby's dad. He'd always been a slightly remote figure, mostly due to juggling raising his daughter whilst running the chip shop single-handed, but still kindly in his way. She nudged him back with a grin. 'Thank you, Mick. Are you looking for something in particular?'

He scratched at the thin layer of greying stubble on his head. 'It's my Libby's birthday soon and she's dropped a million hints about wanting some jewellery, but I'm not sure where to start.' He waved a helpless hand towards the display cabinet.

'Of course.' She reached for the ring of keys clipped to a bungy cord at her waist and unlocked the glass front so she could lift out the trays. After studying the selection, she chose a bracelet of silver filigree flowers studded with delicate agate stones. There was a matching necklace with a single, larger flower and a choice of stud or drop earrings. Laying them out on a black velvet square she'd bought especially to best display items customers wanted a closer look at, she continued to browse the trays whilst Mick touched a tentative fingertip to the bracelet.

'Here, I think either of these rings will go with them. They're not a perfect match, but the stones are close enough in shading to compliment. Take your time and decide which combination of items you want, and I'll gift wrap them for you.'

'Thanks, lovey. You're a lifesaver.'

The bell rang. 'Will you be all right for a minute whilst I see to this new customer?'

Mick waved her away. 'Of course, take your time.'

Beth set her shoulders back and turned with a smile. 'Welcome to Eleanor's Emporium.'

Her mouth dried a little at the sight of the stunningly handsome man filling the doorway. Tall and broad through the shoulders, his figure tapered to a trim waist emphasised by the superior cut of his jacket. Whoever he was, he was definitely not a tourist. The dark hair cropped severely to his scalp gave him a hard edge that the smart clothes and easy smile couldn't quite cancel out.

Approaching with an instinctive sense of caution, Beth asked, 'How can I help you?'

'Are you the proprietor?' When she nodded, he took a long look around the shop before settling his piercing dark eyes back upon her. 'Owen Coburn.'

The way he said his name implied she should recognise it, but she was sure they'd never met before. Owen Coburn didn't have the kind of face you would forget in a hurry. Not that she would admit that. 'I'm sorry, have we met?'

With a look she was going to politely pretend wasn't just this side of a sneer, he pulled a business card out of his pocket. 'Your solicitor should have told you about me.'

The logo in the top left corner brought the memory flooding back. 'You're the one who wanted to buy the emporium.'

He nodded. 'I was surprised to have my offer knocked back. I thought it was very generous given the circumstances.'

She was starting to find that superior tone irritating. 'Circumstances?'

Turning a circle, he held out his hands to encompass the room. 'You're not exactly sitting on a goldmine, are you? Penny sweets and inflatable crocodiles aren't going to make you rich.' Maybe it was the echo of her own thoughts, or maybe it was the condescending glint in his eye, but Owen Coburn was suddenly a lot less attractive.

Bristling, she let the smile she'd been holding fall away. 'As my solicitor informed you, I'm not interested in selling so your opinion on my business hardly counts, does it? Now is there something I can get you? We've had a run on buckets and spades this morning. Maybe you should buy one, help you with that hole you're digging.'

To her surprise, the man threw his head back and laughed. 'Feisty one, aren't you? Maybe you'd like to join me in the pub for a drink later and I'll see if I can do anything to sweeten the offer.' The gleam in his eye told her exactly what form any negotiations with him would take.

Cheeky bastard! First, he insulted her, then he tried to

172

proposition her. 'I could say I'm flattered by your offer, but I'd be lying.' She handed him back his card.

Owen held up his hands in surrender. 'Message received, loud and clear. I won't take up any more of your time.' He turned on his heel to head for the door, paused, then walked quickly to the counter and dropped his business card. 'Just in case you change your mind about selling, or anything else for that matter.' With an outrageous wink, he was gone.

Of all the arrogant . . .

'Who was that, lovey?' Mick Stone interrupted Beth before she could build up a really good head of steam.

'Nobody important. Some developer who offered to buy the place not long after Eleanor died. Wanted to turn the place into luxury flats or some such nonsense.' She dusted off her hands, dismissing all thoughts of Owen bloody Coburn and his smarmy grin. 'Have you decided what you wanted?'

Mick stared over his shoulder at the door for a long moment before turning back to her with a smile. 'I thought I'd get her the lot. She works so hard, and I've not always been good in showing my appreciation. She's not had an easy life, and I hate that she had to grow up so quickly, what with her mum and everything.'

The sadness clouding his eyes threatened to bring tears to her own. It must have been a dozen years or more since his wife's tragic death, but it was clear Mick still carried a torch for her. She cleared her throat, not wanting him to catch on to the sympathy she felt for him. Libby had a proud streak a mile-wide and there was no mistaking which parent she'd inherited it from. 'Let's get these wrapped up nicely then.' She gathered the velvet cloth in her hands.

He followed her as she moved behind the counter, then leaned over it in a conspiratorial manner. 'I worry about her, lovey. I thought the hair and the clothes would be a phase, but she's not showing any signs of growing out of it. I know she confides in you, you would tell me if there was anything wrong?'

He looked so concerned, Beth's heart went out to him. 'She's fine, Mick, although you might have to accept that the way she looks and dresses isn't a phase. I reckon when me, her and Eliza are living out our golden years up at Baycrest she'll still have rainbow hair.'

Mick chuckled. 'I reckon you're right. She's a bit of a peacock, likes to stand out in the crowd, does my girl.'

Beth took some sheets of coloured tissue paper from beneath the counter and wrapped each piece of jewellery carefully before placing them in a red and white striped box bearing the words 'Eleanor's Emporium' in the same font as the exterior signage. 'There's nothing wrong with that, Mick.'

'Nothing wrong at all.' After paying with his credit card, he held up the little paper bag she'd slipped the box into. 'Thanks for your help with this, you're a star.'

'My pleasure. And thank you for giving Libby so much time off lately. I couldn't have achieved half what I have with this place without her support.'

Mick nodded. 'You're welcome. Having you back home means the world to her. The absolute world.'

She surprised herself by replying, 'It does to me too. Tell her I'll wander up for closing and take her for a drink. And don't forget to think about selling me your stones. I'm going to keep asking.'

He left the shop with a nod and a wave, and Beth leaned her elbows on the counter with a sigh. For the first time since opening the place was quiet. Slipping off her shoes, she pressed the soles of her feet into the cold floor, closing her eyes as the burn in her arches faded. She really needed to get some flats.

She pulled out her tablet from underneath the counter and clicked the shopping icon. A vast array of shoes popped up, from glitter-studded mules to the kind of sensible lace-ups her mum had forced her to wear all through junior school. Her finger hovered over a pair of expensive designer ballet flats with a pretty bow on the top. *You're not exactly sitting on a goldmine, are you?* Owen's mocking words echoed in her mind, and she scowled.

Sod him. He'd just been trying to psych her out, nothing more. Time to put Owen Coburn and his cocky smile in the bin where he belonged. But when she searched the countertop there was no sign of his business card. Good riddance.

If she adjusted her search parameters to list the shoes from cheapest to most expensive it was at her own volition.

'Oh my God, you are a lifesaver!' Libby yanked off her hair net and apron and stuffed them beneath the counter. She leaned over to peck a quick kiss on Mick's cheek. 'Are you sure you're all right to close up, Dad?'

'Absolutely. Go out and have some fun, at least I'll get to watch the football highlights in peace. Now, have you got your keys?'

Libby rolled her eyes. 'Yes, Dad.'

'Good girl.' He opened the till and pulled out a twenty-pound note. 'Have a drink on me, you need to celebrate Beth's first day.'

'Aww, you're the best.' She kissed his cheek again, pocketed the money then slid open the warming cabinet. 'Look what I saved for you!' Withdrawing a battered sausage, she wrapped the bottom in a napkin and handed it to Beth, then took the last one for herself.

'I haven't had one of these in years.' Beth bit into the greasy treat with a little sound of bliss. 'Good. So good.'

'I know, right? Come on let's wash these down with some bubbles.'

Arm in arm they made their way along the promenade, giggling and eating their sausages. Beth wiped her fingers on the napkin, then tucked it in her coat pocket. 'You should have seen this guy who was in the emporium this morning. He was gorgeous—right up until the moment he opened his mouth, anyway.'

'What about Sam?'

'What about Sam? You know we're just good friends.'

Libby snorted. 'Are you two still selling that line? I see the way you look at each other.'

'Oh, give over.' Turning away so Libby couldn't see her blush,

Beth pushed open the door to the pub. The smell of good food and the hoppy aroma of beer hit in a warm, welcoming wave.

There were a few locals scattered around the place and a familiar set of broad shoulders at the bar. 'Oh, crap.' Beth made a beeline for their favourite table beneath the window, dragging Libby with her.

'Slow down, where's the fire?' Her friend grumbled as Beth shushed her and patted the seat next to her.

'It's going to be in your pants in about five seconds.' Beth nudged her and pointed towards the bar.

'What are you talking ab . . . oh, thank you, Jesus! I'm sorry for all the times I doubted you, and I'll go to church every Sunday from now on.' Libby put her hands into prayer position as she raised her eyes to the ceiling.

Laughing, Beth pulled the napkin out of her pocket. 'Here, I think there's actual drool on your face.'

Eyes shining, Libby glanced her way. 'That's him, right? That's the guy you were talking about?'

'Uh huh. And if you think the rear view is fine, wait until he turns around. Just a shame he's a colossal arse.' Beth abandoned the pleasing view of Owen's back to where Sam was pulling pints behind the bar. Glancing up, he caught her eye and tipped her a quick wink. She gave a quick look around to check no one was watching then gave him a warm smile in return.

'What about Sam, indeed. You two are about as subtle as a brick,' Libby scoffed before fumbling in her pocket. 'This note is burning a hole in my pocket, I'm getting us the bubbles.'

Open-mouthed, Beth watched her friend stalk to the bar, noting she positioned herself into the eyeline of Owen Coburn. Annie was covering that end of the bar and she gave Libby a quick smile of acknowledgement as she finished up with her current customer. As though connected by an invisible thread, her attention was drawn back to Sam.

Sam, who fixed her plumbing disasters, bought her flowers the perfect shades to match her new décor, teased her, and challenged her, and kissed her until she saw stars. Sam, who was smiling a little too widely at a pretty blonde customer.

Moving before she consciously understood what she was doing, she walked towards the bar, making sure to catch his attention. She cut her eyes to door leading to the back and swung through it. The door opened moments later, and Sam stepped through. 'Is everything okay?'

Closing the distance between them, she grabbed a fistful of his shirt. 'You're mine, Sam Barnes, do you hear me? For as long as this fling between us lasts. You. Are. Mine.' Stretching on tiptoe, she hooked her other hand around the back of his head and pulled him down for a kiss. To his credit, it took less than a second to get on board with the plan and was kissing her back.

The familiar press of his lips spread a delicious heat through her abdomen and she opened to the first flicker of his tongue. His hands closed around her, pulling her closer into his body, taking control. One of these days she might get fed up of his natural bossiness. In twenty of thirty years, maybe. For now, she was content to revel in the way his broad palm slotted perfectly at the base of her spine, holding her steady, keeping her in place when she might float away on a cloud of bliss.

'Not that I'm complaining,' he said, pressing kisses along the edge of her jaw. 'But what brought this on?'

If she hadn't been so distracted by those clever lips, she might not have blurted out, 'You were staring at that blonde.'

His rich chuckled sent delicious vibrations through her. 'You were jealous'.

She pulled back. 'What? No! You were practically face-first in her cleavage.'

'She was the other side of the bar from me!' He stepped into her, one arm clamping around her waist in a possessive grip. 'You were jealous.' She imagined the expression on his face was similar to that worn by the original hunter-gatherers when they speared a sabre-toothed tiger or clobbered a woman over the head and dragged her back to his cave. Primal with a hint of smugness.

Beth rolled her eyes. 'You're going to be impossible now, aren't you?'

Bending to kiss her nose, he grinned. 'Not at all.' He tucked a strand of her hair behind her ear. 'Well, maybe just a little bit. So, I was thinking I could pop over later, help you celebrate your first official day of trading.'

From the glint in his eye, there was no mistaking what his idea of celebrating would entail. Anticipation fizzed inside her. 'Oh, you did, did you?'

He nuzzled her cheek. 'I've missed you, Beth.' She melted against him. 'What do you say? Are you in the market for a little March madness?'

Not wanting to return to the bar at the same time, Sam went first whilst Beth ducked into the ladies' toilet to catch her breath. A quick finger comb managed to straighten her mussed up hair, but having left her handbag in the bar, she couldn't do anything about the lipstick he'd kissed off, nor the rosiness of her cheeks. She'd just have to brazen it out. Setting her shoulders back, she walked back into the bar area, not risking a look to the left lest she catch Sam's eye and blow the whole thing.

Libby waited for her at their table, a bottle resting in an ice bucket in front of her, and a dark scowl across her face. 'You took your time.'

Smoothing her skirt, Beth sat down beside her and reached for the bottle. 'Sorry, I had to pop to the ladies'. Are you ready to celebrate?'

'Hmm? Yeah, sure.' There was a tightness around her eyes, and she sounded distracted. Beth followed her friend's eyeline to where Owen Coburn stood staring grimly into his pint. He drained what was left in his glass, slammed it down then stormed past, casting an angry look in their direction.

Libby muttered something obscene under her breath then snatched the bottle from Beth's grasp. 'Come on, before I die of thirst.'

Raising her hands out of the way, Beth eased back into the padded back of her seat. 'What's that all about?'

Libby glared at her. 'You should have warned me, why didn't you warn me? That man is the most insufferable, arrogant wanker I've ever had the misfortune to meet.' She sent the cork flying with a loud 'pop' and tilted the bottle over one of the slender flutes. The champagne fizzed up the glass, threatening to bubble over.

'Give me that!' Beth steadied the bottle then eased it from Libby's grasp to fill her own glass. 'And I did warn you. You were too busy admiring the view to pay attention.'

Libby sniffed in response and raised her glass to her lips, there was no mistaking the hurt in her eyes. Reaching over to still her hand, Beth squeezed her wrist. 'Tell me what happened.'

Libby shook her off. 'Nothing happened. I don't want to talk about it. I don't want to talk about Owen Coburn ever again.' Slumping back in her seat, Libby closed her eyes for a long moment and blew out a breath. When she opened them again, the tension in her face had gone. 'Right then, let's get back to celebrating. Tell me every single thing that happened in the emporium today.'

Knowing when to back off was an essential part of the friendship code so Beth launched into a detailed description of her day. There were two vital incidents she skipped over—Mick's birthday shopping trip, and the unwelcome visit of one Owen Coburn.

Chapter Eighteen

The friendship code sucked. After that super-hot kiss Beth had laid on him, and their subsequent discussion, Sam had spent the rest of the evening imagining how it might end. He'd pictured locking the bolt on the front door behind the last of the customers then lifting a giggling Beth onto an empty bar stool as he stepped between her thighs and picked up where they'd left off. The two of them would then creep up the stairs and past his parents' bedroom door to tumble onto his mattress in a tangle of limbs and heated whispers. The winning scenario . . . that started with him taking Beth's keys from her trembling fingers and unlocking the back door leading to her flat.

And here they were . . . He reached out to help her.

'Oops, butterfingers!' Beth giggled as her keys tumbled to the floor. It wasn't the sexy kind of giggle he'd been daydreaming about though. It was the 'shouldn't have had that second bottle' kind. At least the dark would hide the frustration he was sure was written all over his face.

'I really need to pee, come on, B, stop messing around.' Libby hopped from foot to foot. And none of his fantasies had involved a drunk, possibly incontinent third wheel.

'I'll get them. Ouch!' Sam and Beth both bent down at the same time, their foreheads clashing hard enough to make his ears ring. He grabbed hold of Beth before she could tumble on her backside and propped her up against the wall next to Libby. 'Leave it, I'll find them.' He crouched down, fumbling in the pitch black. 'It might be an idea to leave your security light on if you're coming home late, sweetheart.'

His fingers touched something cold and slimy and he yanked them back, knocking against the bunch of keys in the process. Thank God. Rising, he unlocked the door, opened it and turned on the hallway light. 'Let's get you both inside.'

'You know your problem, mister? You're too bloody bossy. He's really bossy, Libs, did you know that? Boss, boss, boss, morning, noon, and night. I'm an independent working woman. I can take care of myself!' Her last remark might have carried more weight had she not stumbled over the doorstep and into his arms. 'You caught me.' Her voice carried a dreamy quality which he would have taken full advantage of under other circumstances.

He couldn't help but smile. 'I'll always catch you.'

'I think I'm going to be sick.' Libby elbowed past them to thunder up the stairs.

Beth looked at him, a little of the drunken fuzziness in her eyes clearing. 'You don't think she was being serious, do you?'

Sam winced. 'I hope not, but we'd better go and find out.'

Letting her go first, he placed a hand at the small of her back to keep her steady and they made it upstairs without incident. He steered Beth into the kitchen and flipped the kettle on. 'I'll just go and check on Libby, make sure she's okay.'

Heading down the end of the short hallway, he turned left and stopped dead at the sight of Libby perched on the toilet with her jeans around her ankles. 'Bloody hell!' He turned his back, praying the image wouldn't be burned into his brain forever.

'Oh my God, Sam, go away! What are you, some kind of perv? I'm peeing here!' Her outraged shriek followed on his heels as he hurried back towards the kitchen.

'She's fine,' he told Beth. 'Hasn't mastered the art of closing the bathroom door, but she's fine. Do you want a cup of coffee?'

The bleary look was back in her eyes. 'No. I'm sleepy, I just want to go to bed.'

So did he. But not to sleep. Unfortunately, March madness was definitely off the table. He shrugged to himself. There'd be other times. The toilet flushed and he went to help Beth to her feet. 'Go clean your teeth and I'll get you both a glass of water.'

Entering Beth's bedroom, he navigated using the light spilling in from the hall and switched on the bedside lamp. The flowers he'd bought stood in the centre of her dressing table in one of her new vases. Emma had done a wonderful job with the arrangement; they couldn't have matched her new colour scheme any better. Beth would see them the moment she opened her eyes, and it warmed him to realise she must have positioned them that way. He returned to the kitchen, filled two large glasses with water and placed them on either side of the bed before following the sound of laughter back towards the bathroom. He tapped on the door. 'If you two are all right, I'm going to head off.'

Beth opened the door, a toothbrush sticking out of one corner of her mouth, frothy bubbles around her lips. 'Night, night.' The words came out a bit garbled, but he got the gist.

'Set your alarm before you go to sleep.'

She removed the toothbrush to point it at him. 'So bossy.'

Leaning forward, he avoided the toothpaste foam and pecked a kiss on her cheek. 'And get Libs to text her dad so he knows where she is when he wakes up in the morning.'

'Oh my God, get out of here!' There was amusement in her eyes though.

Sam strolled down the hallway. 'And I left you both a glass of water by the bed. Make sure you drink them.' He raised a hand to wave goodbye, ignoring her exasperated laughter. It was his job to take care of the things that were important to him—and Beth was riding high on his priority list.

After locking Beth's back door and pushing the keys through the letterbox, Sam returned to the pub. He shrugged off his coat, hooked it over the bottom bannister and rolled up his sleeves as he walked into the bar. To his surprise, Annie was still up. The dirty glasses had all been collected and she was in the process of emptying and reloading the under-the-counter washer. 'Mum? What are you doing? You should have left that for me.'

Pausing to pat his cheek, she gave him a sweet smile. 'You don't have to do everything, Sam. I heard you up and about this morning doing breakfasts, and you haven't stopped since. Your dad wasn't feeling too chipper so I sent him up to bed. He's in a right grump because he's been feeling so much better these past few days. I hope it doesn't set him back too much.'

Sam pulled her into a quick hug. 'We won't let it, okay? If he's still laid up tomorrow, I'll spend some time with him going through ideas for Subterranean.'

His mum beamed at him. 'He'd like that, darling.'

'Me too.'

The rest of the week stretched Sam's patience to the limit. He'd barely seen Beth for more than five minutes at a time so there'd been no chance for either of them to grab much more than the odd stolen kiss, never mind anything else. Having got so close to moving things between them to a deeper level of intimacy, his nights were filled with restless dreams.

The more he thought about it, the more convinced he became that one taste of her sweetness wouldn't be enough. A fling might have been his idea, but now he was beginning to regret it. He'd never been this hooked on a woman in his life, it seemed like every waking moment was filled with thoughts of her. And it wasn't just about sex, though God knows he might go crazy if he didn't get her underneath him soon. He wanted to speak to her, to ask her opinion on anything and everything. He just plain wanted to be with her.

On top of his growing need for Beth, he was worried about his dad. Paul hadn't rallied as much as they'd hoped so Sam was back to covering the shifts he'd previously handed back to him. Which left him with even less time to spend with Beth. At least Sam had been able to keep his dad occupied doing research on possible materials for the restaurant. It had been the only way they'd been able to persuade him to stay in bed.

Lavender Bay's Easter celebrations were in full swing, and a band of high pressure had settled over the county, pushing the temperature above seasonal norms. The endless sunshine had attracted an additional influx of visitors. Every room in the pub was booked solid. The first weekend had been focused around events and services at the church, but this final weekend of the holiday fortnight was centred around the beach and the businesses along the promenade.

The plans for the restaurant had been submitted to the council the previous week, and although he knew it was too soon to hear anything back from them, Sam was finding it hard to keep his mind on anything else. If they turned him down, he would be back to square one. Hard choices would have to be made because he could taste success like it was on the tip of his tongue. Coming this close to translating his dream into reality and losing it would break a fundamental part of him. His parents would understand, he was sure of that now. As for Beth . . . well, they'd not made any promises to each other.

A soft tug on his sleeve pulled him back to the here and now. 'What do you think, Mr Barnes?' Amy, one of the children staying in the pub, did a little twirl to show him her fancy-dress costume. From the pink and white bunny ears, to a set of stiff nylon wings and a matching tutu, it was an eclectic mishmash of the contents of a dressing-up box. She looked adorable, and he told her so, smiling as she skipped back out of the breakfast room where he'd been clearing away the plates.

There was to be a children's parade, led by some poor volunteer in an Easter Bunny costume, followed by a treasure hunt. Each of the businesses along the seafront had signed up to participate and the children had to solve clues which would give them a series of letters that needed to be rearranged to find the answer. Once they'd solved the puzzle, the children would return to the starting station on the beach to collect a goodie bag. The event had been organised jointly between the traders' association and the local Round Table group. There would be other activities, including egg and spoon races, musical statues and the like which would culminate in a huge picnic on the beach.

He'd just finished putting the boxes of cereal, condiments and place mats in the bottom of the Welsh dresser when his dad called to him from the doorway. 'Are you about ready?'

Sam closed the heavy wooden doors and nodded. 'All set. Are you sure you're up for this?' Despite his best efforts, his dad had refused point blank to miss the celebrations.

'Don't fuss. I'm fine. Besides I can't let the rest of the committee down, can I?' His dad had been heavily involved with the Round Table for several years.

'All right, Dad, I'll shut up.' At least he had his stick with him, which was something.

Preparations were in full swing when they arrived on the beach and Sam made sure his dad was settled on a fold-out camping chair in the main tent before he headed out with one of the other committee members to help mark out lanes for the races. A large area in the centre of the beach had been coned off the night before and it was his job to bang in stakes with a wooden mallet at regular intervals so strings of bunting could be strung between them.

From the looks of the groups of towels, umbrellas and wind-breaks set up on the margins of the beach, they were in for a good crowd. The heat of the sun felt good on his shoulders as he worked, and by the time he'd finished his T-shirt had begun to stick to the damp skin at the base of his spine. He untucked it to let a bit of air cool him off, and followed the others back to the green-and-white striped gazebo the committee were using as a base of operations.

He stopped short at the sight of his dad perched on a stool at the back of the tent, his arms propped up on his thighs. A man was crouched next to Paul, talking quietly and a cold shiver chased the pleasant warmth of the sun away when Sam recognised Dr Williams, their local GP. Damn, he should have put his foot down and made his dad stay at home. Heart in his throat, Sam wove through the crowded tent towards them.

It wasn't until he was almost on top of them that he released the two men were laughing. His dad broke off the conversation to stare up at him. 'Everything all right, son?'

Sam forced himself to smile through the wave of relief which threatened to overwhelm him. 'Yes, fine. I just wanted to check in with you before I go back and open up.' The raised eyebrow told him his dad wasn't buying it, but he let Sam off with nothing more than a shake of his head. It took the entire length of his walk back to the pub for his hands to stop shaking.

The bar wasn't officially open yet, but he pinned the clue on the wall by the front door and added a basket of mini chocolate eggs before propping open the door. As excited kids trooped in and out, he sorted through the stock he would need for the lunchtime picnic. Along with a few of the other traders, he'd decided to set up on the promenade. The fridge upstairs was full of sandwiches and he'd already loaded the freezer with extra bags of ice.

At just after eleven-thirty, he carted a couple of trestle tables outside and set them up next to the safety barrier at the edge of the prom. Three large tin baths were followed by a dozen trips to lug the bags of ice which he cut open and poured into the tubs. With the help of a sack truck he wheeled out boxes of pre-chilled bottles of beer, cans of fizzy pop and bottles of water.

He got halfway through filling the tubs with drinks before he realised he should have brought out the sandwiches. Damn. Much as he trusted his friends and neighbours, leaving a stack of unguarded booze was asking for trouble. A warm hand rested against the base of his spine, and the heady, warm scent of a familiar perfume filled his nostrils. 'Hey, stranger, need a hand?'

Turning, Sam smiled down at Beth, his smile growing a little wider as his vantage point afforded him a spectacular view down the front of the pretty floral dress she was wearing. 'Hey, beautiful.'

She poked a finger in his ribs. 'Eyes up, Mister.'

Happy to oblige, her stared deep into the soft, chocolate warmth of her gaze. 'Hello there.'

Conscious the crowds along the promenade would include their friends and neighbours, Sam knew he should move back, put a respectable distance between them before they set tongues wagging. He couldn't do it though, he could barely keep himself for reaching for her and dragging her into his arms. Clenching his fists at his sides, he held her gaze, trying to convey the tumult of need inside him. Her eyelashes shuttered down, then up and he could hear a catch in her breath.

'You could set a girl on fire with a look like that, Samuel Barnes. I hope you're ready to back it up because I'm here to kidnap you.'

That sounded like his idea of heaven, but there was no chance of the two of them bunking off work. 'What about the shop?'

'Half-day closing.' She patted his chest. 'Look, I had a great morning thanks to the treasure hunt and everybody's going to be too busy having fun on the beach. So, what do you say, are you ready for a bit of March madness?'

He groaned at her use of those stupid words of his. Why had he ever suggested it in the first place? He didn't want a fling, he wanted to court her properly. Take her out on a few dates, or spend a long evening cooking for her, using his talents to show her how special she was to him. But he'd made this bed, and it was up to him to honour the deal they'd made.

Forcing levity into his voice, he smiled down at her. 'I'd love to, you won't believe how much I'd love to, but I have to look after things here.' He let his eyes trace the sweetheart neckline of her bodice with a look of profound regret.

Beth laughed. 'I'm going to have to wear this dress more often. Right, if I can't tempt you away, then how about I lend you a hand here?' She nodded past his shoulder and he turned to find a small queue had already formed on the beach below them.

'Can you hold the fort for two minutes?' Digging in his pocket he scattered some coins on the table. 'I'll be back in a couple of minutes with a proper float and the sandwiches. Beer is three pounds or two for a fiver, soft drinks are all a pound.'

'Got it.' Smiling in welcome, she stepped past him to greet the first person in the queue. The view from the back of her dress might have been even more sexy than the front. It cinched in tight at the waist before flaring out over her hips thanks to some kind of stiff underskirt. A diamond-shaped cut out between her shoulder blades begged him to explore that tempting glimpse of skin. Hold that thought.

His worries about his dad, and the stress over whether his application for the restaurant would go through melted away in the face of the promise of a gorgeous woman in a pretty dress. Getting to spend the day with Beth might be just the distraction he needed. With his killer schedule, time with her was a precious commodity. He didn't intend to waste a single second.

Chapter Nineteen

The next hour flew past in a blur of chilled bottles, sandwiches and laughter. She and Sam worked together in perfect harmony, handling the queues like they'd done it for years. Sam made two more trips inside to replenish the stock and the ice before things started to quieten down. Taking a breather, Beth leaned her arms on the railing and watched in delight as the first of the races took place. A little girl wobbled her way over the line to huge cheers, beaming from ear to ear like she'd won an Olympic medal rather than an egg and spoon race. The Easter Bunny gave her a high five then raised her arm to acknowledge the cheers from the crowds.

Beth pointed him out to Sam. 'That guy is earning his money, today. He must be sweltering inside that costume.'

Sam popped the top on a beer and came to join her by the railings. After taking a sip, he handed her the cold bottle and settled his arm around her waist. 'It's a nightmare.'

Choking on the beer, she lowered her drink to stare at him. 'You've been the Easter Bunny? What? When?'

He shrugged. 'A few years ago. Dad talked me into it when I was home from university for the Easter break. I'll let you into a secret, it doesn't matter how well they dry-clean that suit, it still smells of sweat.'

'Oh, gross.' Beth cringed. 'I could have happily gone the rest of my life without knowing that. Why would you tell me?'

Sam grinned and took the beer from her. 'I'm sharing, that's what couples are supposed to do, right?'

'Right.' A little shiver of awareness rippled through her. They were a couple. It didn't matter how much they talked about a fling, or that they hadn't taken things beyond hot and heavy embraces, she was falling for him. Sam might believe they could just have a bit of fun, a no-strings attached good time, but she just wasn't cut out for it.

There were so many strings, a whole web of them tying them together. The past, their friends and family, the future they could have. And it wasn't only about him. The emporium, this funny little community where everyone knew everyone else's business and weren't afraid to express an opinion about it. All the things she'd never wanted were suddenly all the things she craved.

'You cold?' Sam rubbed his hand up and down her bare arm, causing more goose pimples to spread over her flesh.

'Not anymore.' Beth turned into him, ignoring the hum of people around them and buried her face in his chest. Breathing deep, she drew in the scent of spicy aftershave, sun-warmed cotton and that indefinable thing that was all him. 'You smell good.'

A chuckle rumbled against her cheek. 'Thank you.' His hand tangled in her hair and he pressed his lips to her temple. 'You smell pretty damn nice yourself.'

'Thanks.' Beth giggled, tried to hold it in, then giggled again. Sam's chest vibrated beneath her and he made some kind of odd choking-cough-laugh. The giggles bubbled free, building until Beth had to step away from him and bend at the waist to try and break the stitch in her side. Beside her, Sam howled with laughter, his hand resting on her back as the two of them fell to pieces. 'Oh, God,' she gasped. 'We are so weird.'

Sam leaned back against the railing. 'Is this what people do? Sniff each other? Is this a thing?'

Beth leaned against him, trying to get her breathing under control. 'Apparently it's a thing. It's our thing.'

'Hey, you two what's so funny?' Annie's question set them both off again. 'Okay, private joke, I guess.'

'Sorry, sorry, it's just . . .' Beth met Sam's eyes and could feel the giggles building again.

Annie's smile widened. 'Don't explain. Private jokes are a good thing, a special thing. They're not supposed to make sense to anyone else.' She rubbed her hands together. 'Right, I can handle things here for a bit. Why don't you two have a break?'

'We're fine, Mum. Why don't you go and rest?' As soon as Sam said it, Beth noticed the lines of strain around Annie's eyes.

'I'm fine. Let me do this for you both, please.'

Sam opened his mouth like he wanted to protest, so Beth hooked her arm through his. 'That's really kind of you, Annie. Come on, Sam, you can treat me to an ice cream.' She tugged him away before he could argue.

'Where are we going?' Luckily, he didn't resist as she tugged him in the opposite direction of the ice cream van parked along the promenade. If he had, she might have lost her nerve. She pulled out the keys to the emporium, unlocked the door and pushed him inside.

'Upstairs.' She pointed through the back of the shop floor.

'Excuse me?'

'Up. Stairs.' Brushing past him, she began fumbling with the button fastening of her dress as she started walking.

'Beth. Beth, wait.'

When she turned around, he hadn't moved. 'What's wrong? Don't you want this?' Her hands fell away from the neck of her dress.

He was there in a heartbeat, one hand around her waist, the other cupping her jaw to turn her face to his. 'I want this. I want this so much it's like I can't breathe properly. But not like this. Not a quickie snatched during a ten-minute break.'

'I was hoping for at least fifteen minutes,' she joked, trying to lighten the mood. When he didn't smile back, she slid her hands up to grip his shoulders. 'If life was perfect, we'd have all the time in the world. You'd take me on an actual date. Candlelight, champagne, good food, a whole evening of flirting and anticipation. There'd be silk sheets on the bed, and a romantic playlist I'd spent hours putting together to set the perfect mood.'

He rested his forehead against hers. 'Exactly, that's what I'm talking about. That's what I want to give you.'

'It doesn't matter. None of that nonsense matters. The only thing that's important is being together. Whenever, however we can. Life's complicated. Our plates are full to overflowing, but right here, right now we have time for this. Time for us.'

'Beth. Beth.' His hands were in her hair, stroking her back, tugging at the fastening on her dress as his lips found hers. She was equally frantic, fumbling the buttons of his shirt open, dropping to tug the heavy length of his belt open. 'Wait. Wait a minute.' Sam gripped her shoulders and set her away from him.

She wanted to scream in frustration. 'No, no, no more waiting.' She pressed against his hold, trying to get close to him again.

Sam laughed. 'Steady on, sweetheart. I only meant we should wait long enough to get upstairs. I know you said the niceties don't matter, but our first time together is not going to be on this bloody shop floor.'

'Oh. Okay. Good point.' She grabbed his hand and they ran up the stairs to collapse laughing on her bed.

His weight came down on top of her. 'I had a fantasy about this.' He trailed kisses along the edge of collarbone, sending ripples of sensation down through her middle.

'Only one?' Her hands slid under his shirt to relish the firm, smooth skin of his back. 'I'm disappointed.'

Sam chuckled against the hollow of her throat, and she had to close her eyes as sparks flashed behind her lids. It had never been like this, not even with Charlie. 'I'm such an idiot,' she whispered.

He jerked his head up. 'What? What's wrong? Did you change your mind, 'cause I can wait.' Little beads of sweat popped out on his forehead, and Beth almost wanted to laugh at his pained expression, but she knew he meant it. Her heart did a little flip in her chest.

'I'm an idiot because I had all this . . .' She ran her fingers over the notches in his spine, delighting in the way he shivered under her touch. 'I had you, right under my nose and I never even noticed.'

'Ah, Beth.' His lips found hers and there were no more words to be said. In their hurry, they'd left the curtains open, and the sounds of laughter and music drifted from the beach below. It could have been awkward, she could have been nervous about him seeing her naked for the first time in broad daylight. But with each inch of her skin he revealed, the heat in his eyes increased and seemed to transmit from his body to hers with every touch, every stroke, until she felt scorched from the inside out. The sounds from outside faded from her awareness. It was only him, only her and the slow slide of skin on skin. Mouths touching, lips seeking, promises whispered, pleasures sighed.

Beth flopped over onto her back, one arm thrown above her head as she tried to catch her breath. 'That was . . .'

'Basic? Mediocre? Adequate?' Sam propped himself on one elbow, fingers teasing along the edges of her ribs.

She squirmed away from his tickling and tugged her pillow free to hide her face in it. 'Did I really say that?'

He pulled the edge of the pillow down to kiss the tip of her nose. 'You know you did. It might have scarred me for life.'

Fluttering her eyelashes, she put on her sweetest voice, 'I'm sorry, honey, I meant to say passably good.' Her laughter was soon muffled as he dragged the pillow from her arms and bashed her in the face with it. When she peeked out, he was sitting with his arms folded, a mock-glare on his face. 'I'm sure you'll get better at it, with a bit more practice.' She sat up, letting the sheets spill down to her waist and watched the glare fade into something far more delicious. 'We could try again now . . . in the shower.'

Teasing him might have been a mistake. The hot water had long run out, but Sam refused to let her out until she'd upgraded her assessment of him to a level of praise acceptable to him. He finally relented when she slapped the wet tiles and begged for mercy. 'Spectacular,' she panted. 'Superlative. Stratospheric.'

Sam flipped off the cold water. 'Now that's more like it.'

They wobbled out of the cubicle into a scene of carnage. The bathroom floor was a write-off. At some point they must have knocked the screen door open, but been too distracted to realise. An inch or more of water covered the lino. 'Not again,' Beth wailed.

Sam dragged the towel off the back of the door and spread it out on the floor, soaking it through in seconds. He scooped it up and into the bathtub, then grabbed the smaller towel hanging by the sink and knotted it around his waist. 'Are the rest of the towels in the airing cupboard?' When she nodded, he splashed out, returning a couple of moments later with an armful of her freshly laundered towels.

They shuffled around the small space, Sam gathering the saturated towels behind her and tossing them into the bath. 'We can wring this out once we're dressed,' he said.

Finished with her own towel, she used it to dab the water off his chest. 'I'll do them later. We should probably get back out and make sure your mum's okay.'

The lightness in his face fell away. 'Damn, you're right. I forgot about her for a minute.' He started towards the door, then turned on his heel to grab her up and kiss her breathless. 'When everything's finished today, we'll sit down with a cup of tea and find a way to make our schedules work. A snatched hour here and there isn't enough for me. I want more than a fling, Beth, regardless of what I said before.'

She flung her arms around his neck. 'Yes, yes please.'

Leaning down, he pressed one more lingering kiss to her lips. 'I need to buy you some new flowers.' On that curious comment, he left the bathroom to get dressed.

Trailing after him, Beth puzzled at his meaning. She'd kept the roses he'd sent for several days past their prime, but she hadn't wanted to throw them away. The card attached to them rested against the empty vase, and her eyes drifted towards it as she pulled on her underwear and tried to shake out the creases in her dress. His silly declaration had made her smile every time she saw it.

Her dress was beyond saving, the layers of stiff petticoats crushed from Sam lying on them. Setting it aside, she dug in her drawer for a pair of Capri pants and a pretty T-shirt. She pulled her wet hair from the neck of her top and wove it into a quick braid, securing it with an elastic tie from a dish on the dresser. Her fingers grazed the edge of the card.

Sam's arms closed around her waist and he nuzzled the side of her neck. Their eyes met in the mirror over the dresser. 'What are you smiling at?'

Reaching back, she stroked the damp curls at his nape. 'Maybe you could buy me tulips next time? They're my favourite.

'Whatever you want.'

Tilting her head, she sought out his mouth for a kiss. 'I already have everything I want, right here.'

Chapter Twenty

Things had been quieter since the happy chaos of Easter, but Beth still had a steady stream of visitors calling into the emporium in the days that followed. The bay was ideally positioned in the centre of a scenic coastal walking route so the local B&Bs and other places that took in guests, such as the pub, turned a decent trade which the rest of them benefited from.

Surviving the busy holiday fortnight had been something of a trial by fire. She'd run out of some stock, had several boxes of things she'd been sure would sell which she now feared would gather dust forever, but overall she counted it a success. Oh, her back had developed a persistent ache which only practical bath salts could ease, and her feet would likely never see another pair of high heels, but she didn't care. Frivolous bubble baths and sexy shoes were a small price to pay for the kernel of pride that had taken root in her heart. She might really be able to make a go of things.

As Beth worked through her day's receipts and updated her stock records, she willed the clock to hurry up and hit five. It was Sam's parents' anniversary that weekend, and Paul's health had shown enough improvement that Sam and Eliza had clubbed together to treat their folks to a break in a luxury manor house a few miles along the coast. Beth had chipped in with a voucher for a couples' spa treatment.

All of which meant Sam was running the pub on his own, so Beth was staying over there for the first time. What he didn't know was she'd planned her own special evening for him, including cooking a meal from scratch. She'd spent the week studying an instruction video on YouTube and was confident she could pull it off. A covert call to the new barman Mr and Mrs Barnes had hired meant the bar would be covered for the second half of the evening shift.

Checking her watch, Beth decided it was close enough to time and flipped the closed sign over and locked the front door. After fetching her overnight case and the sturdy bag-for-life containing the ingredients she needed, she grabbed her handbag, keys and the deposit envelope with the day's receipts. Sam had already offered to drop it off for her in the morning together with the pub's takings, so it was easier to put them in his safe overnight rather than her own one upstairs. With her hands full, she pulled the back gate closed with her foot and crossed the short gap between the two buildings.

'Here, let me take those.' Sam reached for her bags, and although she allowed him to take her case, she hung onto the carrier. 'What are you hiding in there?' he asked, trying to steal a peek inside.

'Never you mind.' She tapped the end of his nose, then stretched up for a kiss before he led the way into the pub and up the stairs.

He pushed his bedroom door open with his shoulder and set her case on the floor—the newly hoovered floor if the tramlines in the carpet were anything to go by. The bedding had that fluffy look only freshly changed sheets could give and the air carried a faint hint of lemon-scented polish. Beth hid a little smile at the spotless room, delighted he'd made such an effort for her. 'You remember where everything is?'

It had been a while since she'd been up there, but she knew the layout of the place like the back of her hand. 'Unless you've made any radical changes, I should be fine.' She hid the carrier bag on the far side of the bed to be retrieved later and followed him into the family living room.

'We've got all the usual channels, plus Netflix so you won't be stuck for something to watch.' Sam put his arms around her. 'Are you sure you don't mind hanging around up here?'

Beth leaned into him for a cuddle. 'I'm sure. If I get bored I can always pop down for a glass of wine, and it'll be nice to be here when you get your break.' His break was set for eight, which was the time she'd arranged for Josh, the barman, to come in and take over.

'I like having you here.' He ducked his head to claim her lips in a mind-scrambling kiss which left them both a little short of breath. 'Perhaps I could just not bother with opening the pub tonight, I'd much rather stay up here with you.'

Beth teased her fingers through the curls at his neck. He'd not had it cut in a while and she liked the way the wild tangles spilled over his collar. 'Can you imagine your dad's face if he found out you'd shut up shop the moment his back was turned?'

He rested his forehead against hers. 'You've got a point. Mum's convinced if their weekend is a success that she can get him to go away for a proper holiday. She's been down the travel agent's looking at brochures.'

Paul going away was a real vote of confidence in his son as well. There was no way Beth wanted to do anything to jeopardise it. Sam would still be here to close up after last orders, and she'd made it clear to Josh he was to shout for help if he needed it. Smoothing her hands down his back, she dropped them lower to give his bottom a playful squeeze. 'You've got a pub to run, get to it.'

Sam laughed, then grazed her lips with a kiss. 'I thought I was supposed to be the bossy one in this relationship.'

She joined in. 'Maybe I've decided to give you a run for your money.'

* * *

198

Beth settled herself on the sofa and switched on the television, making it look for all intents and purposes as though she was settling in for the evening. It was just as well as Sam found myriad excuses to pop back upstairs over the next hour. He'd forgotten his keys; he needed a fresh handkerchief; he wanted her to try a new Sauvignon Blanc they'd added to the menu. Each visit resulted in stolen kisses or a quick cuddle, as though he couldn't bear to stay away from her now he had her under his roof.

Thankfully, once the doors opened at six he was too busy downstairs, and she retrieved her shopping bag from the bedroom and set herself up in the kitchen. A quick survey of the cupboards with a checklist she'd drawn up helped her find all the bowls, pans and dishes she needed. Clearing one of the worktops, she laid out her ingredients in order of use then propped her tablet next to them. A quick swig of wine for luck and she rolled up her sleeves and got to work.

By the time the chicken and mushroom pie was in the oven, Beth's nerves were shot. What on earth had possessed her to try and make pastry from scratch? Sam was a qualified chef and she could burn water. She must be soft in the head to think cooking for him was a good idea.

Heading into the bathroom, she grimaced at the sight of her reflection. There was flour everywhere—in her hair, on her cheeks, spattering the front of her navy T-shirt. Resisting the urge to brush herself down, she washed her hands then stripped off her top and shook it over the bathtub. Bending at the waist, she did the same with her hair, watching the flour sift down like tiny snowflakes.

Dressed again, with her hair brushed and the flour on her face removed with the aid of a soft make-up brush, she checked her watch. She had twenty minutes to spare, plenty of time to pop downstairs and refill her glass. It would also ensure Sam had no excuse to make a surprise visit of his own.

The bar was busy, but she found an empty stool positioned close to the side partition. Claiming the seat, she plonked her glass in front of her and called out cheekily, 'Anytime you're ready, barman.'

Flushed from the heat of the room, Sam glanced over from the optics and flashed her a broad grin. Once finished with the customer he was serving, he retrieved a bottle from the fridge and undid the catch on the bar partition, lifting it so he could stand next to her. 'It's good, huh?'

'I like it a lot. Really crisp and refreshing.' She waved for him to stop when he'd half-filled her glass. 'I might like it a bit too much so go steady, or I'll be fit for nothing.'

Sam waggled his eyebrows and leered at her. 'Maybe I'm hoping to take advantage of you later.'

Biting her lip, she glanced up at him through her lashes. 'What if I told you, you won't need any alcohol to do that.'

He curled an arm around her and she turned on the stool to put them face-to-face. 'No?'

'No.' She beckoned for him to lean down then whispered in his ear. 'I'm a sure thing.' Whatever his response might have been, it was cut short by a friendly shout from further down the bar.

'Duty calls. We'll pick this conversation up when I get my break in . . .' He looked at his watch. 'Exactly forty-three minutes.'

'I look forward to it.' Beth picked up her glass and hurried back upstairs to check on dinner.

The edges of the pastry were just turning golden, so she settled cross-legged in front of the oven door terrified if she looked away it would catch and burn. A bit of the cream and tarragon sauce had bubbled through the central cuts she'd made to release the steam, but overall, she was delighted with the results.

On safer ground making the mashed potatoes and green veg she'd chosen to accompany the pie, Beth pottered around as she laid the table. The bottle of wine she'd bought to go with the meal rested in the fridge, but maybe she'd get Sam to bring the new Sauvignon instead. Everything was on a low heat, she just needed Josh to show up on time, and for Sam to not mind, of course.

Butterflies filled her stomach. She'd been so excited about her little plan it had been easy to assume he'd be equally pleased. She tried to imagine how she'd feel if he made some high-handed decision about the emporium, then wished to hell she hadn't. But Sam was much more chilled out about things than she was, so it would be fine. Probably. She crossed her fingers just in case.

A wash of noise, music and laughter sounded from below, and she took a deep breath as footsteps thumped up the stairs. 'Beth?'

Poking her head around the kitchen door, she gave Sam a quick wave. 'I'm here.'

Looking puzzled, he strode towards her. 'Josh's turned up with some random story about you asking him to provide cover—' His eyes widened as he crossed the threshold and took in the room. 'What's all this?'

'A surprise. For you. I know it was awfully high-handed of me to interfere with the running of the pub, but with your folks away, I just wanted to spoil you a little bit. I'm not the best of cooks, but I needed to show my appreciation somehow . . .' He cut off her babbling explanation with a gentle finger against her lips.

'Shh. It's wonderful.' He replaced his finger with his lips for a tender kiss. 'You're wonderful. Thank you.'

The butterflies fluttered away, and she almost sagged in his arms such was her relief. 'You're not mad?'

'When you've gone to all this effort, how could I possibly be?'

Worried she might have built up his expectations, she hitched one shoulder in a shrug. 'It's only pie and mash.'

'Sounds perfect. Do you need me to do anything?' She sent him off to fetch a bottle of wine whilst she dished up.

The mash was a bit lumpy, and the green beans overdone, but the pastry on the pie melted in the mouth, perfectly complimenting the rich, creamy sauce. Sam had a second helping, declaring it the best thing he'd eaten in ages. He might have been trying a shade too hard, but it was nowhere near the disaster it could have been. They piled everything into the dishwasher, then carried the half-full bottle of wine and their glasses into the lounge.

Sam propped himself up along the back edge of the sofa and patted the seat in front of him. 'Get on in here, woman, I'm in need of a snuggle.' The buttery-soft leather yielded under her body as she lay down next to him. He retrieved a cushion from behind his knees and tucked it under her head. 'Comfy?' He trailed his fingers through her hair.

'Mmm, yes. Although I think I ate too much.'

'Me too, but I can't feel sorry for it.' Reaching across her, he snagged the remote control. 'What are you in the mood for?'

Feeling lazy and replete, she couldn't care less what they watched. It was enough to be there with him. 'You choose. This evening is all about indulging you.'

He brushed his knuckles against her cheek and she turned into his touch. 'It'll be my turn to spoil you for your birthday next week. I'll have to get my thinking cap on.'

'Make me a batch of those macarons, and I'll be happy.' When she thought back to the beginning of the year, of how dark and depressing her life had been it was hard to reconcile the girl she'd been with the woman she was now. That was honestly how it felt, like she was moving into a new era of her life.

And here she was on the cusp of twenty-five. For the first time she had control over her own destiny. She would succeed or fail under her own efforts, not be subject to the whims of others or become a sacrificial pawn in the ugly game of office politics. A quarter of a century on this earth and for the first time she felt like an adult. And damn if it wasn't the headiest feeling in the world.

Her mind drifted from the heist movie Sam had chosen. She'd tried hard to follow the plot for the first half an hour, but as it grew ever more convoluted she abandoned it for the far more pleasurable task of cataloguing each exquisite sensation of his body against hers. The hand he'd curled behind her head stroked idly over the soft skin behind her ear. The steady rise and fall of his broad chest, and the thrum of his heart against her cheek. The untidy tangle of their lower limbs where they'd shifted and curled around each other.

The television clicked off, leaving the room shadowed in the soft light of a single lamp. 'I thought you were watching that,' she murmured as Sam shifted position on the cramped space of the sofa.

'It was okay, but there are other things I'd much rather be doing.' His voice held a rasp that sent shivers of anticipation through her.

'Like what?'

His hands smoothed up the thick cotton of her T-shirt, revealing the vulnerable skin of her belly. 'Like this.' Bending his head, he trailed a row of kisses along the exposed flesh at the waistband of her jeans. Her muscles contracted in response. 'And this.' His mouth moved higher, following the hollows and ridges of her ribcage. 'And this.' He nudged her top higher to uncover the delicate lace of her bra and his lips sought the dusky shadow of her nipples, drawing on her through the material.

Beth arched her back, welcoming the wet heat of his mouth, offering more of her skin for him to claim. Her fingers twined in the shaggy hair at his nape, holding him close as he teased and tasted. 'Sam.' His name came out half-sob, half-sigh. 'Oh, Sam.'

Those hot lips of his never stilled, as his fingers busied themselves at the top of her jeans, loosening the button to make room for him to glide down into the slick passion he found there. He groaned, a deep rumble of sound that vibrated through her, making her cry out in return. Releasing her hold on his hair, she reached down to tug the denim lower, giving him better access and he took full advantage.

'All right?' he asked, the words a heated whisper over her collarbone.

'Yes. God, yes.' And then she was beyond words, beyond anything but the fever rising in her blood, and the urgent press of his thumb driving her up and up and over into oblivion.

Sam's breath gusted hot against her throat, and then he was moving over her, the rasp of his jeans rough on the tops of her thighs. Awareness of where they were seeped into her blissed-out brain. 'Not here, Sam. Not on your mum's sofa.'

'Oh, Jesus, good point.' He wiggled off her, stood and refastened his jeans. 'I'd never be able to look her in the face again.'

'Me either.' She giggled as he tugged her to her feet and helped her straighten her clothing. 'Don't worry about that too much, I'll only be taking them off again in a minute.'

'Another good point.' He swooped down for a quick, hot kiss then grasped her hand and led her towards his bedroom. His shirt flew one way, hers the other. Sam backed her towards the bed, kissing her until her knees grew weak and she tumbled back upon the duvet. 'Hold that thought,' he said, before rushing from the room.

'Sam?' She called after him.

'Keep going, I'll catch up.' Curious, she scrambled out of the remainder of her clothing and crawled under the duvet to wait.

He was back within moments, one hand hidden behind his back. Moving to the bed, he rested one knee close to her hip and leaned over her. 'I said before I needed to give you some new flowers. I wanted to wait, wanted to choose something as beautiful, as perfect to me as you are.' He pulled his hand from behind his back and presented a sprig of fake primroses she remembered seeing in a jug on the kitchen windowsill. 'But I can't wait, I can't wait another single second to tell you I love you.'

'Oh, Sam . . .' Beth reached out to cup his cheeks, drawing him down towards her. 'I love you, too. Beyond anything I ever imagined love to be before.' She rained kisses on his cheeks, on his eyelids, on his lips, desperate to mark every inch of him, to show him everything in her heart bursting to get out.

He pulled free of her grasp, but only long enough to stand and shed his clothing. The silk flowers lay on the quilt, and Beth placed them on the bedside table before they could get crushed. It didn't matter that they were sun-faded, a little ragged around the edges. To her they were priceless, a memento she would treasure forever. Sam lifted the covers to ease down beside her, and then everything was forgotten but the solution to life's easiest and yet most difficult puzzle—the lock and key of man and woman coming together, their hearts and bodies in perfect union.

Chapter Twenty-One

Whether it was the frantic shouts and banging on the metal security gate beneath his window, or the wail of sirens on the air, he didn't know, but one minute Sam was spooned around Beth's soft curves and the next he was wide awake.

'What's that? What's happening?' Beth asked groggily, as he scrambled from the bed to tug on his jeans.

'I don't know. Better get dressed, just in case and I'll find out.' Crossing to the window, he unlocked it and stuck his head out. 'What's the bloody racket?'

'Sam!' The security light illuminated the worried face of Neil Tate, the newsagent. 'Sweet Jesus, Sam, there's a fire next door and no one's seen any sign of Beth.'

'She's here, she's with me.' The impact of Neil's words and the wailing sirens registered, horror striking him like a blow. 'Fire? Fucking hell, we'll be right down.' He slammed the window shut then fumbled for the lamp on the chest of drawers beside him.

'We've got to get out of here, right now,' he said as he yanked open a drawer and pulled out a couple of sweatshirts. Not bothering with a T-shirt, he put one on, and tossed the other to Beth whilst he shoved his feet into his trainers.

She stared at him, fingers bone-white where they clenched the thick cotton of the shirt. 'F . . . fire. That's what he said.' Her eyes were huge with shock.

'Here, give me that.' Taking the sweatshirt, he tugged it over her head and pulled her arms through the sleeves like handling a little child. 'Shoes, where's your shoes? Come on, Beth, we need to get out of here. I don't know how bad it is and it could spread to the pub next.'

His words seemed to snap her out of it. 'Oh, God. Oh, God!' She dashed from the room, and he followed in her wake, relieved to find her sitting at the top of the stairs to lace up her trainers. 'Go. I'm right behind you.' He grabbed his keys and wallet from where he'd left them on the kitchen board and thundered down the stairs on her heels.

The second he opened the back door, he could smell the smoke, see the glow of the flames lighting the night sky. Shit, this was going to be bad. Keeping a tight hold on Beth's hand, he unlocked the security gate and they spilled out into the wide rear alleyway in time to see the fire engine pull up. With Neil at the side, they ran up to meet the officer climbing out of the front seat. 'Anyone inside, do you know?'

'No. No, it's my shop and I'm the only occupant. What happened?' She turned to survey the rear of the emporium and let out a horrified scream. Sam grabbed her as her knees buckled, turning her face into his chest to shield her from the sight of black smoke and orange flames flickering up the building.

'Stand back, all of you.' Another fireman walked towards them, arms spread as he ushered them down the alleyway to what he regarded as a safe distance. Cries of shock, questions and sobs rose behind Sam as more of their neighbours spilled out into the night, drawn by the noise and the shouts of others rousing them.

Chaos reigned, but it was a controlled chaos as the men and women from the fire service organised themselves in short order erecting cordons and unfurling their hoses as one of their number shone a torch up and down the alley to find the fire hydrant cover.

Further up the alley, more blue lights flashed as both a police car and an ambulance arrived.

It seemed to take hours, and yet was probably a matter of minutes before they had the blaze under control. Beth tried to raise her face, to turn in his arms, but he held her tight against him as though he could shield her from the reality for just a few moments longer. A shout went up from the officers tackling the fire, and two paramedics rushed forward.

The officer he'd spoken to crossed to where Sam stood at the edge of the cordon. 'I thought you said the place was unoccupied.'

'It was. Well, it should have been. Beth was with me in the pub, no one else lives above the emporium other than her.'

The officer shook his head. 'Whoever he is, he's in a bad way. His burns aren't too extensive as far as I can see, but smoke inhalation is often the thing that causes the most damage.'

'Can I see him? I might be able to identify him.' Sam turned to Neil who was still beside him. 'Take Beth for a minute?'

'Of course. Come here, sweetheart, I've got you.' Neil led Beth a few paces away, chatting to her quietly.

Sam ducked under the cordon tape when the officer held it up, then followed him towards the ambulance. A quick glance right filled him with sorrow. The fence and gate were gone, completely destroyed and where the backdoor had been there was only a gaping hole, smoke still drifting from it. It was hard to see beyond the range of the emergency lighting, but the once-pale stone of the building looked blackened as far as the roof.

He waited where he was told whilst the officer spoke to the paramedics, and when one of them nodded he was beckoned over. The frail figure on the stretcher was hard to make out beneath a thick layer of soot and with an oxygen mask obscuring his face. Sam tried to avoid anything other than a quick glance at the red-raw skin on his arms. He met the dull-eyed stare of the man and shook his head. 'Sorry, I've never seen him before.'

The female paramedic answered him. 'Thanks for trying. From

the looks of his clothes, he might have been sleeping rough.' They lifted the stretcher, and at first Sam thought the man's arm had rolled off the side, until reddened fingers scrabbled at his sleeve. 'Wait a minute.' He crouched down beside the stretcher. 'It's all right, they're taking you to the hospital.'

The man coughed, tried to reach for the mask on his face, but the paramedic stopped him. 'Sorry.' The dry rasp of his voice made Sam's throat ache in sympathy. 'I jus . . . wanted somewhere to doss down. Didn't mean no harm.' He might not have meant any harm, but what if Beth had been home? Sam shuddered at the thought of it.

Getting angry with this poor, pathetic creature wouldn't do much good though, so he placed a gentle hand on the man's shoulder. 'No one else was hurt. The property was empty. Let these nice folks take care of you, and rest easy.'

The female paramedic gave him a sad smile as he stood to allow them to load the poor sod into the back of the ambulance. The fire officer put a hand on his back and steered him towards the open rear gate of the emporium. 'We'll have to do a proper inspection in the morning, but the cause looks pretty straightforward. There was a stack of folded cardboard stacked behind the bins by the wall. I could smell the alcohol on him, even through the smoke. Is he a smoker?'

Sam shrugged. 'I dunno, I've never seen him before. The paramedic said he looked like a rough sleeper.'

The officer nodded. 'Probably dozed off with a lit fag. It's still one of the most common causes of fire.'

He turned away, and Sam followed him, catching his arm on a sharp piece of wood in the process. 'Ow, bollocks.'

'You all right there?'

Sam tilted his arm to examine the deep scratch on his bicep. The skin looked angry, but unbroken. He could check it for splinters once he was back inside. 'Yeah, nothing serious'.

They walked back to the fire engine, and the officer left him for a few minutes to get an update. 'Okay,' he said on his return. 'Maybe not as bad as you might have feared, the stairs are unsafe, but they've put a ladder up to the upper landing and the top floor is basically sound. Lots of smoke damage, and the sprinklers were triggered so the shop's a mess. We'll be here another hour or so. I can give you the number of someone we recommend who can board up the back door. And you'll need to call the insurance company, of course.'

Head reeling, Sam tried to take in the flood of information. The only thing he needed to sort out tonight was getting the place secured. 'I'll take that number, thanks.' The officer handed him a card and they agreed to meet again in the morning. 'We'll give you all the info you need for the insurers then.'

'Thank you. You've been great.'

'All part of the service.'

Phone pressed to his ear, Sam made his way back towards the cordon. The repair guy was as helpful as promised, and pretty stoic about being dragged out of bed. 'I'm used to it, mate. I'll be there in half an hour, forty-five minutes tops.'

And then there was nothing left to do, but wait. He gave Neil a brief update then left it to him to tell the concerned and curious still gathered around in the alley whilst he got Beth back inside the warmth of the pub. She wouldn't stop shivering and didn't seem to take in much of what he was telling her. Leaving the sweatshirt on, he stripped her shoes and jeans and tucked her into his bed, then went to make them both a cup of tea.

Remembering sugar was supposed to help with shock, he added a couple of teaspoons to Beth's tea. She sat up when urged and her hands seemed steady enough on the mug, so he forced himself to ease down the bed a foot so as not to hover over her. They sipped in silence, and he was pleased to see the shivering fade away as she worked her way down the mug. His phone rang—the security guy letting him know he was next door—and as soon as he'd got Beth lying back down, he went to meet him.

The fire engine had gone and the neighbours dispersed back to their own beds leaving just the pair of them in the alley. He gave the guy his credit card details then watched in admiration as together with an assistant he had a heavy fireproof board screwed into place over the gaping hole. 'All done, mate. We work with a lot of the big insurers, so give me a call if and when you'd like a quote to replace the backdoor. I'm happy to help.' Sam accepted the business card he was offered and waved the pair off.

Just those few minutes standing close to the emporium was enough for the smell of smoke to penetrate his clothing. Not wanting to upset Beth, he stripped everything off, shoved it in the washing machine ready for the morning and jumped in the shower. Within five minutes, he was lifting the covers to crawl in behind her. She hadn't moved a muscle as far as he could tell. From her even breathing, he thought she was asleep, until she spoke, her voice so soft he had to lean over to hear her. 'He'll be all right, won't he? The man they found.'

Not sure what to do for the best, he stuck to the truth as he knew it. 'I don't know. He was lucid and talking, which is hopefully a good sign. He had a few burns on his arms, but the fire officer seemed more concerned about smoke inhalation.'

Her breathing changed, and at the first hitch he tucked himself behind her and held her tight. The wrenching sobs broke his heart, but there was little he could do for her right then other than let her cry it out.

Eventually, she calmed, and he helped her to sit up and remove the sweatshirt when she complained of being too hot. When they lay back down, she rolled to face him, nuzzled into his shoulder and rested the fingers of one hand on his chest, over his heart.

He pressed a kiss to the top of her head. 'It's nothing that can't be fixed.' She nodded against him, but didn't reply. A surge of anger filled him—what the hell had that bloke been thinking? He could have killed himself, could've killed them all if the alarm hadn't been raised in time.

And behind all that anger was a bone-deep fear that the fire would ruin everything. That it would taint the emporium for Beth and cause her to reconsider her decision to return to the bay. Yes, they'd said 'I love you' to each other, and damn it, he'd meant it, but things were still so new between them. And what would happen when her mum found out? She'd jump at the chance to prove to Beth she'd made a mistake by moving back that, and would no doubt exert pressure on her to take the insurance money and run.

His arms tightened around her, causing her to mutter a sleepy protest. Loosening his hold, he tried to calm his racing mind. There was no point in second guessing anything, but he couldn't stop the fear that had wormed its way into his heart though. He couldn't lose her now. He couldn't.

His parents rushed back the next morning, with Eliza hot on their heels as soon as Libby called her with an update. Beth appeared okay on the surface—accepting the support and sympathy of the many well-wishers who called into the pub, and dealing with the insurance adjuster when he arrived the next day. The one thing she refused to do was leave the pub and actually look at the damage for herself, leaving Sam to show the man around and make arrangements for things like a skip to dispose of the damaged stock.

She listened carefully to the report from the adjuster, accepted his assessment and recommendations for repairs. He'd judged it too difficult a clean-up job for them to tackle, and she'd put up no arguments when he suggested a professional firm who would clear the place, salvage what they could and make a full inventory of recovered items. The fire officers had been brilliant, to the point of rescuing some of Beth's clothes from her smoke-damaged bedroom which Annie washed, dried and ironed to ensure there was no trace of smell on them, other than lilac-scented fabric softener.

Sam thanked the insurance agent for his time, then showed him downstairs, Beth trailing at their heels. The agent paused on the threshold to shake hands with them both. 'It'll take a bit of time to get the paperwork sorted, but once we have the fire report to back up your statements, I don't foresee any problems.'

Beth gave him a wan smile. 'Thank you. I just feel so stupid for not locking the back gate before I left.'

The agent stopped in his tracks. 'Excuse me?'

Oh shit. Sam's heart sank as he watched the sympathetic smile fade on the man's face. He wanted to clamp his hand over Beth's mouth before she could say anything else, but he was powerless to do anything as she tucked her hands into the sleeves of her cardigan. She looked so small, and shattered. 'I stopped locking the back gate all the time. It seemed a bit OTT when Lavender Bay is such a quiet place. I thought I was overreacting after living in London.' She gave a little laugh, which trailed off when they didn't join in. 'What? What is it?'

The agent fixed an insincere smile to his lips. 'You've been very helpful, Miss Reynolds. I would suggest you don't do anything next door until you hear from us.' And with that, he walked away.

Beth turned to Sam, a look of confusion on her face. 'What does that mean?'

Reaching out, Sam pulled her into his arms. 'I'm not sure, darling. Let's just wait and see.' There was no dismissing the sick feeling in his stomach though.

It was less than a week later that Sam's worst fears were realised when Beth received a letter from the insurance company denying her claim citing owner negligence. Devastated, Beth allowed Libby and Eliza to commandeer her. His own bloody sister, treating him like a persona non grata! As though Beth spending the night with him somehow made the fire his fault. It was getting on his nerves, but he'd kept his counsel so far, not wishing to upset Beth further. They spent hours locked away in Eliza's room or watching nonsense on the television to keep her spirits up. As a result, he hardly saw her other than at bedtime when she curled up in his arms and cried.

Nothing he tried seemed to help. She didn't want to do anything for her birthday, and the others had leapt to her defence when he'd tried to argue they needed to do something to try and break her cycle of grief.

All his attempts to get her outside the pub's four walls failed miserably. She was too tired to go for a run; it was too cold outside; his mum needed a hand with something. Whatever he suggested, Beth had an excuse to hand to thwart him. And so it went on for the next two weeks.

Eliza had returned home after a couple of days, but Libby stuck to Beth like glue, giving him no option other than to grit his teeth and try and wait it out. She couldn't go on like this forever. The emporium couldn't be left to rot, so Sam had instructed the cleaners that the insurers had suggested, paying them out of his own savings. It put his plans for Subterranean another step out of reach, but to hell with that for now.

They'd left everything they'd rescued piled in the stock room which had escaped almost completely unscathed. Wandering through the empty shop floor, Sam wanted to scream at the unfairness of it all. The security company had been in to replace the back door, the damage to the staircase hadn't been as bad as initially feared and more of his precious savings had gone towards repairing them. He'd been upstairs to open the windows and air the place out, and there was some smoke damage, but nothing too serious. He glanced up past the blackened wood, feeling totally frustrated. The flat was Beth's private domain and without her input, he couldn't do any more than that.

Needing to grab some fresh air, he unlocked the door and stepped out into the yard. The cobbles had been swept and washed clean, all trace of the source of the fire removed and placed in the skip in the alley beyond, together with the rest of the rubbish. The security firm had fixed a new lock to the rear gate free of charge, only mentioning it when they'd handed him the keys.

A new lock . . . Beth said she hadn't locked the gate, so why would the lock need replacing? Sam crossed the cobbles to study the wooden gate and the surrounding fence panels. Other than the panel closest to the building, everything else had survived unscathed. The outline of the old lock plate was visible, standing out from the natural weathering around it. The new lock had been placed lower down to avoid a splintered section on the post where the old staple had been affixed.

The fire hadn't touched the fence, and if Beth hadn't locked the gate, how had it ended up damaged? Closing his eyes, he ran through the sequence of events. He recalled the fire engine pulling up just as they ran outside. The crew piling out and running through the open gate . . . The gate had been open! He rubbed his forearm, recalling the nasty scratch from when he'd caught it on the splintered section of the gate post. If the fire crew hadn't broken the lock to get inside, then who had?

Trying not to get his hopes up, Sam hurried back to the pub to track down the telephone number for the insurance agent. The man sounded irritated when he explained who he was. 'I'm sorry Mr Barnes, but I can't discuss the case with you.'

Sam braced his arm against the wall and fought for patience. 'The lock on the rear gate was damaged. It wasn't anywhere near the fire, so if Beth didn't lock up behind her as she said, how did that happen?'

'As I said, Mr Barnes, I can't discuss the case with you.'

He ground his teeth. 'I'm not asking you to discuss it with me. I'm just asking that if the only reason you rejected her claim was because of what she said about not securing the gate, that you take another look at the reports and see if you can ascertain how it came to be damaged. I remember the fire crew arriving, the gate was hanging open then.'

A period of silence followed, and then the agent sighed. 'I'll check the reports, but you'd better not be wasting my time, Mr Barnes.'

Hanging up, Sam clenched his fist. Best not say anything to Beth in case nothing came of it. If he got her hopes up only to have them dashed again, it might be the final straw.

Chapter Twenty-Two

Beep. Beep. Beep. Beth felt the mattress shift behind her as Sam got out of bed and turned off his alarm clock. She'd just nestled back down into her pillow, when a shock of cold air hit her back as the quilt was ripped away. 'Get up.'

Rolling over, she glared up at Sam. 'Leave me alone, I'm tired.' She stretched out her hand, hoping to find the edge of the quilt so she could tug it back over her, but the rotten sod had stripped it clean off the bed.

He narrowed his eyes. 'You can't be bloody tired, you haven't done anything for days. Now get up. I'm going for a run and when I get back, you'd better be showered and dressed and ready for breakfast.'

He turned his back on her to pull on his running kit, and Beth stuck her tongue out at him. Had she honestly ever thought this bossy side of him attractive? Man, the experts were right, you didn't truly know someone until you tried to live with them. Not that she and Sam were actually living together, it was just a temporary arrangement until she sorted things out. Her thoughts turned to the telephone number scribbled in the pocket diary in her handbag. When she'd called her solicitor, he'd found the contact details for Owen Coburn, the developer who'd previously offered to buy the emporium, in a matter of moments.

It was the right thing to do. She'd tried to run the emporium, had thrown her heart and soul into it once her initial reluctance passed, but the fire had ruined everything. She didn't have it in her to start all over again. With the insurance refusing to pay out, she couldn't bloody afford it, even if she wanted to. Her initial idea of approaching the local artists with a view to taking over the place had flown out of the window. That had been way back in the beginning when she hadn't been sure whether running the emporium would be right for her. She no longer had a going concern to offer them, only a ruined shell, and no one to blame for the mess other than herself.

Just the thought of her own stupidity was enough to make her heart flutter in panic. Worst of all, she'd betrayed Eleanor's legacy, been unworthy of the trust her old friend had placed in her. She hadn't worked up the courage to call Owen yet, but she would. Today. Or maybe tomorrow. There was one thing holding her back from making that call, and that was the thought of telling Sam. She'd have to do it at some point, though. She had no idea how though.

'I'll be back in forty minutes. Get cracking.' Sam zipped up the front of his hoodie and stalked out of the bedroom. Forty minutes. And then she'd have to leave the sanctuary of the pub and face what she had done. Beth threw back the quilt, energized for the first time in days.

Taking the long route around to the station in order to avoid passing the emporium meant she missed the express, so her only choice was to catch the local service which called at every single station between Lavender Bay and Truro. The next fast service was over an hour later, and she needed to be out of the station on the off-chance Sam came looking for her. Not that she expected him to after reading the note she'd left him. It had been the coward's way out, but if she tried to talk to him face-to-face he'd only try and persuade her to stay. And she was afraid she would let him do it.

His tender care of her since the fire had been wonderful. Those quiet hours, when he'd held her long into the night, had soothed the pain in her heart like nothing else. She didn't deserve that though. She'd ruined everything, so it was only right that it hurt.

God! When she'd found out he'd dipped into his precious savings to try and help put the emporium to rights, she'd been furious with him. It wasn't his place to spend money he couldn't afford to lose trying to fix her mistake. And beneath the anger lurked a different emotion—love. Somewhere along the line, she'd fallen hook, line and sinker for Sam, and that had never been part of the deal. A spring fling, that was all it had been supposed to be, nothing more.

Sam had already jeopardised his plans wasting his savings on the repairs, if she stayed she'd only be more of a distraction. A distraction he couldn't afford if he was to realise his dreams. If he lost out on the restaurant because of her, she'd never forgive herself, and in the long run, neither would he. She needed to pay him back, and the best way to do that was to sell up. But if Owen Coburn didn't come through, it might be months before she got an offer on the emporium. She needed to start earning again, and the best place to do that was back in London. Checking her watch, she settled back with a sigh. At this rate it would close to nightfall before she made it back.

Six and a half hours after boarding her connecting train at Truro, Beth bumped her suitcase up the stairs at the underground station close to her bedsit then began to drag it along the uneven pavement. She was an hour later than she'd expected thanks to a faulty signal just outside Reading. Her stomach gave an angry grumble, and she gave it a quick pat. 'I hear you,' she mumbled and diverted into one of the takeaways lining the street.

Swinging the white plastic bag containing her dinner, Beth turned onto the pathway leading to the sprawling Victorian pile containing her bedsit and stopped short at the figure sitting on the front step. The overhead light cast his face partly in shadow, but there was no mistaking his identity. 'Sam? What are you doing here?'

Sam rose. 'Waiting for you. You took your time.'

'There was a signal failure.' She waved her hand, sending the takeaway swinging again. 'Never mind that, why are you here? How are you here?'

'I got your note.' He waved a folded piece of paper then tucked it in his jeans pocket. Her stomach clenched, guilt washing through her in a queasy wave. 'You made some interesting points,' he continued. 'And by interesting, I mean bone-headedly and fundamentally incorrect.' Her jaw gaped, and the plastic bag containing her dinner slipped from suddenly numb fingers, but he didn't give her the chance to respond.

Taking a step closer, he held up a finger. 'One, you claim that leaving is for the best. Best for who? For you, coming back to a place where no one knows you, no one cares about you? Or for me, to be separated from the woman who occupies at least eighty percent of my waking thoughts?'

A tiny spark of hope flared, but she crushed it out before it could grow. 'But don't you see? I shouldn't be taking up so much of your time. The restaurant is your dream, and it's too important for you to risk losing it because of me!'

Taking another step closer, he pressed a finger to her lips. 'Shh. You already had your say, and now it's my turn.' The touch felt too much like a caress, sending a little shiver down her spine. Damn it, she was hopeless when he was this close to her. She tried to shuffle back, but his other arm snaked around her waist, holding her in place. 'Two.' His palm spread against her back, warmth radiating from that point of contact to every part of her body. 'Dreams change. They expand and grow. I'm not giving up on Subterranean, not for one second, but the motivation behind it has changed. Oh, I still want success, still crave recognition from my peers, from the critics. I intend to create the best damn restaurant in the entire county. But not just to satisfy my ambition, but to give us a strong and stable future we can build upon.'

The pressure of that hand on her back increased, urging her

to lean into him, to accept the comfort of his familiar presence. 'Us?' It came out shaky, a bare whisper against the rough stubble on his jaw.

His lips brushed her temple. 'Us. Because none of this is worth a damn if I can't share it with you.'

Her heart turned cartwheels in her chest. 'But what about our deal? What about the spring fling?'

'I want to renegotiate terms. How would you feel about adding some May play?' Ducking his head, he nibbled the edge of her ear, sending little shockwaves rippling through her. 'A little June swoon . . .' His lips trailed lower to tease her neck.

Laughing, she wound her fingers into the curls at his nape. 'You've been working on those rhymes, haven't you?'

'All the way up here in the car. I got a bit stuck when it came to July, though.'

July. How many months did he envisage them being together? He'd said he wanted to build a future for them, and as tempting as his words and—God help her!—his kisses were, they didn't resolve the biggest problem. 'I'm going to have to sell the emporium.'

His mouth left her skin, and the arms around her stiffened. 'No, you don't. The stock can be replaced. The damage upstairs won't take much to put right. You can do this, Beth, I know you can.'

He didn't get it. 'Just stop, okay?' She tried to duck past him, but he took her shoulder in a gentle grip to stop her.

'No. I won't stop. Remember that day when we walked up by Gilbert's Farm? What did we promise each other?'

Oh, bloody hell, he was going to use her words against her. 'We promised to always tell the truth. No matter how hard,' she muttered.

His free hand captured her ponytail, stroking the strands through his fingers in the way she loved. 'I know you've had a shock, but you can't just give up. You've had enough time, but now you need to face up to what happened and make some decisions.'

'I did make a decision, I'm going to sell!'

'That's not a decision, that's a copout. You need to stop running away every time the going gets tough.' His hand settled on her shoulder, his other arm coming around to cradle her from behind. 'You've been through so much these past few months, you have to give yourself time to process it all. I don't want you to have any regrets, and if you let the emporium go without a fight, I think you'll regret it every day for the rest of your life.'

A lump formed in her throat, and tears stung the backs of her eyes. She dashed them away with the back of her hand. She was sick and tired of crying. 'It's so hard.'

Gentle lips brushed her hair. 'I know. Why don't you come back with me tomorrow and at least look around the emporium? It might not be as bad as you think.'

She wished she could believe him, but he was right about one thing. She needed to stop running. Turning in his arms, she placed her hands upon his chest and looked up into his eyes. 'Okay, but I'm not promising anything. I still need to find a way to pay you back.'

He looked like he might protest, but in the end he simply nodded and said, 'Okay, we'll talk about that tomorrow as well.' His hands stroked her back. 'I'm so proud of you, Beth.' He murmured the words so sweetly, it was impossible to do anything other than to rise on her tiptoes and capture his lips with her own.

They broke apart, and Sam rested his forehead against hers. 'I have one more very important question to ask you.'

Butterflies exploded in her stomach. He couldn't possibly mean . . .? Of course not, it was too soon, there was too much still up in the air. Trying to calm her racing thoughts, Beth wet her lips. 'O . . . okay.'

'Did you order enough takeaway to feed us both?'

Traffic the next morning was light, and they made good time. Sam kept the conversation light, and she did her best to respond in kind, but each mile that brought her closer to Lavender Bay tightened the nerves building inside her until she feared she might be sick, and she closed her eyes pretending to sleep. The motion of the car slowed, and she forced herself to sit up. Expecting to see the familiar skyline of the bay, she was met instead with a queue of stationary cars blocking all three lanes.

They crept along for a couple of miles with no clue as to the cause of the delay until they glimpsed the first of many flashing blue lights on the opposite carriageway. An articulated lorry sprawled across the inside two lanes, the wreckage of a bright red sports car wedged partly beneath it. 'Oh, God.' Beth turned her head away.

The lines of Sam's jaw were clenched. 'Don't look. I'll let you know when we're clear of it.' She kept her gaze fixed on the profile of his face until the tightness in his face eased, and he nodded.

Flopping back in her seat, Beth let out a sigh. 'It didn't look good.'

Sam released one hand from the wheel to grasp her hand. He squeezed her fingers tight, then placed her hand on his thigh before letting go to take hold of the wheel again. Understanding his need for touch, she gripped the solid muscle of his leg. 'Those poor people.'

'Life's so short.' His voice was rough, the tension in his jaw back again. 'So bloody short. You think you have it all figured out, and then something terrible happens. Eleanor, my dad, whatever poor sod was driving that car.' His eyes flicked to hers for an instant, and then back on the road ahead. 'I know I can be pushy sometimes, but I want to live the best life that I can. I want that for both of us.'

'I know. I want that too.' And she really did, she just hoped she could find a way to address the guilt twisting her up over the emporium. Her grip tightened around Sam's thigh, and his hand dropped briefly to cover hers. If she had to sell the shop, she didn't know if she could face staying in Lavender Bay.

No matter how much she might want to.

223

When Sam drew up outside the rear gates of the pub, Beth wound down her window and sucked in a lungful of fresh air. The familiar scent of the sea calmed her enough to accept Sam's hand as he helped her out of the car.

They made it as far as the back door of the emporium before she baulked. Sam was having none of it though, and her slight weight was no match for his strength as he picked her up by the waist and carted her inside. He carried her through the shop, before putting her down by the front door, and by then it was too late to keep protesting. Barren shelves and bare walls greeted her, and a wave of sadness rocked her on her heels. 'There's nothing left.'

Sam glanced over his shoulder at the empty room. 'What? Oh, no, don't panic. Everything that was salvaged is out in the stock room. It's pretty cramped in there, thanks to that stupid bloody banana thing, but we can check it out in a minute.'

It seemed ridiculous in the face of everything, but her heart lifted to know at least something that was uniquely Eleanor still remained. A tap on the glass behind her sent her spinning on her heel. 'What the . . .?'

Libby stood on the other side of the door, her flamingo pink hair spiked up in all directions. She pointed at the handle and mimed opening the door, so Beth undid the bolts, and turned the lock.

It was only once she stepped outside that Beth noticed the crowd gathered behind her friend. An arm circled her shoulders, and she blinked up. 'Sam, what is this?'

'Just wait and see,' he said with a wink. Her eyes left his to scan the group. In addition to Libby, she spotted Annie, and Paul, who was leaning on his walking stick, a broad smile across his face. The Tates from the newsagent, the Major and his wife, Gina and Davey from the kebab shop. So many familiar faces.

A man dressed in a suit eased to the front of the group, and Beth blinked as she recognised the agent from her insurance company. 'Ah, there you are Miss Reynolds, Mr Barnes.'

Sam stepped forward to shake his hand. 'Thanks for agreeing to do this at short notice.'

The agent smiled. 'It's a little unorthodox, but I deliver enough bad news in my job that it makes a nice change.'

Completely bemused, Beth looked between the two of them. 'Will someone tell me what's going on?'

The agent reached for his inside jacket pocket and withdrew an envelope. 'This is for you, Miss Reynolds. I'd like to apologise for any distress we may have caused you. On re-examining the facts, we reversed our decision and I can confirm your claim will be settled in full.'

Beth took the envelope when he extended it to her. It was unsealed, and when she opened the flap, her knees turned watery at the sight of the cheque inside it.'

'I . . . I don't understand.'

'Ask your friend, there. He'll explain everything.' The agent checked his watch. 'Well, I must be off, just let me wish you Happy Beth Day!' With a final shake of Sam's hand, the man sauntered off whistling to himself.

'Happy what-now?'

Libby grabbed her arm and turned her towards a large home-made banner hanging over the front door of the emporium emblazoned with the words Happy Beth Day followed by half a dozen exclamation marks.

'What is all this?' Beth asked her friend.

'Sam organised it all. He could tell the idea of trying to get this place back in order was overwhelming you, so once he had the good news from the insurance company, he rallied the troops. You bolting threw a spanner in the works, but he called me last night to say you were coming back so I spread the word. Everyone's here to pitch in and help. You probably won't need all of us today, but we've all pledged to give you at least one day of your choosing to help with whatever you need. Painting, helping to reorder stock, stacking shelves. Whatever you want.

Hester's organised the ladies from the improvement society and they're going to take everything out of your wardrobe and get it washed, or dry-cleaned.'

Speechless, Beth tried to count the number of people gathered on the pavement and gave up after reaching thirty. Everyone was smiling and chatting, organising themselves into little self-assigned groups the way Hester and her friends had volunteered to do her washing.

A familiar hand closed upon her shoulder and Beth spun around to throw herself into Sam's arms. 'What did you do?' She sobbed into his chest, unable to believe what was happening.

He explained to her about his suspicions over the lock, how the insurance agent had reviewed the file and found a photograph showing clearly it had been damaged on the night. That when the police had interviewed the rough sleeper, he'd admitted to forcing his way into the rear yard.

Stroking her hair just the way she liked it, he continued. 'Getting the insurers to pay up wasn't enough. I wanted to show you that you're not on your own, Beth. That you have friends and neighbours who want you to succeed. Want you to be part of this community.'

Sniffing, she lifted her head. 'And what about you? Do I have you?'

Love and laughter shone bright in his eyes. 'For as long as you want me, darling.'

Stretching on tiptoe, she kissed him. 'And what if I want you for more than a June swoon? What if I want you forever?'

His hands cupped her cheeks. 'Sounds perfect. You. Me. Marriage. Babies. I want the whole package. Not yet, but one of these days, I want you to be mine. Forever.'

Heart soaring, she couldn't hold in her joyful laughter. 'Be careful what you wish for, Mr Barnes, you might just get it.'

He tugged her close. 'I'm counting on it. After all, you're a sure thing, right?' Her laughter was swallowed by one of his toe-curling, mind-scrambling kisses and Beth forgot about everyone and everything but the man holding her tight.

Because when it came to him, she was most definitely a sure thing.

Acknowledgements

A new series, who would've thought it? Thanks to everyone who read and raved about Butterfly Cove. Your support has given me the opportunity to introduce you to a whole new cast of characters. I hope you will embrace Beth, Eliza and Libby with as much enthusiasm as you did Mia, and her sisters.

To my biggest supporter, bar none – my lovely husband. Thanks, bun x

To my fabulous editor, Charlotte Mursell. Thank you for helping me find the story that was in my heart. It's been a difficult few months, and your support can not be understated.

To the HQ Digital team – a band of unsung heroes who work so hard behind the scenes. So much of my success is down to your efforts. You are deeply appreciated.

All the friends I have made throughout the romance writing community – you keep me sane, keep me laughing, keep me writing.

And, as ever, to you the reader – I hope you enjoy escaping to Lavender Bay. x

Turn the page for a sneak peek at *Sunrise at Butterfly Cove*, the enchanting first book in the Butterfly Cove series from Sarah Bennett . . .

Prologue

October 2014

'And the winner of the 2014 Martindale Prize for Best New Artist is . . .'

Daniel Fitzwilliams lounged back in his chair and took another sip from the never-emptying glass of champagne. His bow tie hung loose around his neck, and the first two buttons of his wing-collar shirt had been unfastened since just after the main course had been served. The room temperature hovered somewhere around the fifth circle of hell and he wondered how much longer he would have to endure the fake smiles and shoulder pats from strangers passing his table.

The MC made a big performance of rustling the large silver envelope in his hand. 'Get on with it, mate,' Daniel muttered. His agent, Nigel, gave him a smile and gulped at the contents of his own glass. His nomination had been a huge surprise and no one expected him to win, Daniel least of all.

'Well, well.' The MC adjusted his glasses and peered at the card he'd finally wrestled free. 'I am delighted to announce that the winner of the Martindale Prize is Fitz, for his series "Interactions".'

A roar of noise from the rest of his tablemates covered the choking sounds of Nigel inhaling half a glass of champagne. Daniel's own glass slipped from his limp fingers and rolled harmlessly under the table. 'Bugger me.'

'Go on, mate. Get up there!' His best friend, Aaron, rounded the table and tugged Daniel to his feet. 'I told you, I bloody told you, but you wouldn't believe me.'

Daniel wove his way through the other tables towards the stage, accepting handshakes and kisses from all sides. Will Spector, the bookies' favourite and the art crowd's latest darling, raised a glass in toast and Daniel nodded to acknowledge his gracious gesture. Flashbulbs popped from all sides as he mounted the stairs to shake hands with the MC. He raised the sinuous glass trophy and blinked out at the clapping, cheering crowd of his peers.

The great and the good were out in force. The Martindale attracted a lot of press coverage and the red-carpet winners and losers would be paraded across the inside pages for people to gawk at over their morning cereal. His mum had always loved to see the celebrities in their posh frocks. He just wished she'd survived long enough to see her boy come good. Daniel swallowed around the lump in his throat. Fuck cancer. Dad had at least made it to Daniel's first exhibition, before his heart failed and he'd followed his beloved Nancy to the grave.

Daniel adjusted the microphone in front of him and waited for the cheers to subside. The biggest night of his life, and he'd never felt lonelier.

* * *

Mia Sutherland resisted the urge to check her watch and tried to focus on the flickering television screen. The latest episode of The Watcher would normally have no trouble in holding her attention—it was her and Jamie's new favourite show. She glanced at the empty space on the sofa beside her. Even with the filthy weather outside, he should have been home before now. Winter had hit earlier than usual and she'd found herself turning the lights on mid-afternoon to try and dispel the gloom caused by the raging storm outside.

The ad break flashed upon the screen and she popped into the kitchen to give the pot of stew a quick stir. She'd given up waiting, and eaten her portion at eight-thirty, but there was plenty left for Jamie. He always said she cooked for an army rather than just the two of them.

A rattle of sleet struck the kitchen window and Mia peered through the Venetian blind covering it; he'd be glad of a hot meal after being stuck in the traffic for so long. A quick tap of the wooden spoon against the side of the pot, and then she slipped the cast-iron lid back on. The pot was part of the Le Creuset set Jamie's parents had given them as a wedding gift and the matching pans hung from a wooden rack above the centre of the kitchen worktop. She slid the pot back into the oven and adjusted the temperature down a notch.

Ding-dong.

At last! Mia hurried down the hall to the front door and tugged it open with a laugh. 'Did you forget your keys—' A shiver of fear ran down her back at the sight of the stern-looking policemen standing on the step. Rain dripped from the brims of their caps and darkened the shoulders of their waterproof jackets.

'Mrs Sutherland?'

No, no, no, no. Mia looked away from the sympathetic expressions and into the darkness beyond them for the familiar flash of Jamie's headlights turning onto their small driveway.

'Perhaps we could come in, Mrs Sutherland?' The younger of the pair spoke this time.

Go away. Go away. She'd seen this scene played out enough on the television to know what was coming next. 'Please, come in.' Her voice sounded strange, high-pitched and brittle to her ears. She stepped back to let the two men enter. 'Would you like a cup of tea?'

The younger officer took off his cap and shrugged out of his jacket. 'Why don't you point me in the direction of the kettle and you and Sergeant Stone can make yourselves comfortable in the front room?'

Mia stared at the Sergeant's grim-set features. What a horrible job he has, poor man. 'Yes, of course. Come on through.'

She stared at the skin forming on the surface of her now-cold tea. She hadn't dared to lift the cup for fear they would see how badly she was shaking. 'Is there someone you'd like us to call?' PC Taylor asked, startling her. The way he phrased the question made her wonder how many times he'd asked before she'd heard him. I'd like you to call my husband.

Mia bit her lip against the pointless words, and ran through a quick inventory in her head. Her parents would be useless; it was too far past cocktail hour for her mother to be coherent and her dad didn't do emotions well at the best of times.

Her middle sister, Kiki, had enough on her hands with the new baby and Matty determined to live up to every horror story ever told about the terrible twos. Had it only been last week she and Jamie had babysat Matty because the baby had been sick? An image of Jamie holding their sleeping nephew in his lap rose unbidden and she shook her head sharply to dispel it. She couldn't think about things like that. Not right then.

The youngest of her siblings, Nee, was neck-deep in her final year at art school in London. Too young and too far away to be shouldering the burden of her eldest sister's grief. The only person she wanted to talk to was Jamie and that would never happen again. Bile burned in her throat and a whooping sob escaped before she could swallow it back.

'S-sorry.' She screwed her eyes tight and stuffed everything down as far as she could. There would be time enough for tears. Opening her stinging eyes, she looked at Sergeant Stone. 'Do Bill and Pat know?'

'Your in-laws? They're next on our list. I'm so very sorry, pet. Would you like us to take you over there?'

Unable to speak past the knot in her throat, Mia nodded.

...... They're next from now that I'm so very tired, would you like me to take you over there?

trouble to put the logs in that corner, Miss reduced

Chapter One

February 2016

Daniel rested his head on the dirty train window and stared unseeing at the landscape as it flashed past. He didn't know where he was going. Away. That was the word that rattled around his head. Anywhere, nowhere. Just away from London. Away from the booze, birds and fakery of his so-called celebrity lifestyle. Twenty-nine felt too young to be a has-been.

He'd hit town with a portfolio, a bundle of glowing recommendations and an ill-placed confidence in his own ability to keep his feet on the ground. Within eighteen months, he was the next big thing in photography and everyone who was anyone clamoured for an original Fitz image on their wall. Well-received exhibitions had led to private commissions and more money than he knew what to do with. And if it hadn't been for Aaron's investment advice, his bank account would be as drained as his artistic talent.

The parties had been fun at first, and he couldn't put his finger on when the booze had stopped being a buzz and started being a crutch. Girls had come and gone. Pretty, cynical women who liked being seen on his arm in the gossip columns, and didn't seem to mind being in his bed.

Giselle had been one such girl and without any active consent on his part, she'd installed herself as a permanent fixture. The bitter smell of the French cigarettes she lived on in lieu of a decent meal filled his memory, forcing Daniel to swallow convulsively against the bile in his throat. That smell signified everything he hated about his life, about himself. Curls of rank smoke had hung like fog over the sprawled bodies, spilled bottles and overflowing ashtrays littering his flat when he'd woven a path through them that morning.

The cold glass of the train window eased the worst of his thumping hangover, although no amount of water seemed able to ease the parched feeling in his throat. The carriage had filled, emptied and filled again, the ebb and flow of humanity reaching their individual destinations.

Daniel envied their purpose. He swigged again from the large bottle of water he'd paid a small fortune for at Paddington Station as he'd perused the departures board. The taxi driver he'd flagged down near his flat had told him Paddington would take him west, a part of England that he knew very little about, which suited him perfectly.

His first instinct had been to head for King's Cross, but that would have taken him north. Too many memories, too tempting to visit old haunts his Mam and Dad had taken him to. It would be sacrilege to their memory to tread on the pebbled beaches of his youth, knowing how far he'd fallen from being the man his father had dreamed he would become.

He'd settled upon Exeter as a first destination. Bristol and Swindon seemed too industrial, too much like the urban sprawl he wanted to escape. And now he was on a local branch line train to Orcombe Sands. Sands meant the sea. The moment he'd seen the name, he knew it was where he needed to be. Air he could breathe, the wind on his face, nothing on the horizon but whitecaps and seagulls.

The train slowed and drew to a stop as it had done numerous times previously. Daniel didn't stir; the cold window felt too good against his clammy forehead. He was half aware of a small woman rustling an enormous collection of department store carrier bags as she carted her shopping haul past his seat, heading towards the exit. She took a couple of steps past him before she paused and spoke.

'This is the end of the line, you know?' Her voice carried a warm undertone of concern and Daniel roused. The thump in his head increased, making him frown as he regarded the speaker. She was an older lady, around the age his Mam would've been had she still been alive.

Her grey hair was styled in a short, modern crop and she was dressed in that effortlessly casual, yet stylish look some women had. A soft camel jumper over dark indigo jeans with funky bright red trainers on her feet. A padded pea jacket and a large handbag worn cross body, keeping her hands free to manage her shopping bags. She smiled brightly at Daniel and tilted her head towards the carriage doors, which were standing stubbornly open.

'This is Orcombe Sands. Pensioner jail. Do not pass go, do not collect two hundred pounds.' She laughed at her own joke and Daniel finally realised what she was telling him. He had to get off the train; this was his destination. She was still watching him expectantly so he cleared his throat.

'Oh, thanks. Sorry I was miles away.' He rose as he spoke, unfurling his full height as the small woman stepped back to give him room to stand and tug his large duffel bag from the rack above his seat. Seemingly content that Daniel was on the move, the woman gave him a cheery farewell and disappeared off the train.

Adjusting the bag on his shoulder as he looked around, Daniel perused the layout of the station for the first time. The panoramic sweep of his surroundings didn't take long. The tiny waiting room needed a lick of paint, but the platform was clean of the rubbish and detritus that had littered the central London station he'd started his journey at several hours previously. A hand-painted, slightly lopsided Exit sign pointed his way and Daniel moved in the only direction available to him, hoping to find some signs of life and a taxi rank.

He stopped short in what he supposed was the main street and regarded the handful of houses and a pub, which was closed up tight on the other side of the road. He looked to his right and regarded a small area of hardstanding with a handful of cars strewn haphazardly around.

The February wind tugged hard at his coat and he flipped the collar up, hunching slightly to keep his ears warm.

Daniel started to regret his spur-of-the-moment decision to leave town. He'd been feeling stale for a while, completely lacking in inspiration. Every image he framed in his mind's eye seemed either trite or derivative. All he'd ever wanted to do was take photographs. From the moment his parents had given him his first disposable camera to capture his holiday snaps, Daniel had wanted to capture the world he saw through his viewfinder.

An engine grumbled to life and the noise turned Daniel's thoughts outwards again as a dirty estate car crawled out of the car park and stopped in front of him. The side window lowered and the woman from the train leant across from the driver's side to speak to him.

'You all right there? Is someone coming to pick you up?' Daniel shuffled his feet slightly under the blatantly interested gaze of the older woman.

His face warmed as he realised he would have to confess his predicament to the woman. He had no idea where he was or what his next move should be. He could tell from the way she was regarding him that she would not leave until she knew he was going to be all right.

'My trip was a bit spur-of-the-moment. Do you happen to know if there is a B&B nearby?' he said, trying to keep his voice light, as though heading off into the middle of nowhere on a freezing winter's day was a completely rational, normal thing to do.

The older woman widened her eyes slightly. 'Not much call for that this time of year. Just about everywhere that offers accommodation is seasonal and won't be open until Easter time.'

Daniel started to feel like an even bigger fool as the older woman continued to ponder his problem, her index finger tapping against her lip. The finger paused as a sly smile curled one corner of her lip and Daniel wondered if he should be afraid of whatever thought had occurred to cause that expression.

He took a backwards step as the woman suddenly released her seat belt and climbed out of the car in a determined manner. He was not intimidated by someone a foot shorter than him. He wasn't.

'What's your name?' she asked as she flipped open the boot of the car and started transferring her shopping bags onto the back seat.

'Fitz . . .' He paused. That name belonged in London, along with everything else he wanted to leave behind. 'Daniel. Daniel Fitzwilliams.'

'Pleased to meet you. I'm Madeline although my friends call me Mads and I have a feeling we will be great friends. Stick your bag in the boot, there's a good lad. I know the perfect place. Run by a friend of mine. I'm sure you'll be very happy there.'

Daniel did as bid, his eyes widening in shock as unbelievable! Madeline propelled him in the right direction with a slap on the arse and a loud laugh.

'Bounce a coin on those cheeks, Daniel! I do so like a man who takes care of himself.' With another laugh, Madeline disappeared into the front seat of the car and the engine gave a slightly startled whine as she turned the key.

Gritting his teeth, he placed his bag in the boot before moving around to the front of the car and eyeing the grubby interior of the estate, which appeared to be mainly held together with mud and rust. He folded his frame into the seat, which had been hiked forward almost as far as it could. With his knees up around his ears, Daniel fumbled under the front of the seat until he found the adjuster and carefully edged the seat back until he felt less like a sardine.

'Belt up, there's a good boy,' Madeline trilled as she patted his knee and threw the old car into first. They lurched away from the kerb. Deciding that a death grip was the only way to survive, Daniel quickly snapped his seat belt closed, scrabbled for the aptly named oh shit! handle above the window and tried to decide whether the journey would be worse with his eyes open or closed.

Madeline barrelled the car blithely around the narrow country lanes, barely glancing at the road as far as Daniel could tell as she sang along to the latest pop tunes pouring from the car radio. He tried not to whimper at the thought of where he was going to end up. What the hell was this place going to be like if it was run by a friend of Madeline's? If there was a woman in a rocking chair at the window, he'd be in deep shit.

The car abruptly swung off to the left and continued along what appeared to be a footpath rather than any kind of road. A huge building loomed to the left and Daniel caught his breath. Rather than the Bates Motel, it was more of a Grand Lady in her declining years. In its heyday, it must have been a magnificent structure. The peeling paint, filthy windows and rotting porch did their best to hide the beauty, together with the overgrown gardens.

His palms itched and for the first time in forever, Daniel felt excited. He wanted his camera. Head twisting and turning, he tried to take everything in. A group of outbuildings and a large barn lay to the right of where Madeline pulled to a stop on the gravel driveway.

Giving a jaunty toot on the car's horn, she wound down her window to wave and call across the yard to what appeared to be a midget yeti in the most moth-eaten dressing gown Daniel had ever seen. Not good, not good, oh so not good . . .

Dear Reader,

We hope you enjoyed reading this book. If you did, we'd be so appreciative if you left a review. It really helps us and the author to bring more books like this to you.

Here at HQ Digital we are dedicated to publishing fiction that will keep you turning the pages into the early hours. Don't want to miss a thing? To find out more about our books, promotions, discover exclusive content and enter competitions you can keep in touch in the following ways:

JOIN OUR COMMUNITY:

Sign up to our new email newsletter: hyperurl.co/hqnewsletter

Read our new blog www.hqstories.co.uk

🐦 : https://twitter.com/HQDigitalUK

📘 : www.facebook.com/HQStories

BUDDING WRITER?

We're also looking for authors to join the HQ Digital family!
Find out more here:

https://www.hqstories.co.uk/want-to-write-for-us/

Thanks for reading, from the HQ Digital team

**If you enjoyed *Spring at Lavender Bay*,
then why not try another delightfully
uplifting romance from HQ Digital?**